MURDER BY DEGREES
A NOVEL
by
VICTOR E KNIGHT
ISBN: 978-1-9165001-9-8

All Rights Reserved.
No reproduction, copy or transmission of this publication may be made without written permission. No paragraph or section of this publication may be reproduced, copied or transmitted save with written permission or in accordance with the provisions of the Copyright Act 1956 (as amended). Copyright 2019 Victor E Knight.
The right of Victor E Knight to be identified as the author of this work has been asserted in accordance with the Copyright Designs and Patents Act 1988.
A copy of this book is deposited with the British Library.

Published by

i2i Publishing
Manchester. UK
www.i2ipublishing.co.uk

CONTENTS

1 An Odd Way to Spend an Odd Day Off; or,
The Adventures of a Dead Pig   1

2 Odd Jobs   17

3 Hooligan's Sunday   30

4 Scholars and Gentlemen   47

5 A Suspect   65

6 All that's left of a Dead Professor   77

7 Death Is Such a Let-Down   90

8 Even a Conference is Interrupted if it's Murder   107

9 An Atmosphere of Violence   125

10 Suspicion and Fatality fail to Meet   140

11 Media, Mugger, Melodrama, Murder   161

12 Someone Who it Wasn't   184

13 On the Track, and off it Again   199

14 Bolted In, and Dead   211

15 On Watch   221

16 A Matter of Love and Death   240

CHAPTER 1

AN ODD WAY TO SPEND AN ODD DAY OFF; OR, THE ADVENTURES OF A DEAD PIG

'Is that the abattoir?'
'It is, sir.'
'Do you have a pig's head?'
'Only on my passport photograph, sir.'
'Oh, I didn't mean ...'
'Of course not, sir,' came the soothing reply. 'A lot of people ask something like that, and' – he sounded pleased – 'we have our little repertoire of responses.'

The caller realised that even the last explanatory remark, too, was in the repertoire. So, probably, was the continuation:

'I've been asked if I've got sheep's eyes already today, sir, and I said, "Not for everybody, madam, but you *could* get lucky".'

The abattoir man suddenly emitted a laugh more reminiscent of a poultry shed than of his own daily environs, but equally suddenly stopped it as though by a switch, and said:

'You wanted a pig's head, sir. Now, what size did you have in mind?'

'Er ... I'm a biology teacher. It's for my class to learn from. I'll need all the flesh and ... er ... on the top, and so on. To study the muscles. And so on. About the size of a man's head, I suppose.'

'Very interesting subject, sir. Well, we've usually got one or two. Look you out a nice one.'

'Thank you. Could I come round now?'

'Good idea, sir. Any time. Come to the office, ask for Joe, and say you've come for your head.'

The demented fowl out-cackled the formal goodbyes.

2

'What does one carry a pig's head in?' he wondered. He tried to visualise it. 'Surely it wouldn't fit into a supermarket plastic bag? A medium-sized cardboard box would be better. I should take some newspaper as well, to stop it from rolling around ... Would it be dripping blood? And would the blood soak through the cardboard? Perhaps by now it would have dried inside the head, or have all dripped out? How long does pig's blood take to dry, anyway? ... And how exactly do I get to this place?'

He took a cardboard box, a couple of plastic bags and some newspaper, and spread more newspaper over the floor of the car-boot. Then he remembered again that he did not know where he was going, so he sat behind the steering-wheel, took a street-map from the glove compartment, and worked out a route.

He stalled the car in setting off.

*

He had never seen the abattoir, having had no occasion to visit either it or its vicinity before. As he crossed the bridge over the railway he realised, consciously for the first time at any rate, that the American concept of a right and a wrong side of the railroad tracks prevailed in this Victorian city of Pillingham, too. On either side of the main road, the pebble-dashed, semi-detached world of hedged crescents, sparkling and glistening in the sunshine after a spring shower, had suddenly given place to moist, blood-red terraces, severely cornered and opening directly on to the pavement. He pulled in to check the map which lay, folded to display the required section, on the passenger seat, and saw that he should make a couple of right-angle turns round a primary school playground. He was thus again parallel to the main road, but now facing back towards the railway, and he saw the abattoir straight ahead.

It occupied a complete block on the grid of streets, and at first glance seemed to be a gigantic version of the dwellings around it. Houses of life and death with structural decay – on both sides of the road.

Modern wire gates, which stood open, contradicted the general style. He drove through and saw, mounted on a wall, an engraved stainless-steel notice, which jarred typographically in the same way. It offered visitors the choice between OFFICE and – a euphemistic evasion – LOADING. He had hoped to see some slaughtering, but a woman in a spotless white overall came out and waved him into a car-parking space by the office entrance before disappearing into LOADING.

He had imagined the office to be full of blood-stained men presenting blood-stained worksheets to an elderly clerk or languorous typist. He saw, instead, a bright room with a Formica-and-steel counter, behind which stood a bald, rotund man wearing a spotless white overall and exhibiting long, yellow, pointed teeth. He admitted to himself, not for the first time that day, how scanty was his knowledge of life and work outside his own immediate circles – the very deficiency which he censured in his colleagues.

The man soon proved to be Joe, the waggish poultry-impressionist on the telephone. Again, the screech-cackle cracked the air and abruptly cut out.

'Yes, you're a pig's head, sir,' he said, politely, after the manner of a waiter informing a diner that he was a lamb chop or a rainbow trout.

He reached down and straightened up in one movement, and a severed pig's head, peering amicably through heavy-duty translucent plastic, landed with a resounding thump on the counter.

'That'll do you, sir?' The yellow teeth lengthened further, in expectation of approval.

The visitor peered at it for form's sake as part of the scene being played, and answered with forced pleasure, 'I'm sure it will. Thank you ... er ... how much is it?'

'Teaching profession, you said, sir? No charge in that case. Simply ask for a signature and draw your attention to the Lifeboats collection box.'

As the pig surveyed with apparent gratification the price placed on his head by a charitable donation, his new owner signed a ruled exercise-book in which a succession of local teachers and schoolchildren had acknowledged receipt of a variety of amputated or extracted parts of animals. The recent entries did not indicate that a woman had collected sheep's eyes - which circumstance confirmed the purchaser's earlier supposition about the repertoire of responses.

'New to us, I think, sir,' said the yellow teeth, long again in amiability, as his porcine hand turned the book round. 'Mr Omen from the Technical College. You're new there, sir? It's normally Mrs Jones. She's just a pair of lungs and a heart.'

'Yes, but she's ... on maternity leave.'

'What? At her age?' Cackle and cut-out awaited the truth.

'Er, no ... just my little joke. Of course, she's ... I'm there temporarily ... on attachment from the Department of Education and Science.'

'Ah, hum, well, there you are, sir. He's frozen at the moment, so you'll have to get him into the deep freeze soon, or he'll get a bit bloody.'

'I've got a box in the boot outside ... Thank you again. Goodbye.'

'Oh, have you heard about the Falklands, sir? The Argies have packed it in. Knew they would. Got slaughtered by our lot.'

The customer gave a smile which meant whatever Joe wanted it to mean.

In the car-park he opened the boot and shifted the head around in the box to pack it firmly with the spare newspapers. He noticed that some blood was already collecting in the bag. It had found a leak, and a long red smear, like a tongue of blood, had appeared on the cardboard.

Did the pig have more of a sneer than a smile?

He began to think about the next stage as he settled himself in the driving-seat.

'What would be the best tool for the job? A knife obviously *is* too messy ... though rather appealing ... No, the proverbial blunt instrument is better. Interesting that I must have decided on that by buying the head. One's subconscious always knows ... You don't stab a head ... So - a brick, perhaps? A blood-red brick?'

Turning out of the abattoir car-park, he misquoted, spontaneously:

'Red bricks are not so red
As the ooze of blood
from the dead pig's head.'

'Well, I know someone who'll not appreciate that one. But ... as for a brick, even in the world of Red Brick, it's awkward to carry. It really comes down to a hammer. But what sort of hammer? That flimsy little one in the kitchen drawer would not do at all.'

*

It was only ten o'clock in the morning, and he already had the pig's head. So, what about this hammer? Obviously, it should not be a claw hammer: he wanted to cave a skull in, not yank bits off. It should have that rounded part where the claws would be. But should it be heavy or light? Should it have a short shaft or a long one? Going to buy a hammer is far from straightforward with all these choices. Of course, people who normally work with hammers have a variety already. They select the one that's right for whatever they intend to hit. They develop a feel for the weight and length of each one, and they retain the sensation of impact in their muscle-memory, which guides them the next time they strike with it. But he was a novice in such matters ...

'I'll get a selection,' he reasoned, 'and find out by trial and error.'

He drove to the city centre where he had noticed a large do-it-yourself store. ('I'm certainly going to do something myself. Or some*one*!') He would not be remembered there; not so in a small suburban shop. When he found a meter with plenty of unexpired time he felt that Dame Fortune was surely smiling on him and his enterprise: a free head and free parking!

He checked the boot-lock before leaving the car.

In the specialist store his puzzlement as to what to buy returned: the concept 'hammer' defied precise definition. The range on offer was daunting. A philosopher or theoretical linguist would, he reflected, spend hours musing on the definitions of hammers which are nearly bludgeons, hammers which could draw music from xylophones, hammers for pulverising stone, hammers for the precision-tapping of delicate pins ... Some time-wasting fool would write an article about it for a learned journal. One probably has. And they're paid to do it! Correction – they're paid while they're doing it. But all that was wanted now was an honest, everyday hammer to ... well, to hit something with.

An assistant was about to threaten help, so he looked theatrically at his watch and left. Then, to evade the burden of choice, he retreated to the less-sophisticated hardware section of a chain-store, where he bought two hammers of different weights and sizes. There was another hammer on sale which also attracted him, but he did not want to draw attention to himself by buying too many – even the two which he bought stimulated a comment from the sales assistant. He resolved to buy others only one at a time. So he took his purchases back to the car, locked them in the boot, and made for another chain-store.

After a few trips he had amassed a varied little collection. Surely at least one of them would prove to be a workmanlike tool for his purpose?

What an odd day to spend an odd day off!

At every return to the boot he had to resist the temptation to experiment there and then by surreptitiously hitting the head – that would indeed look odd!

He drove home, keyed-up, half-fearful, half-excited. And, in surges, elated.

*

He reversed into his drive. This was not his usual practice with such a narrow gate. But on this occasion he wanted the boot to be as close as possible to the bushes on the way to the shed, for the two deaf old brothers next door spent most of their waking hours observing their neighbours' comings-and-goings or looking for Boko, their wandering pet cat. In bad weather they were reduced to monitoring events from the window, and the cat joined them. On fine days, like today, they tended the front garden as a pretext, while Boko pursued other interests.

Getting out of the car, he responded fortissimo to their inquisitive pleasantries. Yes, it was indeed a nice day. Yes, he did have a day off. Just an odd one. Yes, it was an odd way to spend it, just driving around in all that traffic. The day might get even odder before it was over. No, he hadn't seen Boko, but he always popped up again, didn't he, the rascal!

'Of course I've seen your bloody cat, you silly old fools!' he muttered, as he turned away. 'I locked him in the shed accidentally-on-purpose. He was very partial to a piece of meat pulled from the joint in the fridge. Either the miaows have stopped, or you cloth-eared idiots haven't heard.'

He went into the house, changed into some gardening clothes, and came out again to transport his purchases into the shed which, at the end of a long garden full of shrubbery, was well hidden. He opened the door carefully and slipped in as quickly as he could: he did not want Boko to escape. Unwinking green eyes behind the lawn-mower followed, with a determined exactitude of which those ancient owners would have been proud, his captor's every movement ... as he propped an old sack over the window with a rake ... as he searched around in the gloom for a suitable piece of wood ... as he fixed the wood firmly in a vice on the bench.

He unwrapped the pig's head, now thawed into the consistency of flesh, with black congealed blood around the severed join, and he rammed it on to the wooden pseudo-neck sticking up in the vice. Was the pig-face beaming cheerfully, or was its lip curling in a sneer? The cat continued to peer at these proceedings with curiosity and, perhaps, with appetite.

Now for the hammers. He arranged them in ascending order of size and tried the weight and swing of each before giving the pig's head some speculative blows. With each hammer he started with quite a light, tentative tap and worked up to a powerful crack. The pig seemed to review these assaults with sardonic detachment.

He then reflected that he would do better to attack the pig from behind. This would be more germane to his intentions and would obviate the need to undergo constant quizzical inspection from his victim. He twisted the head round on its mounting so that it laughed in silent derision at the blank wall while the experimental hammering continued.

'Sneer away, you bastard!' growled his assailant; but the victim was not deterred.

One hammer in particular seemed the most satisfactory. Its heavy head and shortish shaft would permit a crushing blow in a confined space. The shaft would inevitably protrude from a jacket pocket, but a raincoat would conceal it effectively.

Now: what did it feel like to hit something alive, and to see it die under the blows?

*

He had already acquired some experience of harming and killing live creatures. As a boy he had pulled the wings from butterflies and watched them walking about as though they were simply confused. He had speared beetles with pins and studied their frantic wriggling. He had cut the heads from sluggish autumnal wasps, and had wondered why the stupid things struggled so, when it was obvious that they were wasting their efforts. He had flogged a large earthworm with a length of thick, waxed string until it was in pieces which writhed individually. He had kicked his sister's guinea-pig and had so plausibly sympathised with her grief at its unaccountable demise. ('Such a *feeling* boy!') And that baby bird which had fallen from its nest had not seemed to notice having its head twisted off. The animal world was, he found, quite inconsistent sometimes. As bad as the human one.

He particularly remembered the cat.

One day when he was thirteen he had been allowed to stay home alone while the others went out shopping. He watched through the kitchen window, and his hopes were fulfilled: a cat which wandered the neighbourhood had entered the tiny, high-walled back yard and was optimistically approaching the back door.

Keyed-up, half-fearful, half-excited, he ran upstairs to his bedroom to fetch a length of stout, smooth twine which he had secreted there. He ran downstairs again, pulled a piece of meat from the cold joint in the fridge, and went gently into the garden. He stooped, making little purring noises, and the cat zig-zagged to its new friend. He stroked the furry head lovingly while the animal investigated the smell of meat on his fingers. He tentatively offered the tit-bit, and as the cat took it with an air of graciously receiving tribute he slipped one end of the twine beneath its flea-collar under the pretence of a little tickle.

His victim, suddenly suspicious, pulled away, but was now on the leash of the doubled-over twine, with his captor holding both loose ends. The cat, panicking, began to bite and scratch at the twine, while the boy swiftly knotted the two ends together.

Hissing and howling, it found itself suspended from the washing-line hook high on the yard wall.

The cat scrabbled frantically up the wall. It might thereby have freed itself, albeit with the twine still looped in its collar. But it was suddenly, jerkingly, restrained: for the hook was a double hook, and the twine, having been wound over both, could not slip up or down. The cat fell and was brought up sharply by the neck.

Though it was still full of fight, it did not know what to do. What it usually did was of no use ...

Hissing, howling, lashing out.

Hissing, howling, scrabbling up the wall, falling, lashing out.

Hissing, howling, scrabbling up the wall, falling, lashing out, writhing.

Lashing out, writhing, shuddering.

Writhing, shuddering.

Shuddering, twitching.

Twitching into stillness.

Eyes protruding; tongue protruding.

Blood in the eyes, nose, mouth.

The reek of fear and excreta heavy in the air.

*

He remembered the wonderful sense of liberation from ordinariness. Surges of elation.

But, all the same, that was different: he could not trap and hang those he had in mind; and that experience was over half a lifetime ago. And it was not a sufficient preparation for bludgeoning something still alive and observing its translation into death from the heavy blows.

Leaving his trusty hammer on the bench next to the head – now somewhat battered and oozing dark blood, but still apparently taking it in good part – he went into the house and returned with a saucer of milk, which he placed on the shed floor. Boko was by now on the bench, sniffing at the pig's head, and wondering perhaps if he were quite hungry enough for this interesting but unfamiliar offering. But milk was a different kettle of fish! Most acceptable. He jumped down and strolled over to it with dignified condescension.

His head, poised elegantly over the saucer, was rammed into the milk by the force of inelegant iron. He twitched and died silently.

Milk and fresh blood – its redness contrasting with the pig's blackened blood – were added to the décor.

'*Dead pigs are not so red*
As the cat's head,
smashed in the garden shed,'
his executioner misquoted.

'So,' he thought, 'living things, hit hard enough, splatter blood, jerk a little, and die obligingly. Messy – but it works! – and I can do it!' He gave the pig's head a valedictory series of blows: to program the swing and the impact into his muscular sensations; and because he enjoyed it.

He put the head – was it really glaring now, and was it really giving a lop-sided leer? – into the box, and rammed it in with newspaper, from which he had removed the newsagent's mark. The warmly oozing cat went into a plastic bag given away by a national store.

He wiped the blood from the bench, floor and walls of the shed with absorbent paper, which he also put into the bag. There were, however, some residual stains. The ingrained dust of earth and years would probably not reveal what they were, but all the same he rubbed some earth into them, then swept it up and threw it on to the flower-beds.

He took the box and the bag to the car-boot (fortissimo: 'Yes, it *is* a nice day. No, I haven't seen Boko') and then went into the house to see to his clothes. They were only gardening clothes, but since they showed a few blood-spots they would have to go as well. He changed, minutely checking his face and hands for any blood-splashes, put the discarded clothes into another anonymous bag, and returned to the car.

(Fortissimo: 'Yes, I'm off again. Yes, all this coming-and-going, certainly an odd way to spend an odd day off. No, my wife's at work all day. Yes, I'll certainly ask her if she's seen Boko.')

*

Damian was on fire for Sharon. He felt that the world was a beautiful place which had been created chiefly, if not solely, in order that he might adore, pursue, flatter, and, if possible seduce Sharon (quite respectfully of course).

Sharon was not quite sure about her own fire. But she liked Damian and liked being seen by her friends to be the object of fervent pursuit by this sixteen-year-old Adonis. When not being lustful, he made clumsy attempts to be gentlemanly; the girls liked both and laughed at both. So she had agreed to bunk off school with him to go for a walk in the country. Surely, he reasoned, that counted as a little more than acquiescence.

He had managed to get them to seem hopelessly lost in a part of the woods which, in fact, he knew intimately from his previous incarnation as a mere mortal boy.

His amorous ambitions foundered on the rock of her womanly caution. She was fourteen and was determined not to get pregnant – not only because that was for mugs but also because she would assuredly get half-killed by her Dad if he found out that she'd ... that is, that she'd been ... that is, been with ... Somehow, being half-killed seemed to be a consequence both more probable and more terrible than being completely killed. She gave Damian a severe talking-to about real love and respect and self-respect – she knew that he would not have read the women's magazine from which she was quoting verbatim – not to mention being half-killed by one's Dad. And, as the Woman in Charge, she then consented with grace and enthusiasm to everything within her legalistic view of the permitted limits.

Damian's hopes that she might relent yet further were dashed by external intervention. Sharon heard, over the rushing of blood and the rustling of the wind in the trees and bushes which concealed their recumbent but not immobile forms, the sound of heavy footsteps on the hard, dry path nearby. Anxiously, she silenced and stilled the ardent Damian with a power of command that one day would quell even a Dad's wrath. Half-turning beneath her amorous slave, she saw, through the foliage, the approach of a stocky, angry-looking middle-aged man. Momentarily, she feared that it was her father, who had followed them, bent on ritual half-killing. It was not.

She knew the man but did not tell Damian.

Silently, they watched through a frame of green as the man, too well-dressed for a walk in the woods, and carrying a cardboard box awkwardly - hence the heaviness of the footsteps – came closer, looking this way and that. He put the box down, took from the top of it two plastic bags, each with something inside, and threw them into different parts of the undergrowth.

When he threw the box, it came straight at them.

14

They flinched as it caught in a gorse bush almost directly over their heads. The man paused, evidently wondering if he should, or could, conceal it better, and then, deciding to leave it where it was, turned and went quickly back the way he had come.

The young couple waited tensely until he was out of sight and earshot, then looked at each other and giggled. For a moment they were little children who had got away with being naughty. Damian gently urged her down again, but her curiosity about the box had now to be satisfied. Still half-sitting, with her slim bare arms around him but not resuming the marathon embrace, she said:

'I wonder what's in it?'

The answer came as if on cue. The bush had been imperceptibly sagging under the weight and allowing the box to turn. Suddenly, a sneering, battered, blackly bloody pig's head landed on the grass beside her.

She was naturally distressed; no longer, in fact, was she the Woman in Charge. Damian's ardour had been cooled by these distractions, but he was not without resource. He supplied calmness and comfort and made his caresses reverential rather than passionate. One part of his mind bragged that this was a stratagem to achieve success. Another part told him that he was trying to dispel fear: his sixteen-year-old fear that were creating a future.

*

The incident in the woods remained unreported. Sharon, while being consoled, analysed the situation. You are fourteen and sixteen, playing truant from school, very nearly disregarding the age of consent, and under threat of half-killing from those who gave you life. Rule One is that you don't draw attention to it. That means you don't go around accusing people of throwing battered pigs' heads. Suppose he denied it? They'd believe him. They always believe adults, and he was an important man. 'What were we doing there?' they'd ask. Anyway, if it's his pig's head – and we don't know that it isn't – is there a law against dumping it in the woods? No. But there are other laws. About truancy. About being, or not being, sixteen.

The head *did* look battered ... So what? Damian wanted to go back and have another look at it, but she did not. Hammer-marks may be very interesting to him as an intending carpenter, but not to her. He could look if he wanted to, but she wanted to go. Now.

Sharon thus saw to it that three people's secrets were kept.

The pig sneered and leered at the scene of erstwhile amorous dalliance. But not for ever. His skull, picked clean by birds, was found three years later during a school outing, and he ended his days smiling benignly – for, being now without lips, he had lost his scorn – in the Nature Study Room of the primary school down the road near where he had met his death.

*

Mr Knowsley always checked his bus at the end of his journey to the depot. You never knew what you might find.

If it had a name on it, or if the loss might cause distress to a child or an old lady, he always handed it in. Principles were important.

Otherwise, anything without a name on it ... well, much depended on whether it was any use, or would do the owner any great harm to be without it. Principles were important, yes, but Mr Knowsley, though not a mean man or an unkind one, really enjoyed finding things.

He knew that he ought to hand the bag of hammers in as lost property. But he was about to go off duty and couldn't be bothered with form-filling. Perhaps more to the point, he really liked this set of brand-new hammers. He proceeded with self-justification. Obviously the hammers had not been bought by a tradesman – a tradesman wouldn't buy a whole set. Now, a tradesman deserved to have the tools of his trade returned to him; that was an important principle. But this must be some suburban do-it-yourselfer, deciding to have a go at the week-end. No principle involved at all. Or perhaps there was some sort of anti-principle.

Mr Knowsley's interest in these ethical abstractions was small, as was his ability to articulate them, and was easily dispelled by two facts: he didn't know who this geezer was; and they were a nice set of hammers. Even if lacking a medium-to-heavy one.

CHAPTER 2

ODD JOBS

Professor Peccary sniffed yet again. The not-quite-dehydrated, incisive inhalation caused some of those present at the Staffing Committee to twitch, or grimace, or clench their fists, or shift in their seats, even though their long subjection to it made their reaction more subdued than it had been.

The head of the University's administration, Registrar John Boyle, found himself wondering, not for the first time, why Peccary was so detested. The man was, of course, detestable in his person, and people usually sought to avoid sitting next to him. Quite apart from his irritating habit, he was physically repulsive: he was fat to overflowing; his skin resembled unwashed hessian; his uncut finger-nails were black; his shirt-front was decorated with food stains; and his jacket collar was greasy from the long hair which dangled from a sparsely fuzzy pate. He looked smelly, though in fact he was not. To quote the Deputy Librarian, Bertrand Pyle, Peccary was fortunate in his appearance because he was behind it. The immaculately-suited Boyle had to allow that Peccary was unusually shabby and unprepossessing even amongst academics, so many of whom seemed bent on demonstrating that their superior minds were above such mundane matters as care with their appearance.

But Peccary was not merely disliked: he had actual enemies. Boyle counted himself one. Prominent amongst Peccary's many targets of vilification were certain of Boyle's staff who had incurred Peccary's displeasure by doing their jobs properly; by, for example, refusing to redraft Minutes of meetings to record what Peccary thought ought to have been said and decided. In his vendetta he had stirred up unparalleled antagonism between administrators and academics. Life, Boyle ruminated, as he fiddled with the heavy dark frame of his spectacles and polished the lenses unnecessarily, would be so much more peaceful without this odious fellow.

Then there was Peccary's own staff in English Literature. He had maliciously blocked promotions to Senior Lecturer or Reader by feigning a generous recognition of the claims of Lecturers in other Departments. Boyle remembered two or three English Lecturers who had tried to persuade the Committee that their cases were being unfairly disregarded. But Peccary's views had prevailed, and the rejected applicants were certainly entitled to hate Peccary's guts. And so was the Deputy Librarian, Pyle. for a rather similar reason. All this was common knowledge in the University, but nobody admitted to knowing it.

There was more ... The Students' Representative Council had been complaining to Boyle that Peccary's marking of essays was helpful when he liked the student and inexplicably terse, hostile, destructive even, when he did not. Peccary's reply to Boyle's letter asking for comments had been a masterpiece of insulting evasiveness. The matter really would have to be pursued before tempers rose any further ...

The Chief Librarian, Dr Brisley, the only other well-dressed person present, had made another mark on his agenda-paper to record the thirty-seventh sniff which the obese Professor of English Literature had perpetrated since the beginning of the meeting exactly thirty-five minutes ago. Brisley had started a little sum in the margin to work out the average time between each, and the predicted total if the meeting took the same time as usual. It gave him something to think about while the Professors were rabbiting on. He was, however, distracted when Professor Peccary, hitherto speechless though not silent, placed the right-hand side of his face in the position which he used for talking (another habit which annoyed everybody) and interrupted the Chairman to remark, with an air of authoritative definition:

'The basic wate per ar *[rate per hour]* is sufficient. We do not hev unlimited funds et ar dispezzal *[at our disposal]* if the twuth wair teld *[truth were told]*.' (Sniff.)

Dr Brisley irritably crossed out his half-completed calculation and began again, dividing thirty-nine minutes twelve seconds by thirty-eight.

The Staffing Committee of the University of Pillingham had spent most its time thus far, chewing over the proposed temporary employment of extra clerical staff during a reorganisation of student records. This item of business had been presented as a minor and purely formal one before the main part of the agenda. But the academic members, who frequently complained that their participation in the University's governing committees took time from their academic work (by which they meant research, not teaching), had perversely prolonged the discussion. They had repeated, in essence, the deliberations which had taken place between virtually the same individuals two weeks earlier in a meeting of the General Purposes Committee. The same preconceptions, the same mutual incomprehension, the same misattribution of unintended meanings and of hidden intentions, the same long-standing personal animosities – all had been paraded again. The same persons had asked the same questions, each of which had been anticipated and answered in the Registrar's background paper distributed in advance. But most of them had not properly read the papers before either meeting, and had not grasped any of the salient facts during the chaotic discussion which had ensued under a Chairman who was as ill-prepared, and as unsuited to the duties of office as they. Today, the Staffing Committee was required only to note the policy decision taken by the General Purposes Committee (themselves, for the most part, though in other roles) and to include the cost in its budget. The Registrar had thrice reminded them of this, but they persisted in discussing it as though they were still free to take a decision.

An incipient digression on the relative value of such-and-such a grade of secretary compared with such-and-such a grade of technician had been truncated by Peccary's intervention. His ignorance and rudeness had chanced to achieve what the Chairman should have done.

Brisley found himself wondering what, if anything, might lie behind Peccary's probably unthinking use of the phrase, 'If the truth were told'.

Peccary's salary – that of a long-serving Professor – worked out at several times the rate which he evidently thought suitable for an experienced middle-aged clerical worker of reasonable skill and sense of purpose. That would be the ratio if one assumed that each worked, say, a thirty-five-hour week. But, for thirty weeks of the year, at most, the learned Professor – if he was indeed learned – gave six lectures a week. These disquisitions had changed little for twenty years and were poorly attended because he was inaudible and left sentences confusingly unfinished. The rest of his time he would read; or write the odd article (for which he would obtain leave of absence or grant himself time off by misuse of his authority as Head of Department); or attend conferences at University expense; or sniff his way through Committee meetings. The dampening effect of his rude interruptions sometimes earned him the gratitude of dithering chairmen who had been concealing their deficiencies beneath a veneer of toleration.

For years Peccary had produced no significant research and had not imparted to his students one fact or pearl of wisdom which they could not have found for themselves in the University Library. He had, however, placed his early and falsely promising book on students' reading-lists, thereby keeping it lucratively in print.

Even a librarian with a regular commitment to his desk, Brisley thought in a mixture of resentment and self-righteousness, managed some research. Two or three people in Peccary's own Department did the real work there and earned Peccary's hatred for it; and if it were not for Peccary, would have been promoted by now, or perhaps even have got a Chair elsewhere (*'Char elswhar'*, as some of them put it).

Yes, Professor Peccary could rest assured that the 'twuth' had not been 'teld'. He could rest with even greater assurance that it would not be heeded even if it 'wair'. It was not in the best interests of the putative heeders – committees of his peers – to heed it, for their lives and evasions were often similar to his own. Not surprisingly, they thought the present arrangements eminently satisfactory, and wished them to continue indefinitely.

Unknown to members, Peccary's remarks had been even more uncharitable than usual because, on the way to the meeting, he had been waylaid in a chance encounter by the President of the Students' Representative Council, and his outrage had not receded one iota. 'Such pwetentious tatles *[titles]* these people give themselves, end insist on using! End the fellow ectualleh ixpicted a weplay *[reply]* to the lettah in which he had vartualleh accused a Pwofessah – *himself!* – of unfair and negligent mawking *[marking]*. Awl on the say-seh *[-so]* of thezz ewwogant, ungifted nonentities in his Literwawy Interpwetetion Class. Well, they'll faynd art *[find out]* how the weal warld warks' *[real world works]* when they gweduate and want weferwences! And that Wegistwar fellow, Boyle, seemed to be teeking it sarwiousleh! – in wevenge because Ay ventured a little just cwiticism of some of his minions. But – to be accawsted by a student in the stweet! Inconsiderwate and impartinent in the extweme!' (Peccary took an entirely different view of his own opportunistic approaches to Boyle or Brisley in supermarkets or by telephoning them at home. 'Thet was to smooth the twensection of impor'n't business.')

Any member of the Committee with sufficient fortitude to think of Peccary, and blessed, or cursed, with sufficient insight to divine his mental processes, would have thought that the sniff with which he placed a full stop to his interruption was unusually derisive, contemptuous, and menacing.

But the members were preoccupied with their own thoughts, which were centred on the prospect of personal or Departmental advantage in the rest of the meeting. Not so in the cases of Boyle and Brisley.

Boyle, with one ear still on the gassing for any breach of official policy or of legality, was wondering how best to bring the whole business of Peccary to a head. Plainly, it could not be allowed to ferment much longer, and a controlled dénouement was always better than a sudden eruption.

Brisley, likewise with one ear on the gassing for any mention of the Library, was wondering, as indeed was Boyle, if the general public would believe that this top 5% of the country's intellect (self-styled, at least, and popularly assumed to be such) would really behave as they did and were now doing. Stupid, petty, vainglorious, treacherous – the very opposite of 'the Professor' in innumerable bad films. No, they just wouldn't believe it.

He made a thirty-ninth mark on his agenda paper and checked the time. His calculation was not likely to yield a result significantly different from the average.

The meeting proceeded to the main item of business, for which the time remaining had been reduced by the prolix bickering over a simple and self-evident matter. Some Professors were proposing that certain Lecturers in their Departments should be promoted to Senior Lecturers, and they and other referees had written on their behalf. An imposingly and dauntingly fat wad of documents supported the recommendations, not quite with every superlative in the dictionary but certainly with some that were not. Professors in the less literate subjects, from the social sciences and engineering upwards, were wont to make strange declarations. One protégé's research publications had, apparently, 'flown from his pen' and 'enrichened' his subject, and the case was worth 'outlining in detail' ('not,' Brisley reflected, 'particularising in general?'). There was reference to 'one of the most crucial evidence' for some assertion or other; the word with the s-sound at the end, albeit -ce, had made the referee treat it as a plural, even though only one item of evidence was being cited. Another colleague was praised for his 'pastural' work with students, even though he had taken on the time-consuming 'secretarialship' of a professional society. Then came the referee who had 'appraised' himself of the 'budgetory' situation and was convinced that the recommended promotion would not have an 'imbalancing' effect on the 'ball-park costings'. This particular protégé had always been willing to turn from his research into the psychological effect of food 'adages' in order to help colleagues with Russian books printed in the 'acrylic' alphabet.

Most of the recommended promotions were nodded through. One case, however, occupied the Committee for half an hour. An entomologist had identified a particular type of mosquito which caused a debilitating fever to the rural inhabitants of the wetter parts of Asia. He had then worked with a pharmaceutical firm on the best method of exterminating the insects. None of the candidates for promotion, not even those from the Medical Faculty, could match this record of usefulness to his fellow man. Peccary, always perversely eager to endorse promotions outside his own Department, pointed this out, with the usual routine of preliminary snort, face-adjustment, and post-rhetorical sniff. Brisley, suppressing his chagrin at having to agree with Peccary, supported him. A small majority on the Committee eventually defeated the proposal, on the ground that the topic of research was not academically comprehensive or fruitful enough. Brisley discerned a reason for this pernickety and callous view. They had to assert the absolute value, as they saw it, of pure research, because they needed to assure themselves that they worked to intellectually exacting standards under a communal self-discipline, the criteria of which outweighed all others. Their research purity, which was their all, would be sullied if they gave weight to a practical value.

But they also liked, on some occasions at least, to think themselves tolerant, even an easy touch, provided that their research ethic was not at stake. So a technician, hauled up on charges of incompetence and absenteeism, which he had neither the wit nor the will to dispute, was given a last chance. The man could easily have been dismissed by now: the facts were not in doubt, the disciplinary procedures had been properly followed, and his Head of Department had already given him several 'last chances'. Indeed, it had been stated that the Department could not carry this passenger any longer without harming the instruction of students.

Brisley, and not only he, thought it ironic, even scandalous, that a person such as Peccary should sit in judgement on the matter. Peccary was, if anything, a worse offender, being more pretentious and more expensive.

The meeting broke up in schoolboy merriment led by Professor Peccary. It appeared that one of his staff was undergoing an operation for piles, and this was supposed to be funny.

'But we all' – snort – 'have Pyle-trouble!' he added.

This was a reference to the Deputy Librarian, between whom and Peccary deep hostility had existed for years. Brisley had never known in detail what the original rights and wrongs had been, and when he had taken up his own appointment the character and demeanour of both men neither made the process of establishing the truth attractive nor gave reasonable prospect of success in so doing. He decided that he had not heard Peccary's remark. Being thought distant and aloof had its advantages when there were things that one preferred not to see or hear.

Brisley, hastily noticing that he should divide forty-nine into one hour fifty-two minutes and that the rate per hour ('wate per ar'!) was more or less par for the course, returned to his office to sign some letters, and then went to the Staff Club for lunch.

*

He made periodical resolutions to lunch more frequently in the Staff Club. Apart from its physical convenience, it provided the opportunity of being known to, and therefore approachable by, staff other than the senior Professors whom he normally met on committees. But his repeated resolutions were just as repeatedly broken. The targets of his friendly overtures would often ignore him, returning a greeting for sure, but with minimum cordiality, and then making obvious their preference for gossip with immediate Departmental colleagues. Some would, however, abruptly exploit his presence by seeking to obtain favours in their borrowing allowance, or by complaining about having been charged a fine on an overdue book. Lunch there was boring, except occasionally, when it became acrimonious. Most of the Library staff avoided going to the Staff Club at all, for the same reasons.

The building was a modern pastiche of a Victorian house. It had a much-frequented bar and a less-frequented dining-room: The University could sell and consume drink at reasonable prices, but could not run an efficient routine catering service, even with a known and stable clientele of predictable habits, and even with its overheads concealed in the University's running costs.

He went past the bar to the dining-area, entered the self-service aisle, and, too late to change his intention, saw the heavy shape and snort-ready sneer of Peccary at a table with two or three others, including the Registrar, John Boyle. The latter, catching sight of Brisley, made a welcoming gesture – seeking, no doubt, to enlarge the circle and thereby dilute the unpleasantness. Brisley accepted the inevitable and, suppressing his distaste for the constant barrage of sniffing and verbal venom which had already bedevilled the morning, joined them.

'Par-suing me to wetarn [return] a book, Libwawian?' snorted the articulate side of Peccary's face.

'I never talk shop at lunch, Professor of English Literature.'

Brisley disliked being addressed by his function, as though this obscured his name and personal identity. But Peccary, for all that his profession required understanding of the nuances of words, took his manner of replying to be mere waggishness, and acknowledged it as such with a blunt nasal intake.

'You were saying something about a play ...,' prompted Brisley, from what he had overheard when he sat down.

'Yes' – (snort) – 'Ay'm geng [going] to see *The Cuntchy Waif* at our Playharse Theeyataa.'

'God help anyone within ten yards of him,' thought his hearers; and, aloud and incredulously from one of them, '*What's* the play?'

Peccary's respiratory *pièce de résistance* momentarily inhibited an answer, and Brisley supplied the information:

'*The Country Wife* – a Restoration comedy – Thomas Wycherley,' and mentally added a promise of unscripted farmyard sound effects from the stalls. Peccary combined the worst features of infancy with the worst features of old age and was only fifty-three.

'You learned fellows!' remarked Boyle, not unappreciatively.

'Anywee,' continued Peccary, 'Ay'm hevving to be a kind of gwass widower thar. May waif has gawn to be a cuntchy waif harself with fwiends. Gort the hice [*house*] to mayself until tomowwow.'

Even as Peccary delivered himself of this statement, Brisley thought that Peccary's implied discontent at being left alone was already being displaced by the pleasure of forthcoming solitude. It was as well that a man such as this could enjoy his own company, for he must surely get more than a normal share of it.

Peccary leered, snorted and vilified his way through lunch. A whole series of people, as individuals and categories, came under his lash.

His staff he held to be, with two exceptions, incompetent or idle, or both - although Brisley was well aware that half a dozen of them, which was a reasonable score in a large Department, were good teachers and had impressive research achievements. They were, if the 'twuth wair teld', superior in all but formal rank and power to this mean, spiteful, odious person. The two individuals strangely honoured by his approval were a young woman, Dr Bellsham, the one case for promotion which Peccary had ever proposed, and Mrs Mountjoy, the Departmental Secretary. Brisley had at first been puzzled by Peccary's support for Dr Bellsham, even though she was one of the good ones, because the old compost-heap was as bigoted about the advancement of women as about any other topic. But her good fortune was the outcome of his twisted mind. How could a man in his position, Peccary would have asked himself gleefully, be accused of any sort of personal prejudice in these days when such accusations are common, if he furthered the prospects of a young woman over those of older men? This promotion which he had engineered was the cloak of liberality and progressiveness beneath which his repressive malice would continue to flourish. His other exception he had selected in a less complicated way. The Departmental Secretary held power because she had knowledge, and because she would be loyal to him if he were loyal to her. To bind her to him was political common-sense. Both women were excellent at their jobs, and Peccary had done the right thing for the wrong reason.

His aggressiveness not assuaged by familiar victims in his immediate circle, Peccary turned on the outside world. Before lunch was over he had shaken out his venom on schoolteachers, lawyers, doctors and tradesmen. He had, it would seem, reproved myriads of these and put them in their place. Teachers were self-important, ill-educated little tin gods, who derived their conviction of grandeur from their lifelong association with juveniles. He blamed 'bed [bad] schooling' for the fact that local children had 'wendered may fwont door inoperwable by the insartion of glue into the fwont door lawk [lock]'; parental responsibility was obviously not a concept for him. And lawyers, those 'unscwupulous obscuwentist cheats', created their own income by their inability to write clear laws or to interpret them properly. Medics were irresponsible, arrogant, dangerous charlatans, nincompoops and ignoramuses, from whom mistakes can be virtually guaranteed whenever an illness goes beyond the sophistication of aspirin or granny's experience, but who cover up for each other more effectively and more unscrupulously than any trade union. On which subject, he had paid good money to have new carpet laid in the hall and had been unable to get the front door open for weeks in consequence. 'But will they send their joinah to adjust the daw [door]? Neh [No], tha're too buseh [busy] wuining somebody else's hem [home], Ay'll be bind [bound]!

When they're warking at all! *End* ixpicting to be peed *[paid]* for it!' {Snort.) ...
'... Blood bwothers of thet Deputeh Libwawian of yours, Pyle!' (Snort.) ... 'Ay'd hev done something abite him yars ageh' (Sniff.) It's mutual, of cawss, but ...' (Snort.)
'Few people are all good or all bad,' said Brisley. 'Let's not talk about all that ... Anyway, I think I must be getting back ...'

*

Professor Peccary is shortly to be removed, and not by a well-wisher, from active participation in our tale. He will be remembered, but not missed, except in the sense of good riddance.

If his remover knew Peccary, he would have disliked him; certainly there was much to dislike. He may even have hated his guts; which sentiment would probably have been reciprocated. But in either person this hatred may not have been avowed or even known to others. Would that putative animosity have been a sufficient motive to bump him off? Not, surely, without a more specific reason: which would imply some sort of private or professional relationship.

On the other hand, dislike, hatred even, may have been absent, or irrelevant. Suppose Peccary had been somehow in the way? Or had unwittingly blundered into a situation which turned lethal? Or mistaken for somebody else? So – perhaps he and his remover were strangers to each other?

Detective-Inspector Terence Hooligan does not often declare himself baffled; but is about to do so. The murderer knew the victim or did not ... hated him or did not ... had a specific reason or did not ...

Most of his investigations augured better than this one.

CHAPTER 3

HOOLIGAN'S SUNDAY

Detective-Inspector Terence Hooligan was still only half-awake, and was hoping that his wife, Jeanie, might soon stir, when a sudden ringing woke him up. In one continuous movement born of long practice, he rose from his bed and reached for the alarm clock where he always placed it – far enough away to ensure that he had to get out of bed to suppress it, and so would not drop off to sleep again. The ringing continued nonetheless and revealed itself to his gathering consciousness to be the bedside telephone. He had not set the clock last night. Today was Sunday. His chance for a lie-in.

Was.

Jeanie, whom thirty years of marriage to a policeman had programmed to ignore all inconvenient telephone calls, was still asleep. He picked up the telephone, grunted a rough-hewn version of his number, and with a sinking feeling recognised the duty sergeant's voice.

'Sorry about your rest-day, sir. We've a little problem, and you're next on the rota.'

'Tommy Balham's next,' mumbled Hooligan, his spirits in free fall.

'Not with appendicitis, sir. Surely you knew he'd been carted off to the infirmary? Operated on this morning, and now out of danger.'

Hooligan emitted noises which might have conveyed recollection, sympathy, annoyance, resignation, and enquiry for details of the crime.

'Not much known, sir. A murder, probably in furtherance of burglary, over on the south side. The local uniforms have the place sealed off, the photographer should be there by now, and I'm in process of rounding up the fingerprint boys and a doctor.'

'And me.'

'And you, sir. Detective-Sergeant Plumb should be there about the same time as you.' Hooligan grunted, 'Plumb, good,' as the duty sergeant continued: 'Will you want a car?'

'No, I'll take my own. Just give me the address again, will you? ... Has the victim been identified?'

Hooligan scribbled the details on a pad by the telephone, tore off the page and put it immediately in his notebook in his jacket pocket. At least he could not leave without it now, even in his Sunday morning condition. He began mechanically to make himself presentable. Jeanie, switching to another program of long standing, rose and drifted away to make coffee.

*

'Why,' thought Hooligan, driving through an amber light while ruminating on criminals in general, 'do they lash out when discovered? It raises the stakes ... Probably more of them are caught than of those who just leg it.'

But he then reproved himself for having already slipped into the duty sergeant's assumption that this was a panic reaction by a would-be burglar caught in the act; and began to review what he already knew. First, the address – *Pretoria*, Gladstone Close ... Large, oldish houses, late Victorian or Edwardian – inhabited by people who were fairly well-off as to salaries, but not with a lot of money to spare or to leave lying around. A higher-than-average number of professionals, including university people. Either large families in the whole house or couples in conversions into flats; and some old people living in whole houses because they had never moved to something smaller after the children had grown up and left.

So much for locale. But – a burglary gone wrong? There were more break-ins on the new estate further along the ring road. That made sense: the salesmen and managers, and such like, seemed to have congregated there, and often dealt in large sums of cash which the taxman had no need to know about. Did that suggest a mere amateur burglar in Gladstone Close – and one who wasn't very bright? Not necessarily. Many quite successful burglars weren't very bright. They need only to be lucky, with a dose of opportunistic bravery, to make a living at it. Nobody is lucky forever, so they come unstuck sooner or later. But was this one a burglary at all? That remained to be seen.

Apart from those musings, Hooligan knew only the victim's name: Peccary, Rupert Gavin. A Professor at the University; one of the city's red-brick Victorian intellectuals, then. Identified by a neighbour.

He drove through a red light, gave himself a caution, and imitated one of his colleagues in a mock announcement: 'Wanted for traffic offences, a fuzzy-haired overweight git, fifty, last seen wearing a tweed jacket and matching eyebrows. Do not approach on Sundays' ... And, in his own persona, 'Not much to go on - they'll never catch him.'

He turned from the main road, drove along a wide street with suburban shops – all closed except the newsagents – and thence into a narrow cul-de-sac. Two immaculate police cars were parked outside a house near the dead-end, as Hooligan began to think of it. Next to them, a battered green Ford, which he recognised as Plumb's latest investment, lowered the tone. A few adults and children had collected, unanimous that there would be something worth gawping at. At least two curtains moved slightly as he got out of his car.

A very young uniformed constable had opened his car door for him briskly. It was his first murder. 'Mr Hooligan, sir. The body's round the back with DS Plumb, sir. This way.'

'Er – no, you just hang on here and keep people out. I'll find my own way.'

He left the disappointed constable and entered the front garden through a broken-down gate between overgrown privet hedges. Ahead, a weed-covered path led through a shaggy dandelion lawn to an enormous front door with several colours of paint peeling from it. The door-knocker was a tarnished brass clenched fist. Huge double-glazed windows, an incongruous modernity in such a context, glared either side of the door, and there were smaller versions on two further floors above. From the main path a narrower one branched off between the garage and the house and led round to the back. Hooligan noticed that the section of the main path to the front door was more overgrown than the rest. Passing the garage window, he peered in and saw a car with a University parking permit and an out-of-date tax disc.

'Was the murdered man's character apparent from his property?' Hooligan wondered. 'Self-indulgent and careless?'

On a paved, un-weeded patio at the back of the house, Hooligan found Plumb and another uniformed constable. They both knew him well and did not intrude even by a greeting while he looked around.

The body of an obese man apparently in his late fifties lay slumped against the back door. Blood from head wounds had run down his sneering face into his collar and jacket and had congealed. Hooligan tried not to be distracted by the sneer – people being murdered seldom look pleased about it – and inspected the rear of the house. A ground floor window had fresh marks on the lower frame. The garden, with several untended bushes, could have provided good cover, but was not a route for entry or escape – the broken glass on top of the high walls saw to that. Hooligan also noted a bunch of keys hanging from the lock.

He looked at Plumb, wondering how he managed to keep his short hair always exactly the same length. Ex-army, of course ... 'Morning, Ted. Constable – Page? I gather we have an identification, Ted.'

'Professor Peccary, sir. A neighbour identified him. I've sent her back to the house next door, along with the paper-girl who found the body. It looks as though someone's tried to force that window – you'll see the marks from some sort of lever, and they're entirely new. Looks like whoever did it was disturbed when the Professor came back.'

'I wonder: Did he expect the Professor to come round the back?'

'I suppose not. That would have made him panic, perhaps.'

'If he'd studied the house, he'd have assumed that they don't use the front door.' Seeing Plumb's puzzled expression, Hooligan explained about the weeds, but added: 'Of course, I'm only guessing about the front door. But a pro would have got the facts straight one way or the other, to eliminate surprises on the job.'

Plumb continued: 'The victim said he was going to the theatre, and by car – all according to the neighbour. The back garden's obviously a trap, so I suppose the murderer felt he couldn't run away and lashed out while the old boy was fumbling with his keys. You'll see the keys are still in the back door, sir. No doubt the murder weapon was the jemmy or whatever he was using on the window.'

'Why didn't he just hide behind the bushes when he heard someone coming?'

'That I don't know, sir.'

'I've a horrible feeling about this one, Ted. The more we'll look, and the more we'll dig, the less we'll know.'

He looked at the marks on the window-frame more closely, and said, 'These look more like a large screwdriver. So what did he hit him with?'

He looked at the body again, particularly the mess on the top and back of the head; but could deduce nothing more. 'Anyone in the house?'

'Not as far as we know, sir. Unless the murder's in there now, of course! We didn't go in on arrival, because it would have meant disturbing the body before the photographer had been to fix the position. Which he's done. He left a few minutes before you were due, so I decided to wait for you to get here. He'll come back again if there's anything you want photographed inside.'

'But the house is believed to be empty?'

'So the neighbours believe, sir. The Professor lives – lived, I mean – with his wife. She's apparently away for the week-end, and we don't have an address for her. And the neighbour says there's a son in Australia.'

'While we're waiting for the doctor, I suppose we might look in the bushes ...'

'I thought you thought he wouldn't have hidden there, sir?' Plumb looked at Constable Page for confirmation; the latter looked bewildered in reply.

'No – I meant "Why didn't he just hide and then scarper once the Professor was inside?" Look, suppose you're a burglar, you're having a go at the window, you hear the car coming into the drive. You only need a couple of seconds to be out of sight. The victim has to get out of the car, open the garage door, get back behind the wheel, drive in, get out, lock the garage, and come round the back. Unless the burglar's stone-deaf, the victim couldn't possibly have surprised him.'

'Then he intended the murder!' said Plumb, brightly.

'Or at least intended to get into the house, and therefore intended to knock the Professor out. By now he would have realised that he had no hope of opening the window. As you see, it's painted shut. Probably he couldn't see that in the dark, but certainly realised it wasn't moving.'

'So we're looking for an incompetent burglar with a panicky nature, sir!' remarked the constable, with an air of definition.

Hooligan, who never told young constables to mind their own business, was silent, and then said: 'Perhaps. But I don't understand ... What don't I understand? If he just wanted to knock the Professor unconscious and get inside, why hit him several times, and that hard? Could just have got carried away, I suppose ... And why did he then make off, if he'd wanted to get into the house? Yes, I suppose he could have panicked ... feeling he'd bitten off more than he could chew ... '

'Suppose,' offered Plumb, 'he had wanted something in the house – something he knew was there or hoped was there – but he thought it risky to leave the body on show? A body on the doorstep wasn't in his plan, so he scarpered.'

'He could have taken the body inside, sir' the constable suggested, still eager to make an impression.

'Then he must be a little chap,' Plumb deduced. 'That could be it, sir. The Professor's a heavyweight, and the murderer's an incompetent little tich of a burglar. Shall I get on to Criminal Records, sir? A list of weedy local burglars would make interesting reading.'

'It's a valid line of enquiry,' Hooligan said, and fell silent again. As he was about to go over to the bushes, as he had intended a little earlier, they heard the sound of a vehicle drawing up in the road. 'At night the burglar would have heard more than we do now,' he said. 'Turning into the drive, the business with the garage door ... and he'd have seen the headlights ... That must be the doctor arriving now. I'd like him to see the body before it's moved - and if we go in, the Professor will fall inside when we open the door.'

As if on cue, a large, cheerful, sandy-bearded man carrying a doctor's bag strutted round the corner. An ambulance man hovered behind him.

'Hallo, Terry!' boomed the stentorian Dr Bossom. The police officers winced slightly but were welcoming. 'A patient for me, I believe? Well ...' – he peered at the late Professor – '*he* won't be complaining to the BMA again!'

'What do you mean? And what's the "again"?'

Bossom discoursed and jovially declaimed as he peered, poked, and made notes.

'That's Professor Peccary. Well known in medical circles. In thirty years as a doctor I have never come across anyone with such a talent for attracting and expressing hostility – directed at anyone and everyone, so I gather, but certainly at the medical profession. An incredible record of sustained, petty bickering and complaint. You know, if someone had saved him from drowning – which nobody who knew him would have done – he'd have complained if his rescuer had pulled a button off his coat in the process ... Anyway,' continued Bossom, pulling at Peccary's scowling eye, 'he's certainly stoking away down below now. It must have happened some time last night, and I imagine that having his nasty brains ventilated was the cause. I'll give you a proper report later today, and obviously the apparent cause of death will need verification. I may not be able to establish the time of death too accurately ... If he's been out here all night, he'll have got pretty chilly at an earlier stage ... On the other hand, if you can find out when he last ate, the contents of the stomach will reveal how long the process of digestion went on afterwards ... So, Professor Peccary's dead, eh? Cantankerous old bugger!'

'You didn't do it, I hope?' asked Hooligan, uneasy at the possibility that the doctor's defamatory remarks were audible a hundred yards away.

'Sorry to disappoint you, Terry ,' chuckled Bossom, still addressing his imaginary distant audience. 'In the first place, doctors always do a more subtle job than that. In the second place, half the medical profession of the city would give me an alibi if I had. In the third place, it might have been one of them, and *I'll* provide the alibi. Can I have him now? Excellent!'

He beamed encouragingly at the ambulance man, who was joined by a smaller version. They loaded the outsize Professor on to a stretcher and departed with the jolly doctor, whose booms and roars slowly abated and were then confined in the vehicle which bore him away.

The silence was almost excruciating in its contrast. Hooligan brooded on what Dr Bossom had said about the deceased's character. One did not expect a Professor to be like that, although Hooligan recalled the difficulty which his daughter Carolyn had encountered recently as a student elsewhere. Her Professor had assured her that she did not need Ancient Greek for the archaeology module, then had required analysis of Greek inscriptions, and had denied categorically that she had raised the problem with him at all.

The constable was the first to speak: 'A revenge-murder!' He savoured his idea like a hungry man smelling a roast joint. Hooligan smiled ambiguously, while Plumb, anxious to demonstrate his masterly caution in front of his chief, shook his head and commented, 'We don't know that either.'

Hooligan moved towards the back door. 'C'mon, Ted, let's go in. It's just possible that the murderer did go in and decided to leave the keys here to create the impression that he's made off in a panic ... might be some relative or other with a reason to be staying here ... would claim to have taken sleeping pills and didn't hear all the goings-on ... improbable, of course ... And suppose the murderer and the burglar are two unconnected people who coincided ... equally improbable, but all we have at the moment is an open mind and speculation ...

'... Constable, keep anyone from touching the door or window until Fingerprints are here. Meantime, have a look in the bushes for anything unusual - anything dropped recently, such as matches, fag-ends, packets – and look for footprints, without adding your own. And if anyone rushes out of the house looking as though he's just thumped a couple of coppers, ask him to wait.'

Hooligan did not expect the bushes to yield any useful discoveries. But you never knew, and in any case it was good for morale to give the constable something to do.

As they entered, stepping over the pool of congealed blood, Hooligan stopped and mused: 'They probably hadn't used the front door for some time, when you consider the condition of the path ... Let's look at the front door. If it's out of use for any reason, that would suggest – though not prove - that the murderer knew Peccary and his movements, and was relying on him to use the back door. And perhaps knew that Mrs Peccary was away.'

They went through the kitchen – the immaculacy of which contrasted with the exterior of the house – and into the dark hall, which smelled of new carpet. The pile of the carpet by the inner front door was slightly scuffed in the beginnings of a semicircle. Through a glass panel they could see a large vestibule, with the huge main door beyond.

'That explains it,' said Hooligan, as he tried the inner door and found that it would hardly move. 'They had new carpets fitted and couldn't open this inner door without damaging the carpet. No doubt, like the rest of the world they're waiting for a man to come and do a job – in this case, to take a bit off the door. So what does that tell us?'

'That they've told paper-boys, postmen, various delivery people, to come round the back.'

'And at least one joiner knows as well,' added Hooligan. 'And, of course, the carpet firm – I don't see the Professor laying this carpet himself. Make a note to check on these things, Ted.'

He brooded for a moment, and then said: 'What do we know so far?' The question was rhetorical, for he continued with the answer, such as it was, himself.

'The murderer could have escaped by simply hiding in the bushes when the Professor returned – but he chose not to. This tells us that either he was a deliberate killer who tried to make it look like a burglary that went wrong – or that he was a burglar who intended to knock his victim out, or even didn't mind killing him but hadn't planned to. If we go for the burglar-theory, perhaps he still hoped, or even knew, that there was something worth stealing in the house, but lost his nerve after he'd killed, and ran off. Or might have thought, for some reason or other, that he was about to be disturbed, with a body to explain away. But this burglar-theory doesn't go with the more frenzied attack. Deliberate murder is more likely, though, again, not proved. And I'm still puzzled about the murder-weapon.'

'Surely, a deliberate murderer,' said Plumb, 'would have used the keys to put the body in the house, sir? That would have delayed the discovery of the body, as well as allowed him to ransack the place to make it look more convincing. And doesn't the same go for the burglar-theory? – if he didn't panic, I mean. We don't know that he *did* panic.'

'That's true as well, Ted. We'll examine the rooms for signs of disturbance, of course ... But, sticking to our present theme ... unfortunately, there's more. Suppose he didn't use the keys in the lock at all. There was no moon last might, there's no light at the back of the house, and whether he panicked or not, he might simply not have seen them. And he may have thought it safer just to clear off, whether he was an intentional murderer whose plan was only to kill and run, which I think more likely but unproved, or just a burglar on the prowl with nothing specific inside to go for. So really we still know nothing.'

Hooligan pulled again at the inner front door. It opened a few inches and was then held firmly in position by the braking effect of the carpet. It could be forced a little further, as the marks on the carpet showed.

'You're fashionably scrawny, Ted. Can you squeeze through and try the front door?'

Plumb edged uneasily through the gap, hardly comforted when his chief made a considerate but unnecessary suggestion – 'Mind your goolies on the lock!' – and crossed a vestibule of broken mosaic and chipped plaster. He opened the front door – this briefly excited the spectators in the street and caused more than one curtain to twitch eagerly – and was on the point of closing it again when he stopped and peered more closely at the lock.

'What is it, Ted?'

'It looks like … glue in the lock, sir.'

Hooligan looked with more than displeasure at the gap which separated them. 'I'll come round,' he said. 'Quicker than a diet, and better than an operation.'

It was obvious, as they looked at the front door lock, that glue prevented the key from being inserted, even though the door remained usable from inside by turning the knob.

'So,' said Plumb, 'the murder was deliberate. He didn't know that the front door was out of use because of the carpet, so he glued up the lock to make the Professor walk round the back – not knowing he would have done that anyway – and faked an attempt on the back window to make it look like burglary. Then he waited for the Professor and hit him while he was opening the back door.'

'Hold on!' Hooligan raised a cautionary hand. 'This could still have been either a deliberate murderer or a burglar, in either case knowing about the door and thinking it a good idea to make us think that he didn't know. The glue could also be unconnected with the crime – kids playing a trick, perhaps, or one of the many people who seemed to have disliked the Professor and wanted to annoy him. It's just another thing we can't interpret. The next thing, Ted, is to look around inside – with just the possibility that the man we want is in there.'

They went back into the house – Hooligan choosing the long way round again, since his reasons were still valid, and Plumb squeezing through the gap, just to show that he could. Hooligan was greeted at the back door by the constable, who announced that there were no clues or footprints by or amongst the bushes.

Meeting inside again, Hooligan and Plumb made a tour of the house. It was a cobwebby mess, with the exception of the pristine kitchen; the Professor's study could have been taken for a seedy second-hand bookshop. But the house was empty apart from themselves, and there were no obvious signs of burglary. The simplest, indeed the only, means of discovering if a burglary had been committed was to ask Mrs Peccary if anything were missing or if any part of the established disorder had been disturbed. She could also tell them which carpet firm and joiners knew about the immobilised door.

Two fingerprint men arrived. Hooligan, called by the constable, directed their attention to the back window, the back door generally, and the front door with particular reference to the keyhole area, but he did not expect their efforts to produce any useful information. If Mrs Peccary could point out any particular places in the house which seemed to have been touched, they could be examined in detail; but that would have to wait until she returned. He was beginning to feel that the whole case so far was a set of blind alleys with red herrings in them.

Meantime there were other routines to follow. An officer would have to remain in attendance to keep not only the public but also the Press away: from the upstairs window Hooligan had seen that the little knot of gawpers had been joined by several men whom he knew to be reporters. Two always hunted as a pair: one had a beer-belly to which he clutched a notebook, and the other, as thin as a rake, held a camera and looked like a two-legged tripod. The officer left at the premises would have to intercept Mrs Peccary on her return, tell her what had happened, and get her to examine the house for signs of disturbance. That meant a WPC; not one of the more pleasant duties, as Jeanie would confirm.

It would be interesting to see if Mrs Peccary could prove that she had been elsewhere all night. The WPC could see to that, too – the question disguised as 'Who could have been absolutely certain that you were away? Might they have told other people?' Though this murder did not look like a marital job ...

It was still possible, of course, that being married to such an unpleasant man as that described by Dr Bossom may have been too much for her. The neglectful and self-indulgent character implied by the combination of a messy house with modern double-glazing and the out-of-date road license ... the contrast between the kitchen and the rest of the house, which suggested incompatible standards ... the deceased's reputation as a nasty piece of work ... all that might have come to a head. But wives don't usually murder their husbands without a more specific reason ... so had there been some kind of critical incident? She would have to be investigated ... But on the other hand, there were signs of planning in the murder. If Mrs Peccary were the culprit, wouldn't she be more likely to have just picked up a weapon in her superb kitchen and done for him there? Unlikely that she would have arranged the scene at the back door to put us off the scent ... And she might even have loved him. Women can be very peculiar sometimes.

Hooligan put Plumb on to interviewing the paper-girl and the neighbour as soon as possible. And house-to-house enquiries would need to be made in the cul-de-sac, if not beyond it.

Sitting in a squad car he telephoned for some assistance with these tasks, and then ran through with Plumb a list of questions. Who lived in each of the houses close by? Were there any recent arrivals? Had the Professor any known enemies? Was he believed to have any money or valuables in the house? Who had visited him recently? Who knew about the front door? Had anyone else had glue put in their locks? Who might have put it there? Had any strangers been seen hanging about?

'Well, Ted, that should cover it. Tell the troops what to ask, and to get a note of the exact names of informants and other occupants of the houses, and we'll check them against the Voters' List and follow up anyone missed out.'

He levered himself out of the squad car and made for his own. 'I'll attend the post-mortem and find out what was in the Professor's stomach and pockets, and so on. And perhaps something about the murder-weapon.'

He made his way to his car and was intercepted by the reporters.

'Nothing to tell. Sorry. It's all very boring and entirely useless at the moment.'

'Was the Professor murdered?' enquired Beer-Belly, enthusiastically.

'Professor Peccary is dead,' replied Hooligan, 'and we're treating it as murder. But the cause of death needs verification, which is where I'm off to now. Nothing is going to happen here except house-to-house routine enquiries: which you will keep away from, please. You must understand that I don't want this investigation compromised by your questioning of neighbours in advance of my officers speaking to them. If you're good, you can follow me down to the morgue and I might be able to tell you something after the post-mortem.'

Beer-Belly and his colleagues knew that Hooligan was more likely than many investigators to help them if he could, and more likely to obstruct them, and efficiently, if provoked, so they always accepted his stick-and-carrot. The prospect of post-mortem results was in any case devoutly to be wished, so they made off ahead of him.

On the way, Hooligan nipped into a newsagent's to get Tommy Balham a 'Get well soon' card, and wrote on it, as to a friend, 'You bastard! You've dropped me right in it!'

Driving on, he reflected ruefully that so far in this untidy crime most items of information had several possible interpretations and could be combined to sustain any one of them. The criminal was either a burglar or a deliberate murderer. In either case he did or did not panic. If he had not panicked, either he did or did not wish to create the impression of having done so. Either he did or did not know of his victim's circumstances – that he was alone, that he was returning late, that he would enter by the back door. The house was or was not being burgled at the time of the murder. The glue in the lock either was or was not part of a plot. The murder, if deliberate, either was or was not an act of personal animosity; in which case, it was either a deliberate killing or an attack that got out of hand.

Dismayed, he realised that he had no obvious way of proceeding with his investigation.

The post-mortem carried him no further. The cause of death was confirmed as a number of hammer-blows to the back of the head by a right-handed person: who may have carried the hammer just for protection or may have intended murder; so the incompetence implied by the choice of a screwdriver to force the window may have been genuine or feigned. The stub of a theatre ticket in the dead man's pocket was consistent with Peccary's late return the previous evening. His wallet, containing about twenty pounds in cash, was still in his pocket. Its presence might suggest almost any theory about the murderer: a panicky burglar or a deliberate killer might well have left the wallet. Hooligan made a mental note to discover if the Professor had withdrawn much cash from the bank recently: perhaps a larger sum had been taken from the wallet and twenty pounds left behind in order to mislead. The contents of the stomach showed that a meal had been eaten about four hours before death. Assuming that he had eaten at a restaurant near the theatre, there was something else to look into: perhaps the Professor had been with someone or had been followed by someone. Hooligan was uncomfortably aware that he was by now scraping the bottom of the barrel. But if that is where you are, what else is there to scrape?

The deceased's will, if he had made one, might indicate someone with a motive, although he had not lived in a style which suggested wealth enough to kill for. No – this case had the smell of dislike rather than acquisitiveness. But check for a will, anyway. The absence of a will would bring Mrs Peccary back into the picture, of course ... and so would a will in favour of someone else ...

The only other thing to do while these various enquiries were pursued was to look for Peccary's enemies. And the best place to look for a man's enemies is exactly where you would look for his friends: amongst his family and his neighbours – they were already being investigated - and his colleagues.

A visit to the University of Pillingham was called for: first thing Monday morning.

Tomorrow morning.

CHAPTER 4

SCHOLARS AND GENTLEMEN

Hooligan returned home for what was left of his day off. During the course of the evening he learned on the telephone that the various enquiries set in motion had yielded neither surprises nor clues. A cheque book in the house revealed that the twenty pounds still in Peccary's wallet represented a reasonable residue of a recent cash withdrawal; Peccary was now known to have dined alone at a restaurant near the theatre before seeing the play; and the stage of digestion of the meal fixed the time of the murder at around 11 30 pm, exactly when he would have reached home if he had left the theatre at the end of the performance. He had not been accompanied or followed, as far as could be ascertained.

The joiner who had been asked to adjust the inner front door to restore free movement over the new carpet was a respected local tradesman. His son, Damian, had accepted the carpet firm's commission over the telephone in his father's absence. But the job was repeatedly postponed because of his father's disinclination to do another job for Professor Peccary.

There were no unexplained fingerprints in the house or at the door and window. Other houses in the cul-de-sac had had glue squirted into their front door locks. But that could have been a childish prank against them all, and nothing to do with the murder; or the murderer's attempt to conceal his targeting of Peccary. In either case, no light was shed on the useless deduction that the murderer did or did not know about the carpet and the obstructed door.

Mrs Peccary, who had returned home, had known about the glue, and so had her husband: in which case, both of them may well have declaimed about this *lèse-majesté* to others. The impediment to using the front door may therefore have been known to people who did not know about the carpet.

The widow had also stated that there was no sign of disturbance in the house. Her alibi had been checked and substantiated: for several hours before and after the murder she had been eighty miles away with three old school friends. Reading between the lines of her reported reaction to widowhood - calm and almost casual - it seemed that her feelings for her late husband were on a par with everybody else's, if Dr Bossom's character-assassination was to be believed.

'If that's how she felt, she should have left him years ago,' Jeanie remarked. 'But you, my lad, are having an early night, and it's starting right now. I've had quite enough of The Body on the Doorstep, thank you. Anyway, you can't do any more until you've interviewed his colleagues at the University tomorrow. If old Harry Bossom's even half-right, probably one of them had it in for him. From my vast experience of police work, I'd say he was done in by a friend.'

Her claim to expertise was only self-irony: she referred to her one year as a policewoman. On marrying the then-Constable Hooligan, she had resigned in order to tackle the more exacting job of policeman's wife, audience, secretary, organiser, and sounding-board, when not being a mother and, for a few years until recently, working for the Citizens' Advice Bureau.

'And,' she continued, 'you'll need all your wits about you tomorrow, so that you can keep up with the learned Professors. Though I'm sure you're as learned as plenty of them. You've got your law degree!'

'Correspondence course ... never actually went ... But there's one good thing,' he mused, changing the topic: 'The crime wasn't on University premises, so that idiot Leslie won't be mucking things up.'

'Leslie?'

'Don't you remember Geoff Leslie? Security Officer at the University. Used to be on the force here. The previous Chief Super gave him the best reference ever, to get rid of him. Rumour says he's even more useless there than he was with us, though it's difficult to see how. I wonder how he manages to hold the job down in a university of all places. The man's practically mentally deficient.'

*

The next morning, Hooligan and Plumb called at the Vice-Chancellor's office, only to learn that the head of the University had gone to London for a meeting.

'I could fit you in next Thursday,' offered his secretary, unimpressed by a Detective-Inspector investigating a murder. 'Or would one of the Pro-Vice-Chancellors do? The senior one, Professor Niprollok, is expected quite soon. I'm sure he could spare a minute or two.'

'That would be extraordinarily kind of him,' commented Hooligan. He had intended heavy sarcasm, but the secretary inclined her head and beamed graciously with more sign of practice than of talent.

There was a brief pause.

'Do we wait here or go somewhere else?' Hooligan asked, patiently.

'I'll take you,' she said with an air of suddenly reaching a difficult decision, levered herself up, and trotted ahead of them along a corridor. Her tight skirt, which struggled to constrain its adipose contents, and her high heels obliged her to use at least as much energy in up-and down movement as in actual progress forwards. She led the way into an office slightly smaller than the first.

'Good morning, dear,' she said to an older version of herself. 'These gentlemen are policemen, you know, investigating that simply *awful* murder of poor Professor Peccary.'

'Yes, dear. Have they caught him yet?' It did not occur to her to ask those present who would have known.

'I don't know, dear. They're here to see Professor Niprollok. Just for a few moments.'

She bounce-dashed away.

'Yes,' said the older version. 'I'm sure he could fit you in.'

'Yes,' said Hooligan, 'I'm sure he can.' He sat down, and Plumb followed suit.

The older version consulted a desk diary and announced: 'This afternoon at ten to four.'

'When is the Professor due in?'

'Oh, any minute now …'

''Any minute now will be perfectly convenient for us to see him.'

The older version was about to reply with some asperity when the door from the corridor opened. A wiry little man in a stained suit bustled in, his bald pate shining under the artificial light, and his long hair back-and-sides projecting limply like coat-tails in the wind.

'Morning, Lucy.' He had a thick, gravelly voice which did not match his appearance. 'Professor Thingummy here yet?'

He did not wait for an answer and, ignoring Hooligan and Plumb, went into his adjoining office. Hooligan, having by now realised that an ounce of direct action would carry him further than a ton of good manners, followed him in and sat down. Plumb, bringing up the rear, waved his warrant card in admonition to the Great Terrible Lucy as she attempted to regain control of the situation, and cut off her Great Terrible Glare by firmly closing the door. Hooligan noted with concealed amusement how his amiable assistant could turn on an implication of thuggishness when necessary. ('I suppose I do the same sometimes …')

Niprollok, outraged, began to say 'Gra … gra …', which must have held meaning for him, if for nobody else. He stopped when Hooligan, showing his warrant card, introduced himself and Plumb, and continued: 'We are investigating the murder of Professor Peccary, and need to talk to some of his colleagues. Can you arrange this?'

'Later perhaps. I have appointments this morning.'

'Professor' – Hooligan whispered, and Niprollok found himself trying to hear – 'you have an appointment now. With me. This is a murder investigation, and the University is going to be helpful. I am going to interview the deceased's colleagues. Today. Beginning immediately. Beginning with you. I want you to help me. You want to help me.'

Hooligan then smiled urbanely and continued in a normal volume: 'We don't want to interrupt the normal work of the University any more than necessary. The easier it is, the less the disruption. I'm sure you can help us, can't you?'

'I *am* very busy. Under intensive pressure, in fact. Gragra. Are you telling me that my protests will be rendered nuggetry?'

Hooligan, beneath his practised persuasiveness, had already been reeling at the rudeness which he had encountered so far, and at the general obliviousness to life in the outside world. He had not been prepared for an illiterate professor, who preferred 'intensive' to 'intense' without knowing the difference except that the longer one sounded better, and who made 'nugatory' suggest some form of processed stone or chilled chicken-pieces.

'Well,' continued Niprollok, 'you don't want me, you want to see the English Department. Well. I'm sure that can be authorised.'

'It's been authorised already, sir – by the criminal law. I'm asking you to make it a little easier for both of us by your co-operation. We do need the co-operation of the public, you know.'

'The public?' Niprollok was confused by this seeming change of subject. 'Gra. What have the public got to do with it?'

'In this instance, sir, the University is that part of the public whose co-operation we need: the public as distinct from the police.'

'Yes ... yes... I think I see ...' Niprollok began reflecting on the idea, which was new to him, that the University could be part of the public. He had always regarded that part of the population which was not the University as the public.

Further dialogue was precluded by a knock at the door, which heralded the arrival of an elderly, immaculate, slightly stooping figure, wearing heavy spectacles. His appearance was distinguished and his manner cordial. He shot a smile at Niprollok, who began pointing and saying 'Gra-gra-gra' as though making introductions.

'Detective-Inspector Hooligan, I believe,' the newcomer said gently, and held out a hand. Hooligan began to hope that he had met a Professor worthy of the title after all, and introduced Plumb.

'I'm the Registrar – John Boyle – Chief Administrator. Anything that happens here is my fault.' Hooligan assumed that this was Boyle's routine opening gambit. 'Now, Inspector, my spies tell me that you'd like to get to our English Department. If you will come this way, I'll make the arrangements.'

After the last five minutes during which some cherished illusions had been shattered, Hooligan and Plumb were pleased to be in such different hands. While they were led to a third office, Hooligan made small talk, partly because they were in a public corridor in which coming to the purpose of their visit would have been inappropriate, and partly because he had often found that it was precisely in small talk that people reveal their true natures. He decided that Registrar Boyle was not to be trusted if cornered and had scant toleration of being slighted. The proverb that 'revenge was a dish best eaten cold' came to mind. ('Or is it a quotation from somewhere?') But he perceived an unusual ability to get things done and to stay out of trouble.

Seated in Boyle's office – and it was the first time that morning that anyone had invited them to sit down – Hooligan came to the point.

'We need to build up a picture of the deceased, sir. What kind of man was he? Who were his habitual associates? How did he get on with them?'

'Obviously you have no particular suspect, or you would not be asking general questions,' observed Boyle. He left Hooligan no time in which even to display resolution not to respond and continued: 'Professor Peccary associated with a large number of people, as one might expect. I would not say that he got on well with anyone in particular.'

Hooligan perceived that Boyle felt it important to be forced to say more rather than to do so voluntarily, and asked, 'Is there anyone in particular with whom his relationship was ... shall we say ... bad?'

'Since you ask me so directly, Inspector, I can only say that virtually everyone in his Department, and many elsewhere, seemed to dislike him. I'm afraid that you would have a very long list. But I really cannot believe that anyone in his Department would go so far as to ... be involved in the crime in any way. And didn't I hear on the news that there were signs of burglary? Surely, then ...?'

'We follow up many possibilities, sir, and some of them turn out to be red herrings. There were, as you say, signs of burglary, but it would still help us to have a picture of the last few days.'

Boyle accepted Hooligan's vague allusiveness; so to do was in his nature and was one of his many professional skills.

Half an hour later, Hooligan and Plumb were in the late Professor Peccary's office in the Department of English Literature. A search revealed no clues.

Boyle had produced a list of Departmental academic and other staff, to which were added the names of a few students with whom the murdered man had had direct dealings; and he had made it clear to the Departmental Secretary that every co-operation must be given. She made up a list of appointments based on gaps in the teaching timetable. Hooligan noticed that they all seemed to have ten hours' teaching a week at most and wondered what they did the rest of the time – let alone during the twenty-plus weeks of vacation.

There was apparently another Professor – J Dunkerley Browne by name – who was the joint Head of Department. He was in the middle of two terms' sabbatical leave to write a book, so he was presumably not required to fulfil these arduous duties at all. He was thought to be in Oxford at present, but nobody was very sure. In fact, nobody expected to see much of him again, because soon after this period of leave he was due to retire. One Lecturer was in hospital, having been operated on for haemorrhoids on the previous Friday. Two Lecturers had to give no lectures at all that day, but one of them was thought to be coming in later for a committee meeting. Nobody seemed to know where this meeting was to be held, or exactly when, or with whom. Plumb telephoned these absentees' homes to ask them to attend the Department. Whoever answered the calls claimed not to know their whereabouts, and only a hint of the joint displeasure of 'my Inspector' and the Registrar yielded a grudging promise to pass on a message. The impression was that they had a sense of entitlement to be left alone.

Hooligan had compiled a list of questions which he wanted each Lecturer to answer when interviewed. The obvious one was whether they could account for their movements on Saturday night. This question had to be direct, with little possibility of softening it. Therefore, it had to come last, because it would, if put earlier, let alone first, risk causing defensive antagonism which would distort the interview. The opening questions would be harmlessly oblique: who knew that Peccary would be at the theatre? that he would return to an empty house? that he would use the back door? that the front door lock had been immobilised by glue? The questions actually put, however, had to be so phrased as to conceal Hooligan's knowledge: so 'Did he live alone? Why was he at the back of the house? Where had he been?'

Then could come the more ticklish question about the relations between Peccary and others – particularly whether Peccary had any known enemies. Next the even more ticklish matter of each interviewee's own relations with the deceased. Finally, 'I need to ask you about your own movements at that time, sir. Just routine, you understand.'

Hooligan had considered asking his interviewees not to discuss these questions with colleagues but decided that it was impossible to prevent. In any case, the murderer, if one of them, would be well-prepared already.

The police officers knew from general observation, and from occasional police business, what students looked like – particularly those who, having gone to considerable trouble and expense to express their individuality, as they thought, succeeded only in looking like many others doing the same thing. Hooligan had mellowed towards students since his daughter, Carolyn, had become one; consequently, the self-imposed type-casting and occasional freakishness of the recumbent or perambulating young whom they had passed on the way over with the Registrar had been no surprise.

Their experience of academics had, however, been limited hitherto almost entirely to idealised or caricature figures from fiction, or the occasional television appearance of a distinguished and fashionable minority. The experience of the morning had dented these concepts. The denting was to continue.

As the day wore on, a succession of academics was interviewed. Plumb put his foot in it with the first one straightaway by addressing him as 'Professor'.

'Ay do not hev the Char [*Chair*]', responded this thin, wispy-haired, sallow individual wearing threadbare jeans, dirty plimsolls, and a brand-new corduroy jacket over a t-shirt with a pattern of roses.

'Of course not, Professor,' agreed Plumb with great amiability. 'Detective-Inspector Hooligan will conduct the interview.'

'Ay mean,' pursued the vision of sartorial elegance, 'that I do not *held* the Char. The Char of English Lichacha [*Literature*]. The tatle [*title*] of Pwofessah is confarred enleh on the Head of Depawtment.'

'Ah, yes, *that* sort of Chair,' agreed Plumb, brightly.

'As a mettah of fect, Ay'm just the next gwade dine [*down*] - a Weader.'

Plumb was sufficiently alert to realise that this had nothing to do with gardening, but, even so, his second foot joined his first: 'I'm sure you are a reader, sir, in a job like yours. Now … er … Mr Simmonds …'

'*Dr* Simmonds.'

Hooligan, fearing that his poker-face would disintegrate if Plumb turned out to have a third foot, intervened.

'Dr Simmonds, you will know that we are investigating the murder of Professor Peccary last Saturday night.' He began with his innocuous lines of enquiry before finally asking Simmonds to account for his movements at the time of the murder. He had expected some resistance to the question and was mildly surprised that it was not resented at all.

The police officers worked their way through the list. They were trained to separate informants' physical appearance from the question of their reliability but did not find it easy in the present instance. The succession of shapeless jeans, scuffed plimsolls, and fingernails acceptable in a manual worker, was occasionally interrupted by incongruities: tweedy plus-fours; or tailored nicety verging on dandyism of a type which would have led to scurrilous comments in a less tolerant age. Of the four ties, two were worn by women. A Senior Lecturer turned out to be a neat, pretty little woman, almost a young girl in fact, with manners to match her healthy good looks; Plumb noted with disappointment that she wore a shiny new wedding ring. Most interviewees, however, reminded the investigating officers, as they agreed between sessions, of ironmongers' assistants, but without the practical, workmanlike connotations of the overalls.

The general run of replies throughout the day was co-operative, but unfortunately not very revealing. Too many for Hooligan's peace of mind could not prove their claims to have been at home except – and then not in all cases – by the corroboration of family or of other occupants whose relationship remained delicately unspecified.

None of the interviewees spoke of Peccary's death other than with casual indifference. It was obvious that he had been universally detested, and equally obvious that nobody was willing to attract attention either by admitting personal loathing or by imputing it to colleagues and thereby risking counter-charges.

On one point, however, they were clear and unanimous: if there was one person in the University who had a particular hatred of the late Professor, that man was the Deputy Chief Librarian, one Bertrand Pyle. Hooligan divined from a remark by their first interviewee, Dr Simmonds, that they all detested Pyle, and would happily see him embroiled in suspicion of murder, whether deservedly or not. Accordingly, he introduced a few innocent-sounding questions about the Library in the rest of the interviews and noted that their inhibitions at naming any Departmental colleagues as Peccary's detractors did not extend to Pyle. They regarded him as a man of acid tongue and with a tendency to regard help as a four-letter word – though Hooligan could not understand their outrage at Pyle's refusal to allow them to borrow books marked for reference only ... It was widely believed, though nobody had any details, that Pyle and Peccary had clashed years ago, and that Peccary had thwarted Pyle in job-applications subsequently, including that for the post in charge of the Library here – for which Pyle had been passed over in favour of an outsider. Whether that was itself the cause of the clash or just a major battle won by Peccary in a longer war was not clear from the gossip.

Whatever the truth in this tangle – if there were any - it would be sensible to interview Pyle as soon as they had finished in the English 'Lichacha Depawtment', as it was called by most of its inmates.

The two Lecturers supposedly working at home could still not be contacted at all, but the Departmental Secretary did not seem surprised at this. Hooligan decided to leave these to be pursued by Plumb later. On present showing, they would add nothing to the little that had been discovered already, and, if guilty, would hardly have drawn attention to themselves by being unaccountably absent now. Unless being unaccountably absent was normal; he was beginning to wonder. Obviously, he would contact the absent Professor Dunkerley Browne as well, but he expected nothing much to come of that either, if only because the man was reportedly left-handed and as blind as a bat.

Not for the first time on this case, Hooligan had the uncomfortable feeling that he was not really investigating it, merely going through the motions ... fishing in the wrong pond. Anything as simple and decisive as murder with a blunt instrument was surely beyond most of these people, although experience warned him to assume nothing yet. At least they had discovered the need to interview Pyle, though the fact that someone had an aversion to the deceased is not enough to go on and is, indeed, often a false trail. The hatreds which spill over into violence have usually been suppressed; and for that very reason there comes the unforeseen explosion.

The Departmental Secretary brought them tea at intervals, referring breezily to the dead man as 'Prof', as though it were his real name. This, Hooligan inferred, was intended to raise her status, partly by reminding everyone of the quasi-aristocratic nature which they attributed to the title in their circles, and partly by underlining the familiarity which she could claim with this great personage. From his kingship derived her courtiership.

*

'These interviews have really led us nowhere, Ted,' remarked Hooligan, depressed, at the end of the day. 'A large number of people could have known from general talk around the Department, and around other parts of the University, and elsewhere in his own street,' – he began ticking points off on his fingers – 'that the Professor was alone in the house because his wife was away – that he was going to the theatre and would therefore return after dark – that he was using the back door because the new carpet had put the front door out of action and the joiner was slow in coming.'

'We also know,' went on Plumb with his own fingers, 'that just about everybody who knew the Professor either hated him enough to do this or is quietly pleased because someone else has.'

Hooligan resolutely avoided looking at Plumb's unconscious imitation of his mannerism with his fingers while enumerating points. His own family teased him about it; and it certainly looked very schoolmasterish on Plumb. He really must stop doing it himself.

'And we also know, Ted, that it might have been a panicky burglar anyway. So we know damn all! Not much to show for two days' work. And frankly I can't see this lot doing anything as practical and straightforward as bashing Bossom's cantankerous old bugger and getting away with it. Remember – if this is premeditated, the murderer has either had astonishing good luck in the chance supply of red herrings or is really very good at his job – which would mean, better than we've been at ours so far. By the way – have you noticed that all the older ones we've interviewed have some sort of curious speech-impediment? Simmonds, for example: "Ay hev a numbah of wesarch interwests …"'

Hooligan's accurate imitation set them both off laughing; which Hooligan truncated by continuing, 'Good interventions in the interviews, by the way.'

'Oh … thanks … sir.' Plumb pulled ineffectively at his collar, which was needlessly tightened by his overtight tie. 'I thought I was being a bit dim.'

'No, you were playing the dumb copper and making them talk. Useful tactic.'

'Oh … er …' Pull.

Hooligan was about to ask the Secretary to contact the Registrar again to arrange to see Pyle in the Library, when she buzzed the extension. Hooligan picked it up.

'Inspector? Mrs Peccary would like a word with you.'

He prepared himself mentally to speak in a tone of reverent sympathy. There were some clicking noises, and then a penetrating female voice said: 'Mrs Pwofessah Peccaweh heah.'

He thought it strange that she should define herself in relation to her late unlamented husband's academic title and wondered if her reported calm betokened strength in adversity. How could he best phrase his condolences? His thoughts were scattered as the postulated grieving widow continued:

'Look heah, did one of yaw men teek [*take*]may Sundeh pepper [*paper*]? Ay cawn't faind it anywhar, and Ay lake to wead the weviews. It wealleh is mest annoying.'

'I have no information about your paper, Mrs Peccary. You will know that the paper delivery-girl found your late husband and informed a neighbour. Perhaps she was too upset to concentrate ("unlike some people I might mention") and didn't make the delivery. Did *she* know that she was supposed to go round the back?'

'Of cawss. We cawn't get to the fwont daw, you kneh. End some silly ess put glue in the lawk [*lock*].'

'When was that, exactly?'

'A few dees ageh, of cawss.' (Everything that Mrs Peccary knew was 'of cawss'; others were expected to know what she deemed important to know but were often deficient in their knowing.) 'Ay've *teld* thet little men [*man*] of yaws alweadeh!' She thus referred to Detective-Constable Dawson, six-four, area champion weightlifter, and holder of two commendations for bravery.

'Look heah, Ay'll hev to get on to the pepper-shop. They'll chawge meh faw it otherwaise, Ay'll be bind [*bound*].'

She rang off.

Plumb had heard her clearly from across the room.

'If we were in a TV play,' remarked Hooligan, 'I would now give a bewildered look into the receiver.' He burlesqued the cliché. 'I've always wondered what they expect to see down there ... But – what do we know about this fellow Pyle? A lot of people have fingered his collar ...'

The general opinion amongst the day's interviewees was that Pyle enjoyed hating Professor Peccary more than anyone else did, and more than any other activity. He seemed pretty well hated on his own account, too, but, though he was feared for his caustic remarks, he was also grudgingly admired for his indiscriminate use of them on the great as well as the small. Interviewees had held this to be the reason why he was still only the Deputy. The head man in the Library, a Dr Brisley, had been brought in from elsewhere over Pyle's head, and was apparently a bit of a smoothie, on good terms with everybody but cordial with none. Hooligan, hearing this, was reminded of the Registrar, John Boyle.

'Shall we see you tomorrow, Prof, I mean Inspector?' asked the Secretary, bringing in some tea at four o'clock.

'I don't think so – though I really don't know yet.'

Hooligan wanted to ask her about Pyle, for secretaries usually knew a great deal, and a little pumping could bring rewards. But he was reluctant to name Pyle to anyone who had not referred to him; she would have to do the naming. He looked out of the window and said: 'That's quite a view. Which are the important buildings, do you think?'

She began a list of bizarre-sounding titles, pointing to each building in turn. The eponymous benefactors and luminaries of the University may have been many things, but they were certainly not euphonious by name.

'Somebody mentioned that the University Library building has an architectural award,' he said, as a searcher after truth. 'Would that be the one over there?'

'An award,' she mused. 'No, I've never heard of that. Perhaps you're thinking of the Ethelred Tower next to it.'

She was about to discourse on that topic, so Hooligan said quickly: 'Then that gigantic egg-box over there would be the Library? I've been meaning to have a look at their criminology section. Whom would I see about that?'

She beamed: 'Our Librarian, Dr Brisley. Or ... well, his Deputy, Mr Pyle. Now, what a coincidence! See that man in the grey suit who is just coming out? That's Mr Pyle, the Deputy Librarian. He does seem to come and go rather strangely. Going home now, I should think.'

'Not,' Hooligan thought, 'quite as workshy as this Department. He has, after all, survived until tea-time.'

He continued aloud: 'Well, I think it's time for us to ... er ... ' – she looked interested, and he realised that his search for a way to end the conversation without leaving Pyle as its last topic had only made her hang on his every word - - 'get back to the station and, er ... see what they've been doing.'

Her face displayed disappointment, to alleviate which Hooligan considerately added to Plumb: 'There's that fake jewellery job to tidy up.'

Plumb registered agreement, for he was learning to react suitably to his chief's whimsy.

'Thank you for the tea and the guided tour from the window,' said Hooligan. 'Would you tell the Registrar that I'll be in touch tomorrow?'

As they left the building, Plumb asked: 'What's all that about fake jewellery, sir?'

Hooligan kept his hands still as he gave his reasons.

'It made her forget that she pointed Pyle out to us, or at least made her think that we're not particularly interested in him. So if, on the other hand, anybody thinks Pyle *is* interesting to us, she'll tell them that we don't seem to think so. She'll also think that we're always busy, which is true anyway. She has ceased to be disappointed that our job is routine – a woman is sure to think that detecting fake jewellery is interesting. And we know that Pyle is not in his office and can get a surprise visit from us tomorrow.'

'Shouldn't we pick him up, sir?'

'He's not going anywhere ... And I doubt if he's our man; he's just sounds like someone who's made the wrong opportunities for himself. But obviously we'll have to investigate him. He might even point us to some unforeseen paths.'

At the station, Hooligan learned from the woman constable that the paper-girl had recently noticed a man whom she did not recognise, walking his dog.

'Did she at least recognise the dog?'

'It's a bit suspicious there, sir. She never saw the dog: only the man on several occasions, carrying a dog-leash.'

'Description?'

'Middle-aged, average height, darkish raincoat. No distinguishing features. But ... the girl thought he looked angry.'

'If it was our man, he certainly was.'

CHAPTER 5

A SUSPECT

The University Library staff room at break times was a place where the official rituals of the Library were set aside in favour of the unofficial ones which had arisen on personality grounds. The longest-established of these was carried out by the Deputy Librarian – Bertrand Pyle – and two other men.

They were not an attractive trio. Pyle, who presided at their favourite coffee-table by right of rank, was a square-built middle-aged man with thinning sandy hair and dull freckles; his habitual dark-grey clothing was a bad match for his colouring. His companions and acolytes were John Mew, the gnome-like foreman bookbinder, and Winston Clark, a podgy, sombre official of the Library, whose duties were a mystery to most people but seemed to require him to wander around with a clip-board. Personal affinity drew them together; antipathy to others isolated them.

Every morning and afternoon they were the first into the staff room at break time and took their seats with the best view of the girls who came in after them. It was the duty of whichever of the three men who arrived first to push the communal sugar-bowl back from the edge of the table which it shared with a coffee-urn, so that it was against the wall; this obliged the girls to lean forward a little when they took their sugar. Of the several dozen junior employees, most were female, many were young, and a few were lovely. Their unwholesome admirers eschewed the audible approval which would have been expected in a factory or on a building site, and they maintained the appearance of decorum. But when they made their appreciative and essentially quite respectful comments amongst themselves about short skirts, tight trousers or see-through blouses, they did not reflect that they would have felt insulted if their wives, daughters or sisters had been spoken of thus by other men. Two other points were likewise beyond their powers of perception: that women usually sense when they are observed and discussed, and usually dislike it; and that the women thought them rather pathetic. The men's behaviour and the women's reluctant toleration of it were of their time.

Girl-watching was, however, only the first stage of the proceedings. As soon as the objects of attention were seated and could no longer be ogled surreptitiously, the three men fell into scurrility directed against their former chief.

The form and course of their morning and afternoon breaks was so ingrained a part of the day that even on Monday the news about Professor Peccary had not entirely displaced their usual practice. By Tuesday morning, the force of habit had reasserted its suzerainty.

'You know,' remarked Clark, 'these gorgeous creatures ... they would have been lost on Our Erstwhile Leader. Lads with lipstick, now, they'd have been more to his liking.'

It was an article of faith amongst them that the former Chief Librarian was a homosexual. Their hostility in earlier life to homosexuality had receded in the two decades since the Sixties, just as they now clumsily attempted discretion in their discussion of the girls. But, the habit of denigration being deeply rooted, an imputation of homosexuality was the standby insult against anyone whom they disliked, if even the slightest spurious justification could be contrived. They would willingly have censured him for having five toes on each foot if they could. Their target's girlish bashfulness of manner and his scandalised gossipiness when confronted by uninhibited speech or behaviour had always been more than enough for their purpose.

'If he actually knew anything at all about the subject – in all its varieties,' rejoined Pyle, and added: 'Perhaps he suspected there was something to do but couldn't quite put his finger on it.'

This innuendo, though not new to their discourse, was greeted with pleasure. It served as the cue for responses in kind: Mew suggested that he should have taken a grip on himself; Clark surmised that he had never learned to take himself in hand and had therefore been unable to keep his end up. These and other similar comments were *de rigueur*, and they ran through a repertoire, the essential ingredients of which were by now traditional amongst them. Pyle's memory, phrasing, and choice of moment were, in these matters, impeccable.

The former chief was lampooned not only for his supposedly dubious sexual proclivities. 'Library management for him,' declared Pyle, 'was a spectator-sport. They should have taxed his salary as unearned income. He was bright enough ... he could pull something out when he was up against it' (a snigger from Clark and Mew) 'but any thought of supporting the people who were doing his working and worrying for him ...'

He left the sentence unfinished. It was an allusion familiar to his companions. As Deputy, Pyle had borne the brunt of the Erstwhile Leader's evasiveness and habit of refusing to take decisions which might offend powerful or troublesome individuals in the University. This had led Pyle, and several others, to retaliate, either by referring all decisions to him to increase the torpor of the system or to apply every rule and procedure with the utmost rigour against powerful complainants in order to create difficulties for the Leader to deal with.

'Anyway,' continued Mew, 'someone's sorted the Other One out for you.'

'You can say that again,' agreed Pyle. 'If it hadn't been for that bastard Peccary, I'd have got Brisley's job when Our Erstwhile Leader left with that nice little ulcer I hope I gave him. If whoever bumped off old Rat-Pig Peccary wants to come to me for an alibi, I'll give him one. My only regret is that he didn't die slowly, in pain, frightened and alone.' He brooded and added: 'The best way someone like him can manure his garden is to lie in it.'

Pyle looked at his watch. 'Time to go and write some more bloody stupid letters to superprats about books they say they need and never read,' he remarked; though he did not move. ' ... "Say they need and never read",' he repeated, musingly. 'That rhymes. Could be a line out of a cheap musical. Not inappropriate for what goes on here.'

'Where's your sense of purpose?' asked Mew, with heavy sarcasm. 'Don't you realise they're pushing back the frontiers of knowledge and you're helping them? It's called "research", you know.'

'Research?' snorted Pyle. 'Research? When I hear the word "research" I reach for my revolver. Stupid bloody jumped-up little pillocks! I wouldn't put any one of them in charge of a broom-cupboard!'

Mew fed him a scripted line: 'Can't call them arseholes,' in order that Pyle could respond, 'That's right: arseholes are useful.'

He was about to rise when his secretary appeared.

'Two gentlemen to see you, Mr Pyle. They say it's important and urgent.'

She went away without waiting for a reply, and Pyle muttered to her departing back, 'Yes, I'll be there. But if it's important and urgent, it's got nothing to do with the Rudiversity.'

To his colleagues he continued: 'Of course, I've got nothing against Brisley. All he did was apply for a job. Mind you, it's not my job to help him do the job that should have been mine, by rights. Still, he's not been bad, I'll give him that.'

'He's a close one,' put in Clark.

'A close one,' agreed Pyle. 'But it's not his fault I didn't get the job. That dubious honour goes to my Rat-Pig friend Peccary, now so joyfully missed. He'll not be bothering anybody else, not where he's gone.'

He went to his office.

Meantime, Hooligan and Plumb were in a waiting-room outside several offices bearing the names of various senior staff, including that of the Chief Librarian – apparently at a meeting elsewhere in the University – and of Bertrand Pyle.

Hooligan was intrigued by some current and back volumes of *Who's Who* and a set of *Who Was Who*. He found Peccary's entry in the current *Who's Who*, with a brief paragraph revealing academic distinction, and noted that Peccary had been only in his early fifties. Somehow, he had seemed older, not only when examined as a murder victim but also when described by everybody.

He had not heard of *Who Was Who* before, though he now realised that it was obvious that important people were often old and likely to become dead, even without criminal assistance. He wondered if everyone in *Who's Who* was automatically transferred on death to the next issue in the *Was* series. Few of the murder victims for whom he had worked vicariously over the years had been in this league, but he had certainly formed the impression that there were too many pseudo-*Who* types already. Surely many of them must be revealed, after death deprives them of power and wealth, to be merely well-connected farts; or successfully self-advertising farts; or cunning, unprincipled farts who could run in any direction as required by the wind of change. And, conversely, might not a few *Was Who* people be discovered who had never been thought of as *Who*-worthy in their lifetime? If the Soviets can rehabilitate people liquidated in error, the least we in the West can do is to admit a few to the Kingdom of *Who*-dom after a lifetime's neglect; it would at least satisfy their nearest and dearest. From what those Lecturers in the English Department said yesterday about their work, they're all writing books about authors who have been unread for years, and perhaps for the best of reasons. That could be how Peccary got in: made a *Was Who* out of a *Was*-fart and became a *Who*-fart himself by hanging on to farty coat-tails.

These reflections were interrupted by the arrival of Bertrand Pyle.

'Important and urgent, apparently,' Pyle remarked. 'She's usually more explicit than that. Come in and have a seat.'

He led them into his nearby office. There was some confusion about coats as Pyle, having removed his own from a hook and put his visitors' coats on it instead, realised that he had dumped his own on the chair upon which he had invited Hooligan to sit. They were eventually seated, and Pyle waited for them to introduce themselves.

Hooligan had seen that Pyle was quite polite, at least in his intentions, but also awkward. He wondered if the surface politeness concealed a lack of self-confidence or whether Pyle merely preferred not to let supposed lapses of formal courtesy distort the substance of the business, antagonistic though the latter might sometimes be. Recalling his experiences in the office of Pro-Vice-Chancellor Professor Niprollok yesterday, Hooligan felt that both explanations might be true, and might make Pyle difficult to interview. That being so, nothing would be gained by beating about the bush.

'Detective-Inspector Hooligan, sir, local CID. My warrant-card. This is Detective-Sergeant Plumb.'

Pyle looked at the card as Hooligan held it out, and said, 'I see.'

Hooligan had hoped for a more interesting reaction, and was further disappointed when Pyle continued, 'Or perhaps I should say that I don't see. What can I do for you?'

Hooligan sensed that Pyle was already mentally writing the Minutes of the meeting and that the tone would favour the interviewee.

'We're making routine enquiries, sir. You will have heard that Professor Peccary of the English Department was murdered late on Saturday night.'

'Of course. And why should it concern me?'

'We're trying to build up a picture of the deceased, sir. So we're talking to a lot of people who knew him.'

'Go on.'

'Did you know him, sir?'

'You know that I did, or you wouldn't be here now. Many people knew him.'

'How well did you know him, sir?'

'Well enough.'

'What sort of man was he?'

'His staff in the Department can tell you better than I.'

'Other views can be useful, sir. What were your relations with him?'

'Why are you asking me these questions?'

'When did you last see Professor Peccary, sir?'

'About ... two weeks ago, I suppose. Look, what is all this?'

'Can you account for your movements last Saturday night, from about eight o'clock till two on Sunday morning?'

'I don't need to. Or are you saying that I do need to?'

'I don't say that you need to at all, Mr Pyle. But it would help me very much if you did.'

'As it happens, I was at home, watching cheap crime-busting on television.'

'Very relaxing, in my experience, sir. And those series tell us what the public think the police are going to do. That leaves us one up when we want to do something else instead. Were you alone?'

'Inspector – I want to know why you are asking me these questions.'

'Just routine, sir, as I said.'

'It may be routine to you, Inspector Hooligan. No doubt you spend half your life asking people where they were at such-and-such a time. But it is certainly not routine to me: I have never been asked questions such as these before. I ask you again: Why are you asking me these questions?'

Hooligan wondered whether to move to the next stage for the encouragement of unwilling witnesses, which was to request, but without making the voluntary aspect clear, to be accompanied to the police station to continue the discussion there. Or perhaps he might use the equally traditional vague threat that evasiveness might be construed as deliberate obstruction by someone with something to hide. But he decided that these tactics would not work: Bertrand Pyle was articulate and almost certainly well-informed about his rights. So he continued gently:

'Obviously, sir, you haven't chanced to be acquainted with a murder victim before. Perhaps you'd like me to be a little more specific.'

'I wish you would,' Pyle said, his sharpness mitigated by the impression that he had somehow won an encounter.

Hooligan put on an air of benevolently confiding in Pyle, so that his voice and manner belied his words: 'It has been represented to me that you and the deceased were not on good terms.'

Pyle reacted as Hooligan had hoped: as though it were a question of logic rather than an occasion for resentment. 'That doesn't mean I did him in,' he replied, as though to a lesser mortal who had jumped to the wrong conclusion.

'Exactly my view, sir. All it means is that I am reasonable in asking you to tell me if anyone was with you at the time in question. That way, it's very convenient for both you and us: you get rid of us, and we can go and pursue enquiries elsewhere with a better chance of worthwhile results.'

Seeing that Pyle could not find a weak point in his explanation, Hooligan softened his manner still further and asked again: 'Do you perhaps want to tell me if anyone was with you? We can be very discreet, you know ... about irrelevancies.'

'There's no great secret about it!' Pyle expostulated. He was now distracted by the idea that Hooligan might think that he had an irregular liaison to conceal. 'If I'd been with a fancy-woman, I'd be pleased about it and tell you. No, I had a house full of them.'

'Full of whom, sir?'

'Full of irrelevancies, to use your excellent term for them. My wife, my mother-in-law, my brother-in-law, his fancy piece of irrelevancy ... Jesus, who bloody wasn't there? Do you know, that stupid cow, my not-quite sister-in-law, talked all the bloody way through that film! Thank God they've gone!'

'No doubt they noticed you during the film, sir. I wonder if you'd write a few names and addresses in Detective-Sergeant Plumb's notebook. We'll need to confirm your alibi.'

Seeing that Pyle looked alarmed and aggressive, Hooligan continued quickly: 'We'll be sure to give them some other explanation, sir. One of my favourites is to say that an incomplete car-registration number was observed at a bank-robbery, so we're having to check dozens of people – expecting to eliminate all but one, of course. Most people are rather amused to be suspected briefly of bank robbery, or at least to let their friends think they were.'

'As long as the suspicion *is* brief,' said Pyle, firmly, as he began to write. 'Of course, they'd probably like me to be done for murder, so they might insist I was out all night. On the other hand, if their fear of scandal prevails they'll say I was in. Which is the truth.'

Hooligan noted which hand he wrote with, and also on which side of his desk he kept his telephone.

'How long did everyone stay up, sir?'

'I don't know. They *seemed* to spend half the bloody night wandering about. Eleven, maybe.'

'And you didn't leave the house the whole evening?'

'No. I've already answered that question.'

'From your home to Professor Peccary's home, sir – how long would that take?'

'I've never been there or wanted to.'

'Gladstone Close, sir. How long would it take by car?'

'A few minutes, I suppose. The question has never interested me.'

'And you were not out of the sight of these people on the list even for a few minutes?'

'I *was* allowed to piddle in peace. Otherwise, no.'

'Thank you very much, Mr Pyle. This really will enable us to go through our routines as quickly as possible. Now, formalities over, and we'll confirm your alibi – but we still need to know as much as we can about Professor Peccary. What sort of man was he?'

'What sort of man? How can I put it? I try not to tread on his sort on the pavement.'

Pyle unleashed a tirade of abuse against the dead man. If only half of it were true half the time, Peccary had been rude, arrogant, overbearing, treacherous, mean and spiteful to colleagues and to his students. The description recalled to Hooligan Harry Bossom's version: an amazing capacity for expressing and attracting hostility.

Hooligan listened to Pyle's reply with particular interest. If Pyle knew himself to have a cast-iron alibi, whether he were innocent of the crime or not, he would be speaking freely. On the other hand, if Pyle were overestimating the strength of a false alibi, his having seemed to speak freely would prove little or nothing about his guilt or innocence. On the 'third hand', which these attempts at reasoning irritatingly produce, a show of recklessness would come convincingly from a man who believed, rightly or wrongly that he had a sound alibi which may or may not be genuine. So much depended on whether Hooligan felt that Pyle was pretending or not. He did not like to rely so heavily on intuition; but this case was so full of contradictions and red herrings, that he had little else.

His gut-feeling was that Pyle was not his quarry. Otherwise, all he had learned from the man's rant was that the list of possible suspects had lengthened. And Pyle had raised the possibility of an aggrieved student: an entirely plausible explanation which lengthened the list many times over. This outcome was depressing, for they all seemed likely to share Pyle's sense of satisfaction at Peccary's death and seemed, on the face of it, no more likely than he to be the murderer. Yet they would have to be checked out as thoroughly as circumstances allowed ...

What was worse, he would also have to investigate other hypotheses which did not involve Peccary's fan-club at all. He had pushed these from his mind until now, in order to concentrate on Peccary's family and colleagues; after all, the timing and location of the murder did suggest someone connected with the victim. But suppose the murderer had been outside that circle and had got the wrong man: what kind of mistake might he have made? Had he (or she; when you know nothing, don't forget the improbable) gone to the wrong house in the right street? Or the right number in the wrong street? If so, would the right number in the right street bear any relationship to Peccary's address? Plumb would ferret something out ... But, our murderer, if he'd made one of those mistakes, would have realised it by now - so would he proceed with the intended crime or abandon his plan in a panic? If he had another go, which might not be immediate, would the police necessarily spot the connection between Peccary's murder-by-mistake and a second, intended murder?

Hooligan seemed to see the dead man's lop-sided sneer, mocking all attempts to find his killer. The mockery was, so far, justified, Hooligan admitted to himself. 'Far from solving all the riddles, I haven't perceived the riddles which must be hidden amongst the facts. But which are the actual facts – the relevant ones, anyway? There are so many possibly relevant ones ... With every case you enter a new world, with its own values, norms, compulsions, irrationalities ...'

CHAPTER 6

ALL THAT'S LEFT OF A DEAD PROFESSOR

The University of Pillingham gradually ceased to discuss the murder of Professor Peccary, or to wonder fearfully if another may be in the offing. There had been some distractions.

This was 1982. The *Sir Galahad* had been destroyed by Exocet missiles; the *General Belgrano* had been sunk; the Falkland Islands had been liberated; Colonel H Jones had been awarded a posthumous Victoria Cross; and General Galtieri had been deposed. The learned and passing-for-learned at the University of Pillingham were sufficiently aware of these events to be able to strike bellicose attitudes, or to display their superior strategic and tactical talents, or to censure from the safe moral heights of their study armchairs.

But real life pursued them all the same: universities were increasingly required to economise. The league of the sapient met this challenge: with heroic disbelief, pushing their heads yet further into the sands of time which were running out; or gnashing their teeth when the Library cancelled a few expensive and largely unread periodicals. To assuage their suffering, they rigorously perpetuated their wonted self-indulgent fatuities.

Typical of the latter during the dusty, hot Summer term of 1982 were their committee meetings. The scheduled cycle of these pursued itself round and round; and round; and round. From a group of about twenty academics – mostly middle-aged to elderly Professors, with a few men below professorial rank and a token woman or two – different committees of a dozen to fifteen members assembled and reassembled. Inevitably, well over half the membership of any committee would serve on any of the others – but this did not prevent testy complaints that another committee had missed the point or had failed to explain itself. They set up Sub-Committees and Working Parties. They consulted others, and were themselves consulted about appointments to each others' membership. They made recommendations to each other about things which they should have decided themselves; they took decisions which they were not authorised to take. A quarter of their Agenda, and half their time, concerned items sent back for reconsideration.

Administrators sat at Chairmen's elbows and took the Minutes. Those were not even draft Minutes until, some days or weeks after the meeting, the Chairmen approved them as a draft; and were not confirmed Minutes until the Committee approved them at its next meeting, perhaps several months later. During that time, anyone who treated the draft Minutes, in their gradual advent towards confirmation, as though they were confirmed Minutes, risked being accused of ignoring the committee system in all its official and democratic glory. On the other hand, anyone who deferred action until the Minutes were at least endorsed as a draft by the Chairman, and preferably confirmed at the next meeting, may find himself reproached for lack of common sense and denigrated as a mindless bureaucrat worthy of the Hapsburg civil service.

These collectives, whether in session or merely infecting administrative action between meetings, displayed the worst, not the best individual characteristics of their constituent members; consequently, they held themselves and the University as a whole, in a state of oxymoronic equilibrium. Timidly headstrong, sentimentally callous, retiringly interfering, they wallowed pleasurably in self-contradictions. For they were secure. Whatever their impetuosity or delay, whatever their chance achievements or predestined failures, whatever their personal animosities or insincere shows of self-sacrifice, their livelihoods and their expenses-paid conferences were not at risk. And their self-esteem would always be enhanced by the opportunity to interfere and obstruct, without having to take responsibility for the consequences. Life was an intellectual game in which everyone allowed to play wins, and everyone not allowed to play is a loser.

The Staffing Committee at Pillingham held an extra meeting – this time without Professor Peccary's vocal and respiratory interventions, for they were to consider the vacancy caused by his death. The Dean of the Faculty of Arts, feeling out of his element as a mere member rather than in the Chair of his own Faculty, urged an immediate replacement by the normal processes of advertisement and interview.

Professor Niprollok, having just completed his allotted period as Pro-Vice-Chancellor, had reverted to his actual position as Professor of Technological Studies. He continued to absent himself from these duties, however, since he had now become a member of many committees in a personal capacity. His new role expressed the general assumption that his experience of seniority had made him very influential and very wise. The former attribute was an article of faith in a reasonable proposition; the latter flew in the face of all empirical evidence. Credited with both qualities, however, there he was – to represent no particular sector of interest, but to think, advise, and help decide for the good of the institution as a whole. Whatever the topic under discussion, literate speech and self-awareness were no more at his command than before, and he reached with boundless self-confidence for his wisdom like an orang-outang for a mouth-organ. Inevitably, his pronouncements on University business bore to wisdom the relationship of that estimable beast's endeavours to music. His hair, streaming back-and-sides from his topmost and only polish, like cobwebs from a doorknob, reinforced the misleading impression that power was directed by sagacity. And it was his duty to make his accumulated wisdom available to all.

'I very much take the ... gra, gra ... Dean's point,' he said; and the ontological proofs for the existence of God might have been summarised with less sign of mental effort. 'BUT' (he shouted the word, perhaps because whenever he essayed what was for him a long sentence his mind's eye needed to see conjunctions in block letters), 'his criteria is unpractical.'

The Dean winced and had to brush from his eye a straggle of silver which had become unfixed in the stress of his amazement. John Boyle's impassivity was eloquent. Dr Brisley wrote, 'his criteria is unpractical' on his note-pad, and looked at it with pleasure, thinking, 'Two mistakes, or is it three – depends how you count them - in four words! Really an excellent score!'

Niprollok was hotly in pursuit of his self-image: he had decided to be the no-nonsense pragmatist, with an uncanny ability, not given to those less gifted, to put his finger on the obvious; a philosopher-king with the common touch.

'Have you any old staff coming up for retirement?'

'Thwee,' the Dean intoned.

'And they are ...' – Niprollok paused inquisitorially before another cheerful dash into his lumber-room mind – '... whom?'

John Boyle was lifeless; Brisley scribbled again.

'And what,' Niprollok persisted, having noted the names supplied by the Dean, 'is the gra-gra staff/student ratio in your Faculty as a whole?'

'The reetio in the English Depawtment is, es it heppens, awlmest aydintical to thet in the Univarsity as a whel.'

'BUT' – another nuts-and-bolts shout – 'what is the ratio in the *Faculty* as a whole? That was the inwardness of my question.'

Brisley's secret glee was in the ascendant. How the semi-educated loved unnecessary neologisms!

There was a prolonged discussion on the subject of too many or too few staff or students in different parts of the University; and despite the absence of the official figures, opinions were forthright and their expression unmodified. There was a heated exchange between Niprollok and the Dean as to whether the Faculty's figure or the Department's should be considered, though neither disputant explained why settling the point would matter in the main argument. A sociologist's contribution included the word 'lamentable' with, however, the stress on the second syllable, whereupon Niprollok and two others found that they liked the sound of it and repeated the error. Brisley wrote 'lamENTable! 3 times!' on his pad. The solecism was followed on tour by 'alternate' wrongly used for 'alternative', 'refute' for 'deny', and 'reticent' for 'reluctant'. Brisley, feeling that his cup was running over as his collection of blunders grew, reflected that malapropisms are not expunged at higher levels of education; they merely afflict different, perhaps more specialised, sectors of the vocabulary. Those who might sneer at 'pronounciation' or 'maintainance' from manual workers think nothing of what had just been perpetrated, or of 'disassociating' themselves from it and 'appraising' others of the fact.

Brisley tried to help the Dean by remarking that the Library's outstanding collections in the subject would attract applicants of high quality. A couple of elderly Professors glared at him for daring to hold an opinion at all, even on the contribution of his own Department to the University, and he wondered if he had somehow damaged the case by supporting it.

The Dean, fond of summarising discussions, although his accuracy and succinctness would have been more appropriate to filibustering than to summary, eventually stated what he regarded as the 'cwux' (Brisley scribbled) of the 'mettah'. But his air of authoritative decanal definition suddenly deserted him when Niprollok declared it to be a 'mute' point.

'Ay wish it wair,' was the Dean's helpless comment; 'vewwy mute indeed.' Niprollok could not tell if this heavy irony were flat contradiction or endorsement and said 'Gragra' in a preparatory manner.

The Chairman, however, had had enough and, being a new Pro-Vice-Chancellor, wanted to flex his muscles. 'We've spent hawf the mawning arning art *[ironing out]* these teething chubbles *[troubles]*,' he said (while Brisley scribbled again and Boyle's impassiveness spoke volumes), 'end Ay'm geng *[going]* to put it to a vet.' ('Vote for a vet,' Brisley scribbled.)

The meeting decided by a large majority to replace Professor Peccary. 'Not too literwalleh, Ay hep *[hope]*,' said someone, and they all laughed.

'We can only pass this as a recommendation to the Planning Committee,' said Boyle, peering at his notes.

'That's us, aren't we?' said Niprollok, and they all laughed again. 'Oh, with Todd Shyce instead of our gra-Librarian.'

'Let's hope the next encombont,' continued Niprollok, 'won't come to the same sticky end.'

'Unlikely, I suppose,' said Boyle.

*

Towards the end of the Autumn term, Dr Brisley was renewing his attempts to persuade academic colleagues to send their reading lists to the Library before they were issued to students. Some of the lists would contain wrong authors and titles, though the librarians would usually spot the errors. But the greater problem by far was the late arrival, or non-arrival, of lists. Yet again, many academics had not sent a copy to the Library at all or had not done so in time for checks to be made and action taken. Already in the first few weeks of the academic year, deficiencies in some lists and the consequences of their late arrival in the Library had, as in previous years, become obvious. Students had been told to read books which were not in the Library at all, and which the Department had never asked for. There might be only one copy which fifty students would come looking for. And then there were the books which students had been told to buy but which were out of print. It only took one student to solve his or her own problem by stealing the Library copy - which, with forewarning, could have been kept behind the desk.

Most lists went to the Library's subject-specialists, but Brisley liked to have a look at those for English Literature from personal interest. He had one before him now, and saw that it still bore the influence, though now only a posthumous validation, of the late Professor Peccary. He noticed in passing that Peccary's surviving professorial colleague – that old fool Dunkerley Browne; sounds like a ginger biscuit – had marked his brief return from leave before retirement by crossing Peccary's book off. But Arlington's, from Drumbridge University, was still listed.

The telephone rang. His secretary was with the dentist, so the line had been switched through. That was a nuisance, but the same could be said of many a substitute secretary. He picked up the handset and was about to greet the caller with his name, when a power-saw voice at the other end cut him short.

'Mrs Pwofessah Peccaweh heah. Is thet Dr Bwisleh?'

He tried cautiously to admit his identity, but the cutting edge continued, unheeding and remorseless.

'Look heah, Ay'm moving hice *[house]*, and there's simply tons and tons of books and peppers of my leet husband's. What shell Ay do with them?'

Brisley reflected that Pyle, Clark and Mew, whose verbal and social rituals daily in the staff room had not escaped his notice, would have had a ready reply. This thought made him a trifle slow in responding.

'Hilloo, are you still thar? Look heah, are they saleable? Does the Libwawy want to bay *[buy]* them?'

She was at last willing to hold her chain-saw voice in abeyance - to hear about money, for the topic was notoriously dear to her heart. Brisley guessed that a fair proportion of the books which she now offered for sale had been received by Peccary free, as review copies; Peccary would then have written the reviews, perhaps for a fee or at any rate while paid by the University. Many of his books, whether those review copies or acquired by Peccary on his own account, would probably be in the Library already. Some extra copies here and there would probably be useful, but not if they had to be bought instead of new, different items. Then there would be whatever items the Library did not have. They might or might not be wanted, and if they were, the price of buying everything would grossly inflate the price of those that were wanted. On the whole, this proposition, which was not uncommon from academics' widows, was likely to produce more bother than benefit. How on earth can one explain these points to people like that? He decided to communicate with her in terms which she could understand.

'If they're on your late husband's subject, they probably are saleable, Mrs Peccary,' he said. 'But we couldn't match trade prices. There are firms that deal in whole collections. I don't know what they would offer, but certainly more than we could. And they would collect them. That would solve the problem quickly, wouldn't it?'

This implication of slick commercial efficiency at her disposal made it easy for her to decide:

'Look heah, what are their numbahs? Ay'll git them to come to the hice.'

Brisley was ready with a directory and began to read the names and telephone numbers out – slowly, because he knew that Mrs Peccary was incapable of the rapid apprehension and response she expected from everybody else.

'Look heah, Ay'll git a pincil.'

Eventually the information was imparted and transcribed, and Brisley was trying to end the conversation when the revolving blade shrieked further in.

'Look heah, there's his peppers. Messes of nets [*Masses of notes*]. Fo' a book, Ay spez [*suppose*].'

Brisley thought it appropriate that a person of that type would make peppers of papers, messes of masses, and nets of notes. The higgledy-piggledy, meshed confusion of such minds had found apt symbols.

'Simpleh heaps of them. Look heah, they mate be useful to someone, but I dart if anyone in the Depawtment would kneh. You'll hev to tek a look.'

He resisted the temptation to tell her that he would decide for himself what he had to do. He felt that he probably should take a look before the 'peppers' were thrown out: her husband had, indeed, been supposedly on the point of finishing another book; and he had been a reputable scholar once, so it was always possible that some erudite gem had been slowly forming.

Mrs Peccary was pleased to learn that the University's van would call and bring these various manuscripts to the Library for Brisley to examine. If publishable or of possible use to another scholar he would return them to her with suggested action; otherwise …

'Look heah,' she sliced in, as though reading his next thought. 'if there's nothing in them, they can be binned.'

Brisley had not come across this verb before. Had he missed a fashionable usage soon to be *passé*, or was he witnessing the birth of a permanent addition to the language?

'Er ... yes,' he agreed, 'as a final resort they could be ... er ...'

She rang off and did not hear 'discarded'.

He tossed Peccary's posthumously updated reading list into a wire basket destined for Pyle's attention. Pyle would enjoy that as surely as the dog loves the cat.

He then opened an envelope marked, with emphatic underlinings, 'Personal, Private and Confidential.' The letter came from two Lecturers, who complained of some comments which Pyle had reportedly made in the Senior Common Room about academics. The gist of it was that they were accused of being, without exceptions, incompetent teachers, fatuous researchers, and generally idle, useless, self-indulgent, pompous, ill-mannered, and moronic. ('Unfair,' thought Brisley. 'Now, if he'd said "*with* exceptions" ... .') Particular offence had been taken at Pyle's alleged remark that the next Three-Day-Week emergency would kill half of them with unaccustomed overwork.

Their objections had been, Brisley found, a bit of a mishmash because of their reaction to a further alleged remark by Pyle to the effect that American academics, unlike British ones, worked hard and took their teaching responsibilities seriously. Perhaps the two complainants had felt some lingering patriotism stirred up by the Falklands War, even though they probably regarded patriotism as a visceral emotion typifying the ignorant. And possibly some rogue strain of anti-Americanism had joined in the mix. Whatever had actually been said, Pyle seemed yet again, to have lived down to his considerable reputation for abrasiveness.

Wearily, Brisley made a mental note to try, not for the first time, to dissuade Pyle from his habit of sounding off. Pyle was right up to a point, and certainly about the Americans ... Though a minority of the British academics were first-class, and some of that minority had good manners ... The real problem was that the run-of-the-mill majority thought they were in the top five per cent and believed their own publicity. But one had to live with these people, and nothing was gained by picking fights like this. Must try to convince Pyle to keep it to himself ...

But what might be going on with the investigation of Peccary's murder? Nothing, it would seem. Pyle had been under suspicion at one time; perhaps still was. Since he had always expressed particular hatred of the late Professor, that was hardly surprising. The hatred was reasonable enough, of course: Pyle would have become Chief Librarian here as an internal promotion if Peccary had not, as the high point of a pre-existing feud, blocked him. Pyle had certainly had a raw deal in some ways, but, instead of trying to deal rationally with academic irrationality, had bitterly entered upon a vendetta of increasing dimensions, which would now often publicly embrace the entire academic staff if he were not held in check ...

As for the murder, the police seemed to be no nearer a solution; the news media had lost interest; and Pyle, whatever the substance of the suspicion against him in the police's view, was still going about his normal graceless business in the University.

Brisley knew by heart an evasive letter which he always used in response to complaints about Pyle. A minor masterpiece of its genre, it would leave the complainants reasonably satisfied and even sympathetic to him as Pyle's boss, while not provoking Pyle. He scribbled it out and was just placing it on his secretary's desk when she returned from the dentist.

'Nothing wrong!' she exclaimed ecstatically, lapsing for a moment in a Good Little Girl Who Always Brushed Her Teeth Properly. 'No work needed! What a relief!'

Spying the letter, she said: 'Oh, what a pity – you could have dictated it if I'd been a few minutes earlier. I got caught by Mrs Mountjoy in "Eng Lit" with the latest gossip.

They've made an internal appointment to Professor Peccary's Chair – Dr Simmonds. Professor Simmonds, now. Isn't that nice?'

'Yes. Some time ago, the Staffing Committee, which I'm on, recommended advertising the vacancy, but farther up in the Planning Committee our recommendation wasn't accepted – by almost the same members! They decided in the corridors of power to fill it internally.'

But his secretary had another titbit: 'And, do you know, Dr, I mean Professor Simmonds was interviewed by the police *again* about Professor Peccary's murder? Mrs Mountjoy thinks that Professor Simmonds thinks that that the police might think he had murdered Professor Peccary, hoping to get the job.'

'Everything's possible, I suppose. But if he assumed that the job would be advertised, he couldn't have guaranteed getting it against outside applicants.'

'Oh, I'm sure he didn't. Murder him, I mean.' She believed the best in people.

'Anyway,' she picked up her thread, 'now they'll get a replacement for Professor Simmonds.'

'That's what we'd hoped, of course. But apparently not. The University has just put a ban on replacing staff who leave unless there's what they call a "compelling reason". It's all to save money. The English Department here is already overstaffed according to student numbers, though that's disputed - it depends on what you count – so they're not going to replace Simmonds. That, between you and me, is probably why he got the job – he becomes a saving. In fact, the job would probably have gone to that young woman, Dr Bellsham, who's already a Senior Lecturer, but she didn't want it. Doesn't want the responsibility – which it is, if done properly. Anyway, Simmonds deserves it, too … Er … um … Will you send Mr Pyle copies of these letters here – the incoming one and my reply – and remind me to have a word with him about … er … again?'

CHAPTER 7
DEATH IS SUCH A LET-DOWN

Pagham University was a green-fields-and-glass young neighbour of the Edwardian red-brick Pillingham. A man wandered amongst its acreage, taking note of anything that might prove useful. When not observing, he reflected ...

University campuses are, in some ways, like medium-sized villages: gossipy, inbred, dependent on funds from elsewhere, distrustful of outsiders, and resentful even of tactful constructive criticism. They have a village layout: there might be a main road through the middle; if not directly between towns, they are reached by a diversion; they have two or three ways in and out.

But, un-villagelike, much of their population is floating, rather as in a long-stay transit camp; and they publish detailed maps of their layout, because they thrive on their equivalent of the tourist trade, conference bookings.

If you want to know how a university is set out, and where people are accommodated during conferences, you first master your map; you daren't carry it openly, let alone be seen to consult it, lest you advertise yourself as a stranger or – heaven forfend! - attract an offer of help. No, you just stroll past the gateman, who, as Siegfried Sassoon nearly put it, 'speeds glum visitors up the line', not 'to death' but to inspect. You go in and look at the place. You don't look in an obvious way, of course: you just wander about, and you look while you're doing it. And you make sure that your face is expressionless; and you avoid eye-contact with anyone you pass. Who notices, let alone remembers, a bloke wandering about? That's what everyone else seems to be doing. This is, after all, a university.

Places like this are everyone's ... Everyman's land ... No Man's Land ... Like the University of Pillingham, where

Professor Peccary sniffed and snorted his last ... Or here, in the University of Pagham ...

Pagham, in the twenty or so years of its existence, had become synonymous, both in the academic world and in the Press, for new courses and for student sit-ins. So had several other new universities, including Pagham's regional neighbour, the University of Drumbridge. This reputation was not entirely justified; but facile minds love and need a label. The academic achievements of these newer universities were sound enough and, although institutions such as Pillingham felt that there was a little too much talk of Modular Developmental Linear Cross-Disciplinary Area Studies, their beautiful settings and the opportunity to start afresh with new systems had originally attracted youngish and enthusiastic staff, some of whom, at that time, had not yet come to regard their innovations as prescriptive. Twenty years on, however, those now in middle age, who had been appointed young, had turned into the oldest inhabitants. A mantle of grave solemnity, as of vastly experienced septuagenarians, lay upon the forty-and-fifty-year-olds, who had become senior only by demographic chance, and who had gained experience only in what they themselves had done, and had then merely done again.

*

One such luminary at the University of Drumbridge was Professor Arlington of English Literature. He had, as he repeatedly put it with an immediacy of response to a stimulus reminiscent of a ticket emerging from a slot-machine, been 'in, not so much with the bwicks as with the concwete, hahum.' In his demeanour he sought to combine the mystic with the pioneer; the far-sighted founding-father with the glorious posterity which alone justified the struggles of the past.

Multi-faceted in his own estimation, and a man of tedious parts in that of others, Professor Arlington, sitting at his desk, fingered his bow-tie. He always did this when feeling the need to be seen thinking, or when alone and picturing himself thinking. It forced him to raise his considerable chins in order that his chipolata fingers could gain access, and this in turn forced him to turn his head slightly, and gaze into the middle distance and upwards. He felt that it made him look like a great man concerned with things beyond the range of others' perception. A visionary.

He had recently returned from several months' sabbatical leave on full pay to write a book, the profits from which would go into his personal account. Inordinately proud of his *Symbolism in the Romantic Poets*, to whom he always referred as the 'Womentic Poits', he had resumed his duties by checking the typed version produced by the Departmental Secretary. He had paused briefly when she had placed before him a leather folder bearing his initials in gold tooling – the purchase and embellishment of which had, of course, been paid from the Departmental stationery account, though entered in the ledger under some other description. The folder contained a letter which he had dictated earlier, and was now to sign, in which he complained to the Personnel Officer about the delay in replacing his Secretary's secretarial assistant. The letter had an appendix, consisting of a detailed list of the duties assigned to each post or shared between them. This list was not entirely fictitious as to its inclusions and did not mention that they typed his books and articles during their paid employment.

His toying with the knot which lodged amongst the mounds at his Adam's apple was, on this occasion, no mere performance for its own sake; it was more akin to a child's reaching for a security blanket. For he was suddenly confronted by a considerable problem: he was in an agony of indecision as to which form of his name to use for this particular signature. Should he be formal or informal? He had, of course, encountered this problem at the beginning, when he had needed to select an appropriate form of name with which to address the recipient. How should one address a Personnel Officer, who, moreover, had such a silly name? 'Dear Noote' seemed a little too friendly. After all, they had not been at public school together. In fact, the man's job and demeanour – the fellow had actually sought to interrogate him about the cost-effectiveness of the vacant post, indeed! – did not attract the complimentary assumption that if had not been an old schoolfellow, he might well have been. In fact, he was quite likely to have been one of those people who regarded being thus addressed as an insult rather than a form of acceptance. But 'Dear Mr Noote' had seemed a shade too respectful. Arlington had therefore avoided, rather than solved, the problem by a vaguely waggish 'Dear Mr Personnel Officer,' only to be confronted by this wretchedly modern problem of names again at the end.

Professor John Robert Polworth Arlington had obviously not chosen the names which he had been given at birth, and so could not be criticised for them. Indeed, he should have conceded that he had been let off lightly, compared with many other bearers of unwanted handles. Cohorts of Cuthberts and shoals of Shufflebothams would have envied him. It was all the more revealing, therefore, that he had ungratefully eschewed John and even Robert, and announced himself as J R Polworth Arlington on his title-pages, while being known as Polworth Arlington to his outer circle, and Pol to his intimates. He flinched involuntarily when he found a relatively unremarkable JRP Arlington in various bureaucratic listings. The initials of three different forenames might have formed a smart-sounding nickname which would serve as well as 'Pol'. It was his cross to bear.

In the important matter of the signature now required, he judiciously settled for the form he used on his title-pages. One should never go too far.

His concentration on the "Womentic Poits" now broken, he thought that he might as well glance at the revised reading lists which awaited his approval before being duplicated and issued to students next year. He noted with satisfaction that both his previous book, *Methods of "Literwawy" Assessment*, and his forthcoming one on the "Womentic Poits" appeared not only on the list for reading, but also on the list of books which students were advised to buy. Their having been listed could hardly have come as a surprise, for a recommendation to Lecturers from a Head of Department who would be asked to endorse their applications for research grants, leave and promotion can only have seemed wise and helpful. In consequence, the University Library would have to buy several copies to cope with the demand, some students may buy his book themselves, and Arlington's standing with his publishers and his periodic royalties statement would both be enhanced. When his own ideas turned up in students' essays and examination answers, he either rewarded good sense or penalised sycophantic unoriginality, depending on his mood and on whether he liked the student or not.

He noticed that the late Professor Peccary's book, *The "Womentic" View of the Middle "Eeges"*, was also on the list for students to buy.

'Poor eld Peccaweh!' he thought. 'It's been a whel yar since ... A tarsome felleh in many wees, but not a bed scholar, by any mennah of means ... witty parfawmah at conferwences ... He awlways teld his students to bay may book, no dart becawse Ay wecipwocated with his. Ah well, there's neh wecipwociteh now.' He deleted Peccary's book from the list. He realised with a brief pang that a reprisal deletion of his own from Pillingham's list was possible. On the other hand, perhaps nobody would notice for a year or two. He left Dunkerley Browne's book on the list to create the basis of reciprocity with him.

'Yes – Peccaweh wen't be snawting his wee through the Easter Conferwence next week ... Wonder who did him in ... They've got a good enough men in his plece, Ay suppezz, theh he's not vewy wadely exparwienced.'

Returning to the typescript of his own forthcoming book, he found that the newly signed letter and the amended – probably improved, since shorter – reading list now prevented him from spreading out his papers as he wished. He was about to buzz his secretary and have her take this superfluous stuff away, when he realised that she was on the telephone. With a pained air of Apollo serving Admetus - and if that damned Noote hadn't been quibbling about irrelevancies there would have been another secretary anyway! – he picked up the offending items and went into her adjoining room.

'No, Dr ... er ... Kemp,' she was saying. 'Professor Arlington wouldn't be able to see you next week because he'll be away at the Easter Conference ... Yes, that's right, the English Literature Conference at Pagham University ... Yes, such a lovely place ... er ...'

She shot an enquiring glance at Arlington, who mouthed 'In a meeting,' but she then gave a series of 'Hallo's' and said, 'He's either rung off or we've lost the connection. How very odd!'

'It's the switchboard again,' remarked Arlington, as one who was no stranger to disaster but had the fortitude to overcome it. 'Did he say whay he wanted to see meh?'

'Well, not really. We only got as far as his asking for an appointment next week. He said his name was Dr Kemp, and when I asked what he wanted to see you about, he said it was to do with herring gulls.'

'Hewwing gulls?'

'Yes, herring gulls.'

'How vewy odd! Parheps he'll wing beck.'

'I could have misheard him,' she offered. 'Or perhaps he'd got the wrong Department.'

'Obviousleh. Nehbodeh would wing me abite hewwing gulls. Dr Kemp, you said? Never hard of him. Parheps he's a lunatic. Some people oar, you kneh!'

*

It was 1983. President Reagan ('Thet ectah felleh!' as Professor Arlington dubbed him) had just called the Soviet Union an 'evil empire' ('He's weight, for once; some law of everwidges, Ay suppezz'). And he had announced his Star Wars Defense System ('The men's gawn med! Of cawss, Amewicans can't spell "defence", you kneh!').

But the learned Professor Arlington had more important things on his mind.

In the train from Drumbridge to Pagham – first-class, of course, because he was on University business and therefore not paying for himself – he sat as though presiding, chin up, fingers on bow-tie, and glanced with satisfaction at his much-travelled and multi-labelled suitcase above him, and his brief-case and conference papers before him. The Easter Vacation was always welcome to him, and he felt as though he had been rescued from an ordeal. The cessation of ten hours' weekly teaching - he had an unusually heavy load – brought a degree of relief more akin to the removal of a weight from some tender part. But it had been doubly spoiled for him this year: Noote's trouble-making had been bad enough; but that wretched Hooligan girl had been quite insupportable.

Surely the fact of her neurotic importunity must be obvious to any rational person? A postgraduate student who hands her extended essay to her supervisor when he is thinking of something else is inconsiderate and quite without sense. A postgraduate student who expects her extended essay to have been marked not three weeks later has no understanding of the practical necessities of daily life.

When that postgraduate student, reproved for these misdemeanours, points out that, since he, her supervisor, is also the Head of Department, she can only approach the Dean for assistance, as the next stage upwards – then that postgraduate student is unmannerly. When that postgraduate student then makes so bold as to enquire whether the Professor still has the extended essay safely in his possession, then that postgraduate student is guilty of entertaining an ignoble suspicion. When that postgraduate student is not merely unimpressed but scandalised by the Professor's assertion that the extended essay was not handed in in the first place, then that postgraduate student is calling him a liar. When that postgraduate student's father is unreasonable enough to write to the Registrar, asking why the Professor, claiming not to have received the extended essay when due, did not then insist on its submission from a supposedly neglectful student … when that postgraduate student's father asks the Registrar to explain how the Professor reconciles his earlier complaint that it should not have been handed in at an inconvenient time with his later denial that it was handed in at all … when that postgraduate student's father wants to know what the official arrangements are for handing in and safeguarding students' written work and asks for a copy of the regulations covering that matter … when these undeserved plagues can fall upon a busy scholar striving valiantly to do his best for the world of learning, then that postgraduate student's father is obviously the living and breathing explanation for that postgraduate student's manifest deficiencies of character and attitude. ('They're beth demned hooligans! Hooligans bay neem end hooligans bay neechah!')

Ms Carolyn Hooligan had gone home for the vacation. The Dean and the Registrar, who ought to have 'binned' the offensive letter straightaway, had promised her father some sort of waiver of the infringed part of the degree regulations, and an independent external examiner. It was disgraceful, but a sign of the times, that the categorical assertions of a Professor, no less, could be challenged and disregarded in this way.

But the sense of merciful release from the burden of teaching and from being harried by Noote, Hooligan and his dreadful daughter, was now accompanied by the anticipatory pleasure of the English Licha-cha Conferwence.

This event was an annual delight for its participants, whether they were delivering a lecture, taking part in the official business, or merely one of the assembly. Like most of the long-serving members, Professor Arlington had been, at various times, a stalwart, a star, and a spectator – although rather than be thought of in the latter role he preferred now to regard himself as an elder statesman. For he knew how to yield graciously and to unbend with the next generation, while making his vast store of wisdom freely available to it. He conveyed his gracious yielding by prefacing every intervention with such remarks as, 'Well, of cawss, you kneh, Ay dare say one must mooove with the tames, but you'll forgive meh if Ay meek heeste slehleh [*slowly*].' His urbane condescension was surely apparent when he benevolently smiled and intoned a slurred 'Erss' of assent, or at least of tolerant comprehension, at the opinions of newer members. He was just fifty-four.

It was also his custom, which was practised in one form or another by most of his academic colleagues, to complain at home of the inconvenience to which attendance at conferences put him. An air of duty done and merited repose relinquished for the greater good was not to be forgone.

Professor Arlington did not know – indeed, only one person knew – that he was to forgo all pleasures of the conference except that of anticipation.

*

The Conference membership was drawn from the academic staff of a variety of ranks from most of the disparate universities in the country. They were fully united only in one respect, when at the Arrival Dinner the Chairman proposed a motion 'cawling upon the Gumt *[Government]* to ellocate maw funds to finence schol'ship in awl its fawms'. This item appeared as a matter of course and without prior notice, much as *The Blue Danube* was played at the New Year's Day Concert from Vienna and received similar welcome. The resolution was minuted and sent to official circles as though it were the outcome of extended and weighty discussion. But most other tendencies at the Conference were centrifugal, and a few of them internecine: for they had come to play several incompatible conference games, which were begun during conversation at the Arrival Dinner and developed over the next few days.

The most public of these games was played between two small bodies of members. The group most in evidence consisted of the Conference's office-bearers – the kind of individuals who would have aspired to and held office, while complaining about the burden of it all, in whatever association they might have joined. Some other individuals, who did not function as a group, wanted to be in office, but protested vehemently that they did not. These two sets of people caused to be done what little was done at the Conference and were simultaneously responsible for its paucity and for the inordinate amount of time it required. Volumes were spoken on the minutiae of the accounts, points of order, and the remits and constitutions and membership of Sub-Committees, Working Parties and Advisory Groups.

While this game of 'pillars *versus* wannabe pillars' was in process, with, metaphorically, its own pitch, ball and set of rules, another group of players, overlapping with the first two, was playing its own game of 'wannabe stars.' These wannabe stars were members who saw the Conference as a means of furthering their personal standing as scholars. For this, it was necessary to contrive the opportunity for performance, to be heard and seen, to strike up acquaintanceships, and to impress. The recipients and target-audiences of these activities would be anyone who might be on an interviewing committee for a job, or useful as an external referee in the promotion-stakes or asked to endorse a proposed publication; they might be officials, aspirants to office, or elder statesmen detached from the manoeuvres. The risk attendant upon attempts at self-advertisement and self-ingratiation was that the aspirant to favour may get off on the wrong foot if he seemed to have supported the wrong side or had failed to grasp what the topic of a dispute was. This was sure to happen, because the game played by 'wannabe stars' complicated the main game by confusing the alignment and membership of teams. And it obscured the issues at stake, because the wannabe stars had, in essence, brought their own balls unrecognised as such by the main players, but sometimes used the main ball, while playing on their own imaginary pitch at an angle to the main one. Everyone felt that he alone was playing by agreed rules. Participants in these games had to remember which game they were playing and to deduce which game the others were playing – including those in a cryptic third game of biding one's time before suddenly joining in, or a fourth game of playing both games at once, or a fifth of switching from one to the other.

These gentlemen-players sometimes seemed to carry with them the aura of their institutions. Pagham, for example, their present venue, and its sibling, Arlington's Drumbridge, were Sixties' 'new' universities, no longer new but still inclined to regard their civic red-brick elders of the Midlands and North, such as Pillingham, as city-bound neo-Victorian prisons of the intellect. The latter responded with the disdain of the well-established for the Johnny-come-lately, even though many subjects were as 'new' in the 'old' universities as in the ageing 'new' ones. It really all depended on whom they were trying to influence and why: to government money-givers they proclaimed their modernity or solidity; to teachers of sixth-formers, their progressiveness or tradition; to parents of sons, the opportunities of cities; to parents of daughters, their safe rural environs. You reads your brochure and you takes your choice.

*

Professor Arlington's destiny was no longer compatible with participation in these mystic rituals.

Dismissing his taxi on arrival at the Pagham campus, with his dignity still painfully impugned by the onslaughts of Noote and the pair of Hooligans, he ignored younger acquaintances and sought solace by falling in with old Roach from Melbury, who had come by car. He needed to be a Grand Old Man consorting with the like-minded this afternoon.

'It's enleh a couple of hars on the mettahwee [*motorway*],' said Roach, 'seh Ay deceded to jive [*drive*]. Did you come by chain?'

"Arse. The Inter-shitty is vair convenient.'

There was a panting pause as they deposited their cases in the road and looked around them for signposts.

'I see fwom the pwogwemme,' remarked Arlington, with distaste, 'thet we are to heah tomowwow anothah lecsha on the sessiologeh [*sociology*] of lichacha.'

'Tarsome,' Roach assented. 'Ay think Ay'll cut it and look up an eld welative. End Ay den't wealleh car [*really care*] for awl this faynencial [*financial*] stuff immediateleh awfter tea, ayther. But unfawtunateleh Ay'm in the char.'

'Commiserwations! ... Seh you hev welatives heah? Ah, yiss, Ay wemembah your saying that you wair bwought up nearbay.'

'Arse. We awl cem heah fwom Cembwidge in the depths of wintah when Ay was thwee. In fect, may farst memweh [memory] is of when we chiljun wair awl given bollock-lovers.'

'Awl given what?'

'Bollock-lover hilmits. We awl pwetended to be Scawtt of the Entaw'tic.'

'Arse, Ay see.'

Lugging their suitcases about the campus – for they were defeated by the clear campus-plan next to them and by foolproof signposting - they eventually found the student hostel where they were to stay, collected their keys from a porter at an office by the entrance, and installed themselves in their respective rooms.

Arlington fell into his one armchair and began a spell of bow-tie fingering, chin-jutting and lip-pursing, all of which fulfilled for him the function of thumb-sucking for an infant. This had been difficult to do while out of breath and pulled off-balance by a heavy suitcase. Restored to life, he heaved his case on to the bed, unfastened the lid, and took out a tough, thick glass and a new bottle of whisky. He uncorked it by a slow twisting pressure, for he liked the sound of it, poured himself a generous measure, added a dash more by way of judicious afterthought, and sat down again in the armchair.

The seat was a trifle too low in relation to the height of the armrests, and his one previous decline into it had not impressed this fact sufficiently upon him. Consequently, he knocked his elbow and spilled some whisky over his hand. His vast knowledge of literature and of esoteric vocabulary prompted him to hiss, 'Fuck it!' He pulled his bow-tie in desperation, re-enacted the pouring and the supplementation, sat down again, this time with elaborate care, and drank.

He leaned back, every inch the great man at peace after and before his labours.

The building was, indeed, peaceful. The students had gone down for the vacation, though one or two always remained, and the Conference participants were spread over the building, leaving every two or three rooms unoccupied in order to avoid congestion at lavatories and bathrooms.

Professor Arlington let the whisky flow into him, soothingly, caressingly. A miscellany of isolated sounds came from all directions to his drowsy ears. A distant shout intoned from the far edge of the campus; a car-engine spluttered down on the access-road; the central heating radiator hummed *sotto voce*, soporifically. The plumbing, somewhere, joined in, and then fell silent again. Footsteps approached in a gentle crescendo along the corridor. He expected them to pass his door and go into diminuendo, but they stopped, and he heard a knock.

'Come!' he called, sleepily and after a brief pause. He never called 'Come in!' The single word was far more imposing, both as an imperative and as a vehicle for a full-throated vowel. And the pause had two useful functions: it made the caller uncertain; and he gained a second or two to ensure that he did not, as he had once done, shout 'Titties!'

The person outside tried the handle, but the door would not yield. Arlington realised that he had left the automatic lock active on entering and began slowly to rise.

'Arse? Who is it?' he said, as he shambled to the door; but more out of impatience and a desire to fill in time and space than really wishing to know before opening.

'Janitor, sir. Urgent letter from BBC Television.'

Arlington instantly saw in his mind's eye his own performance as an expert interviewee or presenter on a popular but learned series, with his name prominent in the credits at the end. And such a series was often the basis for a book, which would then go into paperback! Already admiring his prospective celebrity, he seized his bow-tie with one hand and, jutting his jaw and pursing his lips, opened the door with the other. A middle-aged man wearing a cap and a khaki overall, and very thick glasses which reflected the window, handed him a sealed envelope. Arlington noticed in passing that the man wore gloves on a warm day.

He was about to close the door, when the man, edging in, said, excitedly, portentously, 'You're to read it and give me an immediate reply for their Special Messenger, sir.'

Arlington would normally have ordered the man to wait outside. But the fellow was his only contact with the BBC Special Messenger, wherever he was, and was obviously impressed with his important errand. In any case, that envelope really had to be opened! He turned and processed towards the window to read it, with his future eminence as a TV pundit still dancing before his eyes.

Suddenly, he was aware that the janitor had closed the door and followed him. He made to turn in annoyance, but before he could do so he received a rapid succession of hammer-blows on the top and back of his head. The first probably killed him.

But his assailant enjoyed the rest of them. The luscious squelch as each time the hammer landed on the victim's scalp; though it was not as juicy as on the fleshy padding on the pig's head ... The way the skull itself simultaneously split and emitted a dry, sharp crack, which the pig's had not ... The combination of sounds was akin to having the first violins doubled by the oboe ... It was accompanied by a different squelch as the hammer forced its way into the brain, displacing some greyish matter with an eruption of blood as though horse-radish sauce and cranberry juice were in a *pas de deux*. And he noticed that the room was increasingly pervaded by the sickly-sweet, metallic smell of blood. That came of killing in a confined space rather than in the open air ...

The murderer gathered up the envelope and paper, both of which were blank, and took the paper money from the dead man's wallet, which he threw down empty. He then took from his pocket a page torn from a book and placed it in the dead man's hand.

He removed his overall, which now bore splashes of blood and brain-tissue. His dark clothing beneath would not show any minor flecks of blood which might have found their way in. From his pocket came a chain-store plastic bag, into which went the blood-spotted overall, neatly folded, the glasses, and the cap. He went to the wash-basin and sluiced the blood and matted hair from his hammer, which he likewise placed in his bag.

A quick check in the mirror reassured him that there were no blood splashes on his face. A Conference badge in his lapel revealed him to be Dr I Omen of the Joint Research Councils.

He was elated.

He said to himself:

'My subject is Pigs, and the Killing of Pigs.
The Killing is in the Piggishness ...

I must write all this up one day. Call it *The Memoirs of a Pig-Hunting Man?'*

The door closed behind him on its own spring-lock; he placed his gloves in his bag; on leaving the building he took a different route.

He maintained a slightly unusual gait which he had adopted since first reaching the campus. One stride was a little longer than the other, as though his legs were of unequal length; but it was not a limp. Anybody who noticed him would remember how he walked.

The building was still.

Professor Arlington was still.

The combined effect of the blows and his fall to the floor had made his jaw jut, while his hand, caught beneath him, rested at the edge of his bow-tie to replicate his favourite mannerism. Blood flowed from his head wounds on to his neck, then, still under gravity's pull, followed the dry gulches of his fatty wattles on to the corner of his tie, and soaked its way up the material before congealing.

A carrion crow squawked as though in resentment at being denied access to a meal. The squawk echoed in agreement with itself.

CHAPTER 8

EVEN A CONFERENCE IS INTERRUPTED IF IT'S MURDER

Detective-Inspector Groyne's Christian names were Barry Oliver Gilbert, and his reaction to his unfortunate initials and other potentialities of this inheritance were quite unlike those of the more fortunately endowed late Professor Arlington. Neither Groyne's attendance at council schools nor three years' service in the military police had induced him to contract his signature. He was not noted for an ability to savour absurdities which concerned himself, although his apparent insistence on appearing so frequently as BOG Groyne might have suggested otherwise to the unwary. And there was, from time to time, the unwary new constable ... It was only after his promotion to Inspector that he seemed suddenly to realise that he had a funny name, for he was heard to remark:

'Every stupid little prick thinks 'e's the first to notice.' He mimicked his detractors with more passion than thespian skill - 'Inspected any interestin' groins lately?' - and continued: 'The next Funny Man will need *'is* bleedin' groin inspected.' Absurdities directed against others were far more to his taste.

Altogether, his promotion seemed to have brought him little but a higher salary to offset the increased irritation. So, following a rather slack period of routine cases enlivened only by the theft of a number of brand-new word-processors from nearby Pagham University – men in overalls had turned up with a plausible story, and the porters had helped load a plain van – Groyne was really quite relieved to be called to the murder of a Professor.

As he was driven off in a squad car, the report of a murdered Professor rang a bell with him, and he was still trying to place the reference when he arrived at the University.

He noted that uniformed constables were keeping the approach routes to it free from casual or inquisitive trespass, barring entry to the building, and obtaining the identities of people leaving. Before going to the scene of the crime he sent a constable to check that the emergency exits were similarly guarded.

The cleaner who had discovered the body was sitting in the little kitchen at the end of the corridor of study-bedrooms, and was being plied with sugary tea, sugary sympathy, and sugary questions by her colleagues. Groyne decided to leave her there for a while. Her initial statement had been taken by a constable from the patrol sent in response to the emergency call, and this would indicate any imaginative additions she might make to enhance her stardom. On the other hand, she might remember something else useful when she had recovered …

Accompanied by Detective-Constable John Robinson – 'Sounds like a bloody alias to me,' he grunted, resentful of such an innocuous and mock-proof name – he went to the victim's room. The University's Security Officer, whom Groyne recognised from previous contacts, including the recent farce with the word-processors, stood near the open door. Groyne nodded to him and glanced in at the body. The congealed blood showed that the criminal was long gone; consequently, time now spent on procedures would be a better investment than a display of energy would. In any case, the cleaner was evidently making little sense at present, if the group performance at the end of the corridor was any indication.

Without touching anything, Groyne looked minutely at and around the body, noting the discarded wallet, and a crumpled piece of paper in the dead man's hand. The wallet was of finest leather and might yield some fingerprints; its contents or lack of contents might also be instructive.

He decided to start with the piece of paper, and, putting on a pair of gloves, eased it from the chilly grasp and smoothed it out. He took a transparent plastic bag from his pocket and inserted the sheet before examining it. It was a page torn from a book, which the running-title at the top revealed to be called *Narrative Styles*.

A sentence had been underlined: 'If ambiguity was the intention, was the style a mere device or the inevitable expression of that ambiguity?'

'What the fuck does that mean?' muttered Groyne.

With the idea that the murdered man might have been reading when attacked and somehow seized the page spontaneously, Groyne looked round for the book. It was nowhere to be seen, and, sensing an irritating puzzle, summarised it: 'Bollocks!'

'Begya pardon, sir?' said Detective-Constable Robinson, uneasily.

'I said, "bollocks," lad. 'E was clutching this, *as* you see, so go an' find out which book it came from.'

Robinson looked blank.

'Ask in the bleedin' Library over the road, lad. They got books in there, 'aven't they?'

Groyne decided to settle in for investigations on the spot. The Security Officer used his master-key to open some of the adjacent rooms which, with most of the students away for the vacation, were vacant and so could be used as offices or interview rooms. The public telephone in the foyer was requisitioned for police use. The University's Conference Bookings Office was contacted to obtain a list of occupants of the building.

The doctor, the fingerprints officer and the police photographer coincidentally arrived together. While they set to work, Groyne installed himself in the room next door and sent Robinson to fetch the cleaner who had discovered the body. Robinson's hollow footfalls faded into silence and began a gradual reamplification accompanied, as though on a separate sound-track, by the shuffling of many slippers and a subdued hubbub through which cups and saucers rattled like the chattering of teeth.

A doleful middle-aged woman appeared in the doorway. Her long, thin face, streaky with dried and replenished tears, perched, neckless, on narrow shoulders; but she was incongruously wide from the waist down. Altogether, she looked like a battered violin. She stood there, her head on one side as though playing a violin herself but supported by a friend at each elbow. Their uncoordinated triangle of movement had obviously placed in constant jeopardy the tea which each held.

Groyne firmly dispossessed the backing-group of their star and led the lone sufferer to the one easy-chair. He sat on the hard chair by the desk, and Robinson sat on the bed.

'Ooh!' she began, looking at the dividing wall as though it were transparent, ' 'e's nex' door! Carn' we go somewhere else?'

This was not a promising start, and soothing troubled minds was not Groyne's *forte*. Offering tea was the limit of his repertoire, and in this he had plainly been copiously forestalled to no effect. But he soon realised that she had nothing more to tell. At around 10 am she had entered the Professor's room to clean it, assuming him to have been at the Conference, 'an' there Oi found 'im aw stiff an' cowd!'

'Did you touch 'im?'

'Oooh, no – Oi coon't 'ardly look!'

'Then 'ow – how did you know 'e was stiff an' cowd?'

'E was dead, wasn't 'e? Wiv awl 'is 'ead loik 'at! Poor man!'

Groyne soon released the Battered Violin, for, having learned that she had then summoned her friends to see the corpse – 'You woon't let 'em come in wiv me!' she reproached him, parenthetically – he wanted to hear what they had seen and whether or not they had touched anything. He soon established that neither of them had dared look at what they had plainly viewed intently while supposedly not looking, and, more importantly, that nobody had touched anything. He was also able to confirm that the Security Officer had mounted guard until the arrival of the patrol car.

He realised with sinking enthusiasm that he would have to interview all regular and temporary occupants of the building. Before doing that, he needed to know, as closely as possible, the time of death – because each interviewee would have to be asked where he was, what he was doing, and what he saw and heard at the material time. But the doctor could only offer a supposition that death had occurred 'some time before midnight,' and turned huffy when pressed for greater precision until the post-mortem examination.

Groyne sighed. This promised to be one of those enormous, long-drawn-out jobs. A few students were still in residence, even in vacation. ('Aven't they got 'omes to go to? Jus' clutterin' the place up!') A hundred Professors or whatever were holding a Conference, and some of them were accommodated in this building. Any of them who had tried recently to get into the building or to move about within it would know that some kind of flap was on. But only the murderer, if still around, would know what it was all about. If the guilty party was attending the Conference, he would be on a list somewhere, and probably still in the vicinity; he wouldn't be so daft as to draw attention to himself by vamoosing. But if an outsider, he'd be well away by now.

There was a knock, and a constable peered round the door, gesticulating to Robinson.

'Don't wave your digit about, lad,' grated Groyne. 'Use your tongue to excite us.'

The constable hastily redirected his attention to Groyne.

'I've found out which book it came from, sir. I went to the University Library, and they identified it somehow.'

'Torn from their book?'

'No, sir. But that young lady librarian pointed out that it looked brand-new, apart from being crumpled up, and wondered if it was from the University bookshop. So I went there, and it was! But they didn't see anyone tear it out. Anyway, this is the book it was torn from.'

He thrust a book in a paper bag at Groyne, who peered in without touching it.

'*Narrative Styles* by J L Simmonds. Never 'eard of 'im. Anyway, good work, lad. We'd better 'ave it fingerprinted - see to that, Robinson – check the pages either side of the one torn out, and the shiny cover. Though I s'pose that's covered in 'undreds of dabs. Oh, Jesus, why is nothin' ever simpoow!'

The constable was still there.

'Now what?'

'It's the night porter, sir. Mr Robinson said I should bring him up.'

'Yes, sir,' Robinson confirmed. 'When I was downstairs, sewing up the building, I heard of something that might be interesting. Last night – an unidentified male person of janitorial appearance.'

''A what? You mean, 'e looked like a set of janitals? No, lad, that was A Joke. Oh, wheel 'im in. I'll try anythin' once, except shit wi' sugar on.'

The porter's story was of a man wearing thick glasses, some sort of cap, and an overall, who had asked for directions to Professor Arlington's room. Groyne sat up.

'When?'

The porter ruminated: 'Welw ... it was after *The Archers* but before my late break.'

Groyne, realising that concepts of accuracy and ways of measuring it varied greatly, essayed a number of questions, and fixed the time of this visit at around 7 15 pm. So: What was the time of the Conference dinner? And had the murdered man eaten? If he had eaten after 7 15 pm, the stranger was in the clear, as far as the murder was concerned, though he might still have been up to something else; or might be a useful witness. But, on the other hand, if the murder took place on an empty stomach ... The post-mortem would settle that doubt.

The porter ventured a really positive statement: 'The cap was definitely a sort of browny colour. I think.'

Groyne waited for another gem.

' 'E was wearin' one o' them overalls,' his informant sought to elaborate with an air of helpful lucidity, and explained, under duress, that he meant a coat-length khaki overall.

'It looked new,' he added. 'But, then, it would, wouldn't it? 'Cause 'e'd jus' started. You can always telw.'

' 'Ow d'you know 'e'd jus' started?'

' 'E said so. Said Mr Bootle 'ad sent 'im. Wiv a confidentchule messidge.'

Robinson, seeing Groyne's mute interrogation, interposed: 'Mr Bootle is the Head Porter, sir, who informed me upon my enquiring at 11 16 am that no new staff had been engaged for four months and that no person answering to the description was employed by him. Sir. Or has been discharged or left of his own accord in the past few years. Sir.'

'Anyone see 'im leave?'

'No, sir. He must have gone out by the North door.'

Groyne grunted and ruminated:

'So we know about 'is cap an' we know about 'is overall, which 'e'll dispose of, an' we know about 'is glasses which might be a disguise anyway, and we know sod-all about the man 'imself. Except that a genuine new man would have gone out the way 'e came in. Which tells us that very likely 'e'd spied out the lay o' the land earlier on.'

The porter had been chewing the inside of his mouth in order to stimulate a thought, which now struggled to be born: ' 'E 'ad a funny walk, sir.'

'Funny? What kind o' funny?'

'Sort o' lop-sided. War-wound, I'd say. I've seen 'em, o' course.'

Groyne surprised Robinson by his sudden amicability as the witness began to reminisce about his lucky escapes from injury in the Western Desert and Italy ... The Inspector seemed almost regretful that he had to steer the talk back to confirmation of the evidence collected.

The detectives returned to Arlington's room – the fingerprinting and other forensic work having been concluded - and went through the dead man's pockets and wallet. They noted that he had no paper money on him. This was not surprising, since the wallet had been taken out. But what did that really tell them?

They sat down and reviewed the case thus far but succeeded mainly in identifying what they did not know. Groyne surprised Robinson again by wanting to know what he thought on many points.

It made sense that, if Arlington had not eaten ... and if the murderer were not a permanent resident, which seemed likely, because he would not have risked recognition by the regular porter ... then this porter-impersonator was more of a suspect than a witness. And if he were the murderer, how would it have worked? He gets the Professor to open up with some story about a message, and just thumps the old boy. Seems like he wasn't a porter here at Pagham, ever. So how does he know about Bootle? Could just have found out, I suppose. Hardly a state secret. But why pick on Arlington?

It sounds like an inside job, with a personal grudge as the motive – except for the missing money. Did he want us to think that it was a robbery gone wrong? But Arlington's flash gold watch wasn't taken. Perhaps he didn't notice it. Perhaps he was in a hurry ... But if it was an inside job, why did he need to find the room number? If he knew the set-up here, why not just wait until the porter's away from his desk and look at the Conference list? Unless he wants us to think he's an outsider ... But suppose it really is an outside job? Nothing really says it's inside. For example, he could have known Bootle's name from some other source ... And what use is our best lead? Middle-aged, darkish, an odd walk that might be a war wound and might not, average height, average-to-heavy build, except that you can't really see under an overall like that ... New overall – so he bought an overall ...

'Check the shops for that, sir?' ventured Robinson.

''Yeah. No bloody use, probally, but we'll 'ave to. It might have been bought by a bloke with that kind of walk. Though 'e'd probably 'ave bought it somewhere else. An' we'll 'ave to interview all these Professors. Jesus Christ!'

Robinson said: 'On that point, sir, the Conference meeting in the next building will be breaking for lunch about now. The porter said some of them will want to get into their rooms to dump papers and things.'

'Yeah – an' we're keepin' everyone out ... So what's best?'

Groyne had to take a snap decision as to how next to proceed. There was no point in keeping the entire building sealed, for the murderer, whether local or an outsider, had had all night to eradicate clues or lay false ones. Most of the uniformed constables could therefore be released to their normal duties, but a couple of extra Detective-Constables would be needed to help with the interviewing. Nothing would be revealed to the Conference members, who would be allowed into their rooms, though Arlington's room would be kept locked and guarded. Refuse-bins all over the campus should be checked, beginning with those for the building and those on the way to exits from the campus. The killer, no doubt with normal clothing beneath his overall, would have removed the overall and perhaps dumped it as soon as possible – though he had given the impression of being too bright for an elementary mistake such as that. For the interviews, a list of Conference participants would be wanted; the Security Officer had this to hand. And whoever was in charge of the entire Conference should be spoken to first, without being given any information in advance.

Robinson disappeared to make these arrangements.

Within minutes the building began to receive its temporary tenants. A few footsteps, some fumbling with keys, minor comings-and-goings, and the mysteries of plumbing.

In the lull, Groyne remembered more clearly that the previous year in the University of Pillingham a Professor had been attacked and murdered, also with a blunt instrument. But that was at his house, surely? This one was different.

*

The Conference Chairman was Professor Roach. Irving Harrison Roach was known to his colleagues as a distinguished scholar. To his students he was known – by reason of a reputation for amorous escapades which, considering his age and apparent condition, ought to have been, but was not, a slanderous and unjustified product of scurrilous young minds – as Cock Roach. Groyne informed him of the events thus far, watched his reaction, and observed it to be convincing enough: that is to say, it consisted, no less than did that of the Mrs Mopps, of cheap theatre, but in an erudite falsetto. The phrase 'another one – just lake poowr eld Peccaweh – end awlmest to the yar' was a leitmotif.

'Probably not connected, sir,' said Groyne, glad to have been reminded of the previous victim's name. 'That one was at 'ome, and was to do with a breakin'-an'-enterin'. This one looks different to me.'

Roach had, as soon as Groyne had started to speak, begun a long, slow nodding with the upper half of his body, as though he were on a horse. He now seemed to simmer down, and said, 'Ay'm sure you kneh best, Inspictah.' Groyne seized this moment to get to the business in hand.

'I'll have to interview a number of your colleagues, Professor. For most of them it should be quick and simple: where they were at the material time, who they were with, whether they noticed anybody who didn't seem to belong ... we might need to reinterview them if anything crops up ... I'll probably need longer chats with those from this University and from the dead man's University, and any other obvious connections. Now, see this list – 'oo are the ones I need to see?'

'Oh, deah me!' intoned Roach, beginning to gee-up. 'Ay doo seh hep this wen't interwupt the Conferwence!'

'We'll do our best, sir. Now, if you would jus' tell me the ones from the two Universities.'

Roach took the list, peered at it, and asked, with elaborate humility, 'May Ay put mawks [marks] on it?'

'Please do, sir,' Groyne assented, silently adding, 'Anything to get your finger out!'

Roach theatrically produced a silver fountain-pen, and sorrowfully rejected it in favour of a matching propelling-pencil, which he twiddled into readiness with an agreeable smile as though performing a conjuring trick for the entertainment of the mentally deficient. He placed a letter by each of several names, and then added a little tabulation: 'C = Cantab, D = Drumbridge, P = Pagham.'

'Thar you are!' he said: 'Ay've shen [shown] the two Univarsities you wequar and Ay've edded Cembwidge – elphabeticalleh et the beginning, of cawss.' Pleased with his initiative, he explained: 'Poowr eld Awlington took his farst degwee and his doctorwate at Cembwidge, and now helds a pest *[holds a post]* – that is to say, he *did* held a pest until yesterdee – at Jumbwidge. But he continued to lecsha et Cembwidge occasionalleh. You *did* say "any other awbvious connections, Inspictah!'

'Very helpful, sir.' And, as Groyne peered more closely, he queried: 'Cantab?'

'Cembwidge,' returned Roach, impassively.

'Ah ... I didn't know you could spell it that way too.'

Roach shifted in his seat and was obviously mounting up for another cantering discourse.

Groyne put a halt to this: 'Professor, I shall have to ask where you yourself were last evening.'

'Oh! Whay is thet?'

'Because you're my line of communication, sir.'

'Your lane of ...? Oh, yes, Ay see. How vair interwesting!' Having perceived Groyne's logic, he felt obliged to explain it to him: 'You cleah *[clear]* me, and enleh then cen you cheat *[treat]* me as cwedible when Ay speak of colleagues end welated mettahs. Ixcellent!'

'And, of course,' – Groyne pressed home his advantage – 'when I interview the rest, I'll be able to tell them that their chief went in to bat first. That always makes it easier in such cases.' ('Christ, I wish this old bugger would sit still!')

'Oh, haw! haw! Hawdly a chief, you kneh. W'ar awl colleagues heah. But Ay suppezz that et the memment, as Conferwence Charman, Ay cunt as *pwimus inter parwes [primus inter parves]*.'

Robinson had been writing in his notebook with an air of being ten years old and at the bottom of the class. He had always been good at English but was unfamiliar with its more obscure dialects. He would have appealed for clarification (though 'Cunt as what into what?' would not have helped); but Roach was trotting ahead so purposively, and

Groyne would not have relished the delay of an interruption.

'May wharabites lawst evening: a simple mettah. Ay went on a pwayvit visit to the woad warks.'

'The ... er ...? Ah, er, yes. And what interested you in the road works, Professor?'

'Neh, not thet sort of woad warks. Ay parceive thet we are et cwass-parposes. I mean the Encient Bwitish woad warks. Woad,' he continued, twiddling his silver propelling pencil again as though about to correct an inferior essay, 'was an Encient Bwitish body-decorwation. Blue, you kneh. Ay hev a pwayvit interwest in Encient Bwitain. Ay faynd thet it pwovades me with wefweshment fwom may pwincipal pweoccupation with English Lichacha.'

'Of course, it would do that,' Groyne agreed, for want of something to say. He was dimly aware, while Roach cantered gently in his chair again and beamed at him, that Robinson was amending odd letters in his notebook. He attempted to take up the lost thread: 'So you were at the – ' – he concentrated hard on his consonants – '– the woad works.'

'Arse. Seh Ay'm awfleh sowweh to disappoint you es a suspect, Inspictah, but, you see, Ay hev en ellybay, as Ay believe you cawl it.'

'You know bleedin' well that's what we call it, you shit-brained pillock!' snarled Groyne, but only somewhere in the back of his head.

'The Cuwator kayndly weceived meh, end will be eeble to confarm thet Ay was thar et thet tah-im *[time]*. In fect, we hed dinnah togithah. Ay hed to visit him, becawse Ay'm one of the Chustees *[Trustees]* end hed to cuntersane the cunty cunts.'

Robinson looked up in despair, and saw that Groyne, too, was baffled. Surely, he thought, the old duffer didn't say ...? Or perhaps he was quoting Latin or something; people like that seemed to do so a lot. Emboldened by that idea he said: 'I didn't quite hear, sir. To countersign, was it? the ...?'

'The cunty cunts. We weceive a numbah of gwawnts [*grants*], end adopt vair stchikt accunting systims, beth for cunt end for deposit. The cunty cunts obviously wequar more fwequent vewification than the deposit accunts.'

Groyne tried hard to smile in agreeable assent, and almost succeeded.

'Charity law demands it, of course, sir. And the times of your arrival and departure?'

Robinson noted the details, with occasional false trails, but Groyne paid little attention. This fluent but incomprehensible chairbound bouncing old fool was only one of so many to be interviewed, and that unidentified porter still sounded like their best lead – except, perhaps, that mysterious torn page.

The ticklish questions about personal relationships he saved until last, but he learned nothing useful. Roach had 'knen the dead men [*man*] intimitly for tharty yars,' and spoke fulsomely of his 'feem' [*fame*] and 'parsonal' qualities ... 'Neh, Mr Wobinson, he wasn't a parson or any other sawt of clargymen, but, hed, Ay suppezz, the qualities one mate seek in one. Such a pewagon could hev hed no parsonal enemies at awl. The mardarwah must hev been a medmen.'

Roach had, by delivering himself of that judgement, covered the back-straight at a sprint, and now reigned himself in.

'Changing the subject, sir ... I've noticed a name on the Conference list ... Professor J L Simmonds, University of Pillingham. What can you tell me about him?'

'Um, now what cen Ay say? Peccaweh's successah. Bwilliant felleh. Not heah at the Conferwence – femileh beweavement – his bwother, ekshleh.'

Other interviewees, though less tiring to watch, less eulogistic and, in some cases, even comprehensible in the native language which was their professional speciality, brought Groyne and Robinson no further forward. No enemies were reported. The witnesses seemed to have eaten, drunk, and gossiped together all evening and half the night. Arlington had not been seen since his arrival.

That bogus porter ... The description was virtually useless except to eliminate anyone who walked normally, who was not of medium height, who was not dark ('I think'), who was not clean-shaven, who had an accent, and who did not wear thick glasses and a new overall. Robinson had telephoned the obvious local shops which sold overalls, and that enquiry had been the predicted waste of time: if this crime had been well-planned, as all the information so far available suggested, the overall would not have been bought either locally or recently. And the refuse bins on the campus had yielded nothing of interest.

Groyne decided – but only on the no-stones-unturned principle – to contact the Pillingham force to compare notes on the earlier crime. His only real purpose was to avoid the criticism of not having done so. That could wait until tomorrow, by which time he would have received the post-mortem report.

The report confirmed the apparent cause of death and stated that the victim had not eaten for several hours. This fact, combined with the 7 30 pm start for the Conference dinner, pointed again to the bogus porter with the odd walk as the murderer. The wallet unfortunately bore only Arlington's fingerprints. And the murderer was right-handed.

Groyne also received a message, forestalling his intention to telephone Pillingham CID, asking him to contact Detective-Inspector Hooligan. The conversation, while Groyne intermittently picked his teeth and Hooligan admired a Vermeer reproduction on his office wall, took them little further. The bogus porter did not sound like the angry-looking man seen walking his unseen dog near Peccary's house, and neither of them sounded like Bertrand Pyle. But, of course, if the angry-looking man and Pyle had nothing to do with each other or with the murders, these resemblances should not be expected. The glasses and the gait were probably a disguise; already people remembered those rather than a face. The interval of around a year between the two murders would make the comparison of identifications, such as they were, imprecise at best.

Hooligan suggested that the crimes might still be linked in some way, because both victims were in their early fifties, both were Professors of English Literature, and both had been struck on the head by a right-handed assailant. He conceded that the coincidences did not create a firm logical case, and that the only people in common – the Pillingham staff – had now twice proved to have unshakeable alibis. What was more, maintained Groyne, the Pillingham case was connected with a burglary.

'We're not sure about that,' said Hooligan, but Groyne was not listening.

'And, 'Groyne added, '*my* man rifled Arlington's wallet, but *your* man just hit Peccary and skedaddled.'

Hooligan was silent, wondering how to explain, to a colleague who was very good at his job but unimaginative, the notion of a false trail laid by a devious and possibly eccentric criminal.

'And,' Groyne continued, 'Arlington was asked for by name in broad daylight; *your* bloke's a night-bird. And, according to you, there's the possibility of a mistaken identity anyway.'

Hooligan wanted to point out that the differences could be the product of a single mind sowing the seeds of confusion. But he contented himself with the suggestion that each should go through the other's files, in the hope of spotting ... something ...

'Did you ever interview someone called Professor J L Simmonds?' Groyne asked and explained the mystery of the torn page with the sentence underlined.

'Twice. Once originally, and then when he got Peccary's job. He seems to be completely in the clear. I'll check for you, if you like, about this funeral he's supposed to be at instead of going to the Conference at Pagham. But this business with the torn page and the underlining ... I can't help wondering if the murderer's done this just for fun ... '

'Bamboozle us, you mean?'

'Yes, but only in a way. As a red herring it seems so clumsy ... I meant, almost as though he's mocking us ... like the glue in the doors ... And that does hint at a connection between the two victims ... and makes me wonder if he's happy for us to think so ... again, mocking us ... I take it you've found no clear motive so far? Personal malice, for example?'

Groyne summarised the praise he had heard of the late Professor Arlington.

'There's one other point you might find interesting,' said Hooligan. 'This business of Arlington as an unsung saint with no enemies ... I happen to know, by pure chance, that he had one or two human failings: like gross neglect of responsibility and deliberate lying. Please don't think I'm interfering, but you might want to look for an enemy somewhere.'

Hooligan recounted the story of his daughter, Carolyn, and of his own intervention, and added: 'She was very upset and furious at the time; we all were. But neither of us is much use as a suspect, I'm afraid. She's in New Zealand, and I'm too pure in heart, as well as having an alibi. Anyway, I mention all this because if you or the Drumbridge force dig around Arlington's Department for clues, you'll presumably come across her name and mine as people who might have wanted him bumped off.'

'Look forward to it. Do you want to come over here at all? Or meet me in Drumbridge?'

'I don't think that will do any good, as long as we exchange files and any information that turns up.'

Just before the call ended, Detective-Sergeant Plumb came in, and Hooligan gave him a full account of the conversation. Plumb had, of course, heard the last few sentences of it himself.

CHAPTER 9

AN ATMOSPHERE OF VIOLENCE

Dr Brisley drove off in good time for a meeting twenty miles away with two of his opposite numbers, who were Chief Librarians of other universities in the region. These meetings, held at irregular intervals in each Library in turn, were usually about nothing in particular and everything in general: they provided exchanges of experience and mutual support.

Today's gathering, intended for the middle of the Autumn Term, had been postponed for a couple of weeks from its original date, because the host for this occasion, Jack Thurlow of the University of Melbury, had been assaulted by a postgraduate student. The affair had attracted more attention than it might have done normally, because local public opinion immediately assumed that the attacker was the double-murderer. However, the police had soon established that the young man in question was left-handed, whereas the blows that had killed Peccary and Arlington had been dealt by a right-handed person. He was also too young and too thin to have been what the Press had called the Phantom Porter of Pagham. The attacker had been charged with causing grievous bodily harm and remanded on bail.

Melbury, a Red Brick cousin of Pillingham, had long ago sold off its inner-city premises and removed to the edge of the city when it expanded and needed new buildings. These, surrounding an old manor house, the gift of a benefactor, Lord Dunsinane, already looked unlikely to survive their venerable headquarters.

Brisley knew this campus. He drove unhesitatingly round its ring road, which presented a changing perspective of buildings in a mad jumble of architectural styles or architectural bad taste and parked at the back of the Library. A few minutes later he was being shown into Thurlow's office, where Thurlow was drinking coffee with Bill Dottie from the University of Stockchester. Brisley immediately saw Thurlow's still badly bruised face and heavily bandaged hand.

'We'd almost given you up,' said Dottie.

An interrogatory gap in the conversation seemed to require more than an apology by way of reply. Brisley said, with vague helplessness, 'I got lost.'

'Got lost!' they chuckled in derision. 'In his own home town! Local boy can't find the way home!'

'Yes,' confirmed Brisley. 'I thought I was taking my usual short cut – but it's all changed since I was here last. Next time I'll go round by the motorway and through the city centre – it'll be easier.'

'And you once boasted about having a good sense of direction!' scoffed Dottie, enjoying Brisley's discomfiture.

'Put it down to premature old age,' said Brisley. 'No, put it down to planners. It was perfectly all right until they decided to develop it.'

''But where were you?' Dottie persisted.

'I don't know. If I'd known where I was, I wouldn't have been lost, would I?'

'Have some coffee,' said Thurlow, weakly. 'We left you a drop.'

'That part of the city just south of the park still looks a pleasant area,' Brisley remarked as he sat down. 'Is that still where a lot of the University people hang out?'

'So you haven't lost your sense of direction all that much,' Thurlow commented.

'Not for the bits they've left alone. It always seemed a nice sort of area. We lived in the other bits, that *have* been developed, and, to be honest, needed it. But the egg-boxes go upwards nowadays, instead of sideways.'

Brisley's late arrival, as a topic of conversation, seemed to have drifted through local topography into planning blight, and there was a sudden silence. Thurlow resumed: 'Yes, that's quite a favoured area. A lot of the academics live over there: which is why I've moved out of it.'

It was Thurlow's turn to encounter a gap to be filled, and he continued:

'It got to the point when I couldn't go out without meeting one of them, and there was a good chance that he'd start farting on about the Library, or want me to let him in when it's closed … We all get that sort of thing, of course … Life is more peaceful a few miles further out. I don't walk as much, and I've put on a bit of weight – but I listen to Radio 3 on the drive to and from, instead of having to walk with some professorial ponce putting the world to rights.'

'Professor!' Dottie scoffed. 'One who professes to know but doesn't!'

Thurlow was seized by a sudden distraught anger.

'They're completely bloody irrational!' he seethed. 'Some members of the Library Committee here actually said I should have been more "reasonable" with that little skunk, Peabody – as though I'd somehow provoked him merely by enforcing their bloody Regulations. Which they'd passed in the first place and said should be enforced strictly.'

'What did he do?' asked Brisley. 'His breach of the Regulations, I mean.'

'Prevaricated for months about bringing some books back. I told him he was not to use the Library again until he complied, and then he started vomiting on about being in his final year, and how he can't get the books on his reading list, which is probably true because his supervisor's a prat and lists books he's never asked us to get in the first place, and we're not bloody clairvoyant, but that's by the way …'

Thurlow seemed to have run out of steam, or perhaps to have choked on an excess of it, and there was another brief silence.

'Anyway,' he added, 'they – the little sheep-shagger-demics who reign over all – said I'd been too hard on him, and the student rep started farting away about bureaucracy, and so on. The usual fashionable crap. They also said I should have called University Security, not the police, to him after he attacked me. Well, screw that for a lark. I want that bastard behind bars, not petted by some unwashed sociology poof, who'll tell him he'd under examination stress and needs loving care and attention, poor little cunt!'

There was another silence, reinforced by his colleagues' surprise, not at what they had heard about the Committee's moronic perversity or even at the level of Thurlow's righteous anger, but at the venomous vulgarity boiling over from this normally urbane man. It was plainly the eruption of a long-simmering resentment and hatred – emotions to which they, too, were no strangers.

'What did you … er … do when these things were said?' Dottie asked.

'I just got up and walked out. It was either that or murder the nearest one. Whoever's going around bashing these buggers' heads in is doing a public service. He can come to me for an alibi any time.'

'Your Committee does seem to have been more than usually obnoxious,' Brisley remarked. 'But, apart from a few individuals of merit, basically all academics are the same. They think they're unutterably wise … take snap decisions without getting any facts, except those that happen to be lying around or suit their prejudices … or they go to the opposite extreme and mistrust anything simple and self-evident. The idea that they might need advice, from a mere librarian of all people, about a library of all things, is some sort of offensive novelty to them. Whenever I express an opinion about university libraries, which we've each worked in for twenty years or more, they seem to react like some old Deep South plantation-owner, who sees a Black wearing a tie and thinks he's getting uppity. I suppose most of us are hardened by now to having our opinions about our own speciality disregarded by some academic ignoramus. And they're bloody rude almost as a matter of routine, don't you find? Take no trouble to express themselves with common courtesy, but if they get anything less than obsequiousness back, they go all high-and-mighty. And at least two of my present Committee members seem mentally deficient …'

'That was long speech,' said Dottie, 'but not unfair.'

'Too bloody fair,' Thurlow rasped. 'That was obviously the polite version. If it hadn't been for the money I'd have chucked it all in long ago and become a road sweeper or a kitchen hand in a Chinese chippie. At least my opinions about libraries might have been listened to. Anyway, I'm taking early retirement next year. I can't really afford it, but even less can I afford to carry on working for these … '

Words failed him, and he continued over the lacuna: 'And there's no point in thinking things would be better anywhere else, even if another University would have me. From what you say, your lot are just as bad.'

Dottie remarked: 'Yes, there's always a couple of obsessionals for whom the Library can do nothing right. The trouble only starts when they're taken seriously, as they too often are, instead of being told by the moderates to shut up. As usual, it's the moderates who do nothing, and think a mere librarian has no right of reply, who let the trouble happen. I suppose it's naïve to hope they might risk souring relations with colleagues they work alongside and whose good opinion they might need on a committee somewhere, just to be fair to someone they don't need to keep happy.

And their rage when I expose how daft their ideas can be! – when a librarian has accidentally failed to be inferior!'

The others grunted assent, and Brisley filled in another silence by returning to Thurlow's retirement: 'So you'll spend your retirement looking for the murderer to offer him thanks and assistance?'

'Too bloody right I will! And suggestions for future activity - career advice! It shouldn't be Peabody they suspect – I'm a better bet. One good thing – I hear that neither of them, those who were done in, I mean, is being replaced – staff savings to be made. Shows how necessary they were in the first place.'

'Something curious about the two murders though,' Dottie mused. 'Both Professors of English Literature, both hit over the head …'

'Could be coincidence,' said Thurlow, struggling to regain an abstract interest. 'After all, there must be – how many? a couple of hundred? - of these Professors, in the sense of holders of Chairs, of "Eng Lit" in the UK. The fact that the two victims have those points in common could be a meaningless statistic. Suppose, for example, you meet an old schoolfriend in some remote town, or are dealt a perfect hand of cards. These things are highly unlikely, but plenty of people experience them just once and occasionally more than that.'

'But,' Dottie persisted, 'in the same subject? Same rank? Same means of killing?'

'Late middle-age,' Brisley ruminated, 'look reasonably prosperous, probably not in good physical condition … the answer to a thug's prayer, I would have thought.'

Dottie was still not satisfied: 'It doesn't seem to have happened before, or with other subjects – the coincidence, I mean.'

'All the more reason to think it could have come about by chance now,' said Thurlow.

Brisley nodded. 'That's right. That's all a coincidence is: something with no statistical significance and no inner connection, happening once in a blue moon. After all, what else did they have in common? Only the professional similarity. I don't suppose, for example, that they moved in the same circles all that much – less than we do, anyway. And the murders were a year apart. They've got noticed because the media like university stories. For all we know, two bus drivers or two plumbers have been murdered the same way in different places a year apart, but it hasn't been noticed or built into a story.'

'Well, he's certainly got academics here worried,' Thurlow chortled through his healing lip. 'I've seen several with walking-sticks they never had before and shrinking away from porters they don't recognise.'

His darkness flooded back in, and he added: 'Whatever the explanation, before he packs it in he can have a go at Roach, who's a pain in the arse on our Library Turds Committee.'

'Roach?' Brisley repeated. 'Ah yes, old 'Cock' Roach and his monumental *Sexual Roles in the Eighteenth Century*. It takes someone like him to make sex boring.'

'Rumour has it,' Thurlow said, 'that his sexual interests are not confined to literature. The occasional whisper about female students given extra help and promised better grades on the continuous assessment part of the course. It's said that he was in favour of introducing continuous assessment here – entirely out of character, because his teaching's hopelessly old-fashioned otherwise – precisely because he saw the chance of some skirt-chasing. 'Cock' Roach, as you say, and for entirely unentomological reasons.'

He savoured the innuendo through loose teeth.

'But you would have known that,' said Dottie to Brisley. 'You're an Eng Lit man yourself.'

'Amateur, and very much part-time,' disclaimed Brisley, 'and not eighteenth century either. I'm stuck in the nineteenth. But, yes, one does hear little breezes blowing ... And Roach isn't the only one abusing his position in that way. So perhaps we're wrong in thinking of the murderer, or murderers, as male? Could they be those seduced and discarded young women seeking revenge? Or their fathers or jealous boyfriends getting it for them? Especially if the sexual favours had been granted and then hadn't led to the promised exam successes.'

'Perhaps next time our murdering benefactor will do for Roach,' said Dottie, 'who is still alive.'

'Unfortunately,' rejoined Thurlow. 'But were Arlington and – who was the other one? – Peccary up to that lark with female students?'

'Not that I've heard of,' said Dottie. 'Anyway, I would have thought them a bit too old for more than sordid impropriety.'

'Actually,' said Brisley, 'Peccary may have been too old, and certainly too repulsive, to get much of a chance, but he did have the interest – after a fashion, at any rate. His widow – awful woman, voice to crack a brick wall – dumped his private manuscripts on me to see if there were any great scholarly treasures in them. Lots of perverted fantasies and rituals! Had to shred 'em. And old Pendlebury, the bookseller I referred her to, to get rid of Peccary's books – I chickened out, wisely enough – found some books nicked from your Library, Jack, and mine. I've brought the three that are yours with me. All about sex, of course.'

'Distinguished scholars pinching library books,' Thurlow commented, 'par for the course, I'd say. Offhand I don't remember any bequest of a distinguished academic's books that didn't contain one or two that had to be returned to their rightful owners.'

'But we were being prurient and scurrilous about the victims' sex-lives as though they were likely to be impotent,' said Dottie. 'Were they really all that old?'

'Only early fifties,' said Thurlow. 'Younger than me,' he added, with some asperity. 'Anyway, 'Cock' Roach *is* old. And he's a widower, so there's nobody to keep him in order. Lovely person, Meg was. Can't think what she saw in him.'

'So now,' Dottie summarised, 'he's on his tod, except for any young groping-companions he can find.'

'Yes – and you're right, 'Cock' Roach is quite a bit older than I am… But why are we talking about that bastard? Do either of you know the size of your book-fund for next year yet?'

*

Detective-Inspectors Terence Hooligan and BOG Groyne had hoped that a consideration of the two murders together would illuminate at least one of them.

But Inspector Groyne's investigation of the murder of Professor Arlington had come once more to a dead halt. The recently promoted Professor Simmonds had, as stated by Roach, been at his brother's funeral at the time of the murder, and too far away to have committed the crime surreptitiously from there. After Hooligan's latest interview with him – the third - Simmonds was feeling persecuted. He could shed no light at all on the mystery of the page torn from a copy of his book, or upon the sentence which had been underlined {'Surely it's cleah in cawntext? But Ay see neh welevance to your enquarweh'). His conclusion was that an 'unknen thard pawty is twying to implicete meh'. Hooligan calmed him down by asking what the underlined sentence actually meant and found himself interested in a lucid account of the relation between style and content in literature. He noticed that the note of 'lichacha' previously discerned in Simmonds discourse was now considerably augmented, presumably to go with the new accolade of Professorial status.

Hooligan was confirmed in his view that they were looking for one murderer, not two, for they shared another common feature: the murderer had intended to mystify them gratuitously if he could, and otherwise to have the pleasure of taunting them.

It was also possible that the murderer hated Simmonds and was trying to throw suspicion on to him. But this explanation seemed implausible to Hooligan. Simmonds was too insignificant a personality to be a likely victim of personal malice to that extent. It was more probable that he had simply become a convenient fall-guy by mischance. The murderer would know him either from the same University of Pillingham or because he was in the same subject elsewhere. Which brought the investigation not one inch further forward.

Pyle's alibi had not been quite perfect for either murder; but the same could be said of a number of other potential suspects, and there was nothing to connect Pyle with Arlington. The possibility remained that the murder of Arlington was Pyle's elaborate cover-plan for his desired murder of Peccary; but this explanation, too, could apply to others in one form or another. In any case, secret plotting and ingenious red herrings did not go with Pyle's openly abrasive character.

At the time of Peccary's murder, Pillingham University's Security officer, the infamously inept Leslie, had, at the third time of asking, procured copies of the passport-style photographs which appeared on the staff identity cards of Peccary's Departmental colleagues and Bertrand Pyle. These had been shown to the newspaper-girl who had discovered Peccary's body. She had remarked pertly that she would not like to be stuck in a lift with any of them and had not recognised the angry-looking man whom she had seen supposedly walking his dog. She was now shown an artist's impression of the bogus porter at Pagham, with similar outcome. The night-porter at Pagham was shown the set of Pillingham photographs and could not identify his phantom colleague.

Thus were the hopes that the two murders would bring light to at least one of them dashed; indeed, the darkness had thickened.

Hooligan and Plumb still occasionally chewed over the two crimes while working – and with much more success – on other cases. They had been interested in the report of the attack on Thurlow, and disappointed when the extreme improbability of a connection was established. Hooligan increasingly valued Plumb as a sounding-board and as a source of ideas which, though sometimes discounted when analysed, could lead to better ones.

Hooligan began to notice that Plumb asked him, more often than might have been expected, what he thought that the murderer – assuming that a lone double-murderer might evolve into a serial killer – might do next. Plumb's earnestness had always amused him, and so had the younger man's overestimate of his own subtlety. He took care to reply with some gravity:

'I've said before, Ted – I do think they're connected, but it's more a case of feeling rather than thinking, let alone knowing. Though there are sometimes other ways of knowing ... without knowing what it is you know ...'

Perceiving Plumb's bewilderment, he went on:

'I suppose I'm saying that I think Groyne's too literal about the facts we have. Two old guys – well, not that old; in fact, no older than I am, but they seem old – anyway, two the same age, same line of business, same kind of killing - an apparent attempt to put us on the wrong track – living in an unreal world where everything that's odd to us might seem normal to them ... You know,' he went off at a tangent, 'until I had more to do with these academics I could never understand how that bumbling idiot Leslie could fit in as Pillingham's Security Officer. Now it's obvious. Reminds me of Hamlet's madness in England.'

Perceiving Plumb's furrowed brow, he added: 'Not noticed, because everyone else is as mad as he is. Shakespeare.'

'Oh, yes, sir. Of course, Shakespeare ... Yes ... But our two murders, sir. What do you make of the differences - different settings for the murders, and so on?'

'Yes, different settings, of course, but that doesn't necessarily mean he contrived those settings. It could be just that he knew where his victims would be on each occasion, and was a good opportunist ... making plans quickly ... He's either very clever or very lucky, or both. And I don't think we've come across him in our investigations. Not even without knowing. So – why don't we try to get ahead of him?'

'But – without knowing his next victim – if there's to be one – or where - how can we - ?' Plumb trailed off, nonplussed.

'Ask yourself: Why were both victims in the same category? And what might now prompt him to have another go? And where?'

'The "same category" question's easy enough, sir: he doesn't like late middle-aged Professors of English Literature.'

'Thanks for the "late", Ted. But OK, we assume he's some kind of Jack the Ripper - but Bert the Basher, and Profs instead of toms.'

'Unless,' Plumb demurred, 'he only wants to kill one of them and the other's a blind.'

'A blind, you mean, because he wants us to look for someone out to kill off a category rather than the one victim he really wants? So this is personal malice with a smoke-screen? Could be. I can't prove your "personal malice" theory wrong, Ted … But, for the moment, it doesn't matter which of us is right. If *you* are, he might want to provide a few more red herrings for us, and perhaps he hasn't even got to the one he wants yet. On that line of reasoning you might want to say that Peccary and Arlington are both decoys. But if *I'm* right, and he's out to get people in a particular category, for whatever reason, then presumably he'll stick at it. Either way, his next port-of-call might be – where? Melbury, I would guess. Where they're already jittery, because of a red herring from that young fool Peabody, and where there's a good chance that a murder there would unleash general panic. He can hardly have failed to savour the alarm he's caused so far. And if he hates a category, that will only add to his pleasure.'

'Won't he realise we've twigged all this, sir? – and stay away, or pick somewhere else?'

'I like the "we",' thought Hooligan, again amused at Plumb, and continued aloud: 'Yes, he might. But if he's really been teasing us by planting false clues, he might relish the challenge. And, frankly, I can't think of anything else to do. Can you?'

'So – can we guard some obvious victims in Melbury, sir?'

'That would be a job for the force over there. I've asked our dear Chief Constable to try and persuade his opposite number at Melbury. But apart from that, you and I will go over to the University of Melbury as soon as we can and spy out the land. Of course, it will mean that the two Chief Constables and the University there will have to get a move on to set it up …'

'What exactly will we be doing there, sir?'

'Nothing much. Just to get to know them a bit better and keep our eyes open. We are going to be distinguished visitors from New Zealand.'

'Oh? But what would we do? And why New Zealand?'
'Don't look so worried, Ted! All will be revealed. After the interest you've shown in this case, I thought you'd be more pleased.'

*

A small hat, to reveal the whitened hair (it would wash out in the motorway stopover). The hat had a checked pattern, to go with the rural affectation of Melbury's countrified outer suburbs, and to go with the dog. Or at least to go with the idea of a dog, since dog there was none; the idea of the dog was adequately conveyed by the dog-leash. Fair enough, no real dog, and no real country either, just an erstwhile railway line now made into a bramble-lined cinder track on which joggers zigzagged amongst dog-turds. And a walking-stick, to go with the limp. He liked his limp. It went with the hair which went with the hat which went with the dog-leash with went with the idea of the dog.

And a thick overcoat, because it's cold in January, and because the coat has deep pockets to contain the proverbial blunt instrument when the time comes.

'So that's where the old fool lives.' Confirmed by the telephone directory and the Voters' List.

All was peace. The countrified outer suburb slept.

The wanderer with the whitened hair, and the contextual hat, and the dog-leash, and the limp had already observed that there was an aviary at the back of the adjacent house. A delightful mystery was forming in his mind. 'Useful creatures, dicky-birds.'

Arranging this Professorial vacancy might be a bit *hors série* - but fun.

'Better check he hasn't moved house.'

The verifying telephone call was greeted by: 'Pwofessah Wooaa-ch heah. Hilloo? Hilloo? Is anehbodeh thar?'

'How will you lie with your brains ungainly addled,'
the caller queried, misquoting again,

*'One arm bent across your lusting old debaucher's face?
It pains my guts to see you,
For, live or dead, you remind me of a pig.'*
'Wealleh!' squealed Roach. He rang off, feeling himself to have been cruelly tortured.

CHAPTER 10

SUSPICION AND FATALITY FAIL TO MEET

A man who no longer had white hair, and who had never owned a dog, but who did own a dog-leash, and a choice of hats, and a walking-stick that had belonged to his grandfather, and who did not limp unless he wanted to, was practising a new gait in his study. He leaned forward as he walked and bent his knees a little more than was usual at each step, so that he seemed to rise and fall as he progressed. Workmen accustomed to muddy ground often walked like this; though not only they.

*

It was still 1983. US marines landed on Grenada in the West Indies to counteract a coup. This violation of British territory passed largely unnoticed in the UK at large and in academe, even amongst those whom the Falklands War had stimulated to passion or superior head-shaking. It seemed that comparatively few people had heard of Grenada, or known where it was, or known that it was British.

'What on arth are the Amewicans doing in Speen?' demanded Professor Roach. 'Doesn't thet ector-fellow Weagan kneh whar Gwanada *is*?'

A new academic term began, and every university in the land resumed its internecine war of words, which glared, spluttered and smirked its way into Summer.

*

Decades of bloodless blood-letting, esoteric wit, phenomenal erudition, astounding ignorance, *grand guignol*, and petty gossip had soaked into the very oak panels of the Dunsinane Board Room, where the Faculty of Arts at the University of Melbury had held its meetings for fifty years. An array of framed past eminences-in-oils, all grey or white, some tonsured by process of nature, all exuding a visionary dignity and oracular penetration conferred by artistic tact – these beings looked variously upon, past or through the Faculty's living eminences who, clutching their papers for the meeting, ambled in, testy and untried, bent in spine, round in belly, and withered in spirit, their indestructible immortal soullessness likewise destined for eventual reincarnation in dead institutional art. On the wall behind the Chairman's seat shone the vigorous baldness and the fiery eye (the other being eyebrowed over to lend its power to the one that looked) of the late Lord Dunsinane, scholar, soldier-poet, and above all, benefactor - in which latter role he had collected several doctorates *honoris causa* in subjects of which he was eyebrowfully ignorant. He now presided in two dimensions as he had once presided in three, proclaiming qualities which they of the present insisted that he had possessed, in order that they might pose as heirs to greatness.

To these hallowed precincts in the Summer Term of 1983, Detective-Inspector Hooligan and Detective-Sergeant Plumb, each equipped with a bundle of replicated documents, were led from the Faculty Administrator's office up and down several creaking wooden staircases with carved newels, in order to become both spectators and silent bit-part actors in the performance about to begin.

Although retaining their own names, they were masquerading as administrators from the University of New Zealand on a study-tour of British universities. Hooligan's suggestion that the murderer might be attracted by the tension and possibility of misunderstanding and panic created in Melbury by Peabody's attack on Thurlow had been as a straw at which the two Chief Constables, short of facts, interpretations and stratagems, had finally clutched frantically.

Arrangements had therefore been made for the imposture. Even to get the feel of the place which might house the next victim, and to stand a chance, however remote, of solving two murders and perhaps forestalling a third, was better than doing nothing. Melbury's Chief Constable was unfortunately not willing to put guards on the staff in the English Literature Department there on the basis of an unknown Detective-Inspector's intuition but had promised to reconsider the possibility in the light of Hooligan's report after the visit. Hooligan did not know what he was looking for, but the Professor at Melbury – Roach by name – and the rest of the staff, one of whom might even be the murderer, would be at the meeting, and Hooligan's only hope was that he or Plumb would spot something ominous … somehow … if anything ominous were there to be spotted …

They were introduced to the meeting by Professor Roach who was, by chance, the current Dean and was therefore in the Chair. He had received from the Vice-Chancellor an apparently genuine notification about their visit – the Chief Constable at Melbury had done that part well – and he read out a series of welcoming and approbatory platitudes about them. Both visitors enjoyed, it appeared, a 'hay [high] weputeetion' in the Antipodes. Hooligan had been credited with a fictitious doctorate, and he had decided that it would be in criminology, after his law degree: close enough to the truth for him to be able to flannel if need be. Plumb had secretly hoped for a doctorate as well, but his comparative youth left him as plain 'Mr.' Forty pairs of variously curious, bored, intrusive or vacant eyes focussed on them briefly before falling again to the papers or drifting back into the distance. In the very middle of this exposure to scrutiny, Plumb's concealed amusement at the idea of introducing 'Dr' Hooligan back in the nick was decoded by the spurious doctor and quelled with a gaze which would have been envied by Lord Dunsinane himself.

Preliminaries over, there was a general shuffling and rustling of papers. Hooligan received the distinct impression that many of the members present were reading the papers for the first time, despite their having been circulated well in advance.

Professor Roach was in whispered conversation with the Administrative Officer at his elbow, nodding slowly with his whole body as though riding a horse. Hooligan, waiting for something to happen, and with a vague sense that nobody seemed to expect this very soon, affected an interest in the papers while surreptitiously looking round at the assembled company. It was not essentially different from his recollections of Pillingham, but now presented itself *en masse* rather than one by one.

Opposite him sat a thin, sallow man of about fifty, wearing an old dark-brown jacket from the sleeves of which protruded large, bony, red hands with dirty finger-nails. His hair was slicked down without a parting, and this made his head look like the shiny newel on the banister outside, though not as well finished-off. As Hooligan ruminated on this curious resemblance, all the assembled company's heads, ranged immobile round the vast polished table, became as newels displayed in a mad workshop: tall newels, short newels, fat or thin newels, newels in an assortment of designs. Differences of skin-texture and hair-style only made them seem to be in varying stages of completion: a committee uniformly wooden-headed, with superficial individuality imposed only by the whims or imperfections of craftsmanship.

'Symbols of those one passes, ascending a stairway to the truth,' he thought, followed by a panic-stricken, 'Christ! I'll get like them if this goes on! Surely it's not an infectious disease? ... Call it newelitis? Inflammation of a wooden head?'

Furtively, he slightly disordered his hair, as a talisman for immunity against the condition, and marvelled at his developing perception of what was before and around him. These people were supposed to be not just the cream of the country's intellect, but responsible for training the cream. Yet they could include the morally worthless ... looked like a gaggle of peasants out for the day - scruffy or unwholesome, or dandyish and affected ... He was intrigued by a specimen further along the table who, on being spoken to by his neighbour, opened his mouth silently, closed it again, and held his breath in an ecstasy of merriment before hissing in and out violently through clenched teeth. The general impression was of a tickled loony hippo. Could anyone who looked like this lot, though especially him, have any brains, or at least be able to use them wisely?

The Dean, Professor Roach, brought his canter to a halt and abruptly announced that he would 'sane the Minutes of the lawst meeting es beeng a cowwect wecord.'

A newel opposite Hooligan suddenly came alive and objected.

He hed, he said, enterteened dites [doubts] from the farst [first] abite the new jaft silbus [draft syllabus]. He hed, indeed, expwessed thezz dites et the pwevious meeting, end hed not ixpicted to beeg gnawed [be ignored] in the Minutes. He was now oblaged to wepeat his dites and to insist on their beeng incorporwated. It was still enleh a jaft, end tharfaw neh unfawseen pwinting cawsts would be incarred if alterwations war' pwoved [were approved] et this stege.

He proceeded to articulate his dites. The lishting of cawsses [listing of courses] in poitchy [poetry] ought to be separwated fwom thezz in jama [drama] and in the novl. In the eethinth centcheh [eighteenth century], foxample [for example], poitchinjama [poetry and drama] war beth vempawnt [very important], ee chinnit sen weight [each in its own right], end a joint cawss cad enleh scwatcha sarfisss [could only scratch the surface]. In conchasht, nentinth centchinglish [nineteenth century English] poitchinjama war quate a nequal [unequal]. The poitchy, lake the jama, could stend alen *[alone]*, with the jamabsawbd inta'agenwal cawss *[drama absorbed into a general course]*: which would, of cawss, include meejah jemmetishtsh *[major dramatists]* shuch ash Sean Wailed *[Shaw and Wilde]* – beth vempawnt – endo mit *[and omit]* lessah figgahs, however impawnt et the tame, such es Awthah Wingpin Airwo *[Arthur Wing Pinero]* and Barebum Chee *[Beerbohm Tree]*. Thisty stinction *[this distinction]* between thim pawtnce *[the importance]* of vairce literwawy fawms *[various literary forms]* et differwent parwiods would beeg gnawed at gweat cawst, for it was jarmene *[germane]* to the study of lichacha.

He shook his head at the end of his discourse, in the sapient sorrow of a sensitive, penetrating genius worried by problems which ordinary mortals could not even discern. He would have been better advised to worry about the fact that even those of his hearers who themselves mangled the language as he did found him difficult to understand.

The two impostors from the police force looked at each other in amazement. Hooligan, to whom the 'Wadio Thwee' type of soppy voice affected by some older academics was already familiar, was reminded of the apparent conviction held by his English teachers at school that poetry - known to its advocates variously as powetreh, poitry, poitchy or poitreh, and to its detractors as po-tree or pomes or 'all that poofy stuff' – must be read thus. Whole generations were thereby repelled from the subject – all for the sake of a speech-affectation no less absurd and intrusive than the current attempt by every pop singer to sound as though he suffers with his adenoids and comes from Tennessee. Why people need to cultivate a speech-impediment was a mystery beyond the reach of police work.

As for what had actually been said, Hooligan felt that most people would need sub-titles to cope with this strange dialect, and that a specialist in English, of all subjects, might be expected to speak his native language with acceptable clarity and spare his listeners the effort of translating it. He inferred that some, at least, of the man's colleagues shared his difficulty, despite their long practice at this futile art - for the Administrative Officer, dead pan, apologised for not having understood before, and suggested that Dr Pine-Coffin should write a letter about it, in order that the Faculty's Working Party could examine the issue in detail.

This suggestion was eminently practical: there was no point in delaying the meeting, and Dr Pine-Coffin's meaning must surely be less impenetrable in writing than in speech. But it still seemed to generate discussion, and one newel after another sprang temporarily into wooden animation, if not to life itself, while Dr Pine-Coffin made several unsuccessful attempts to be heard. Roach satcantered through it all – slowly to show understanding of a point, quickly to show agreement with it.

As they droned on, Hooligan's concentration on the discussion was disrupted by two other factors. One of these was Pine-Coffin's unusual name. Now, people's names were sometimes thought to influence their choice of job or … other activities. Jung said something of the sort … And the gym mistresses at Carolyn's school had been, improbably but truly, Miss Armstrong and Miss Bendall … Would a man stuck with a name like Pine-Coffin have a preoccupation with death? Death in the form of - murder? As a way of identifying a suspect, this is scraping the bottom of the barrel, if only because the influence of names can sometimes lead to the opposite. A doctor called De'Ath; a policeman called Hooligan. But scraping the bottom of the barrel is what we're doing at this meeting anyway … the bottom of a barrel within a barrel … And Pine-Coffin is in the right line of business to be a suspect … It would do no harm to have his alibi checked, just in case … Though he's not the type, mentally or physically, as far as I can see. Wouldn't even make a convincing undertaker.

The other breach in Hooligan's concentration on the gas-baggery was the sudden realisation that these people were not old duffers at all. Duffers, to be sure, but some of them were quite young – old only in manner and attitude. Peccary and Arlington had been in their early fifties; the Pine-Coffin newel looked a bit younger. Old Roach, of course, obviously was old, and looked pretty decrepit as well. An easy target for a killer ... But if the local force wouldn't put a guard on people, then they wouldn't, and that was that. One could see why, to be fair. They have a manpower shortage like the rest of us, and it's only a hunch ...

So how would I explain the theory to our dear Chief Constable? If he understands something, anybody can ...

... Two old duffers murdered ... Not much of a statistical sample ... Would we say, as Ted Plumb suggested, that one killing's personal animosity and the other a red herring for our benefit with perhaps more red herrings to come? But it can't be personal animosity for two or more: if the murderer hated them as individuals, and hated them that much, then surely we'd have found the link by now. Must check that point again: look further into their private lives; schools, perhaps. If that's the explanation, maybe there won't be any more murders: the hit-list would have been a short one. But – suppose someone *is* murdering Professors of English Literature more generally because he hates the category, and therefore intends more killings – that's impossible to track down. Of course, if the two so far had been Blacks or Jews or Catholics or whatever, we could look for a racist nut or a religious nut. But that doesn't seem to be it. It'll have to be something more specific ... What would be the consequence desired by the murderer? Suppose it were a consequence of a type which, once brought about, would cause him to stop ... Somebody wants a victim's job? But these jobs are advertised, and they get applications from all over the country. Even from abroad. Of course, they sometimes promote the next-in-line ... but sometimes there seem to be two or three possible successors already on the staff, so, again, he couldn't rely on being picked. Anyway, he'd only want the one job, so he wouldn't go around the country creating more vacancies. Unless the second murder was committed by someone who failed to get the first vacancy? But no, we've eliminated them already ...Hell, I can't see our dear Chief Constable liking this – but I'll have to tell him *something* ...

Hooligan was aware that Plumb, tugging unconsciously at his overtight tie, which usually indicated a state of perturbation, had been looking at him, and had ceased to do so on being noticed.

Plumb did, indeed, have his own private distraction. An idea, monstrous in its implications and perhaps for that very reason suppressed hitherto, had intermittently signalled for his attention during the last few days. Now, in the enforced lull, as meaningless points of order and burbled nonsense buzzed like a background sound-track, this idea insisted upon rising to confront him. It had been given renewed impetus by a seeming triviality: Hooligan's decision that in their present masquerade they should be New Zealanders. This in itself was sensible enough: the distance would make chance exposure highly unlikely, and the odd nostalgic mention of their British origins relieved them of the need to attempt an Antipodean accent – although Plumb felt that Hooligan could have carried it off. But Plumb remembered that Hooligan's daughter, Carolyn, had just got married and gone to New Zealand with her husband. It was this chance connection that brought to his mind that Carolyn had had a great deal of trouble with the late Professor Arlington. In fact, Plumb had never seen Hooligan so upset, so calmly, dangerously angry. Angry enough, and under control enough, and equipped with a virtuoso's ways and means enough to ... to what?

Suppose the Boss had flipped - he *was* a bit odd sometimes! - and murdered Arlington out of revenge? Would that mean that he had killed Peccary as well? Not necessarily; he could have suddenly realised that the Peccary murder by person or persons unknown was a good cover for his own 'real' one of Arlington. After all, not everyone shared Hooligan's view that the two murders were committed by the same person. Usually, Plumb gave great credence to Hooligan's hunches and was, like many of their colleagues, rather in awe of his guesswork. But this case was, or at least could be, different - very different!

Could that be why they had made no progress over Peccary? The duty sergeant had commented that Hooligan had, contrary to the impression he gave, really known that Detective-Inspector Balham, whose rota position would have sent him to investigate Peccary's murder, was off sick? Was that just an uncharacteristic memory-lapse? Or was it deliberate ignorance as a smoke-screen? Suppose that Hooligan had not murdered Peccary, but had decided spontaneously to use that crime as his own cover-plan, knowing that he would head the investigation and would be able to ensure its failure - in order that he could murder Arlington and insist on his theory that one murderer was responsible for both?

Did Hooligan's stated belief that more murders might follow therefore mean, not one of his famous flashes of insight, but merely his own knowledge that he would kill again as a further elaboration of his cover-plan?

And what of Carolyn Hooligan, anyway? Was she really in New Zealand? Was she really married? Instead, was she - demented by nearly having had her degree lost to her because of Arlington - now on the rampage, with her father covering up for her? Or aiding and abetting her? Had they both flipped together as a father-daughter Bonnie and Clyde?

But, Plumb objected to his own speculation, if any of this is true, why had the Boss told Groyne about his having intervened in Carolyn's problem with Arlington? Hardly the act of a guilty man! Plumb then responded to his own objection: Groyne, looking for motives within Arlington's circle, would have turned up the information sooner or later. Failure to have mentioned it earlier would have aroused suspicion later, whereas its revelation at the outset – and in so convincingly amiable a manner! – was thoroughly disarming.

Plumb stole another look at Hooligan, and, with his conviction that he was on the right track now growingly headily, was at once inclined to read signs of homicidal lunacy into those familiar features. Or were they familiar? Had he ever really seen Hooligan before?

He looked away when he saw that his scrutiny had been observed.

Dr Pine-Coffin had just lost his temper. 'But Ay've awlweadeh witten to yo'!' he fumed to Roach. 'Couldn't yo' see Ay was weading fwom may copeh of the lettah? – with appwopwiate staylistic and syntectical maynor cheenges for the spoken medium, of cawss. It's heah! Do wead it for yoursilf!'

He passed a sheet of paper along the row of newels to Roach, who glanced at it. His physical manifestations of assent had been reduced by the exertions of the meeting to a very slow canter indeed. This was fortunate, for, nearing the end of his tether, he handed it, over a brief whispered exchange, to the Administrative Officer, who read it out in standard English.

Several of those present, including the policemen, and including also some of those who themselves spoke in Pine-Coffin's contorted dialect, looked at each other, silently expressing such varied comments as: 'Thet's what *Ay* think, toooo'; or 'Why didn't the silly bugger say so in the first place?'; or 'I still don't understand what he means'; or 'Knew it was rubbish!'

The meeting continued in similar vein. Apart from noting that nobody showed any particular antagonism to Roach, even though he was exasperating in several ways, Hooligan felt that their masquerade had brought them no further forward in identifying a possible third victim or credible murderer. Indeed, the absence of any criminal note in the enmities expressed - it was all too boring or silly to be dangerous – left him even more puzzled to know whether Roach was a suitable candidate or not. Apparently not. But he felt uneasy.

*

Later that day, Professor Roach was in his office. Like many a fellow Professor, he had given more than passing thought to the possibility of being attacked. In the Staff Club he maintained as his public stance that each of the two crimes at Pillingham and 'Jumbwidge' *[Drumbridge]* was of local and independent significance, not a pair with an undetected connection and consequent potential for 'wepetition'. It was, of cawss, he would continue, a sane of the tames *[sign of the times]* that Pwofessahs wah not entarleh seef, but one's wegwet at each of the two chejedehs *[tragedies]* should not be elevated into a gen'wal alarm. Nevertheless, he remarked that he had once in his youth sustained a sarwious enkle injweh *[injury]*; he began complaining that it would ketch him unawars when he stwode vig'wousleh, though he had never been seen to attempt this; and he referred to the medical pwudence of getting out his late father's favouwite walking-stick. In fact, the walking-stick had, until quite recently, spent two months in the local Oxfam shop; Roach had visited local hardware shops, and had discovered that, since the second murder, a sudden epidemic of Professorial lower joint infirmities had caused an unprecedented dearth of walking-sticks for sale in the area.

After the Faculty meeting, Professor Roach had felt quite distraught because of the fuss which Pine-Coffin had made about the new syllabus. Of cawss, he reasoned, Pine-Coffin was upsit at the memment becawse he'd feeled *[failed]* to get Awlington's job at Jumbwidge. They'd made an intarnal pwomotion, and then not filled the consequential vacanceh. Awl to seve moneh.

But Roach's attention soon drifted off to his favourite subject, which, at present, took the form of the blonde girl at the front in his weekly lecture. He wondered, not for the first time, what colour her pubic hair was, and a familiar, pleasurable heat was starting to flow through him, when the telephone intercommunication buzzer brought him sharply, almost painfully back to reality. It was his secretary, who neither appeared nor wished to appear in the Professor's fantasies, though her grandchildren thought her beautiful.

'Ar … r … se?' he hooted.

'A Mr Krishnaswami is asking to speak with you, Professor Roach – urgently, he says … '

'Wa… a…al, Ay *em* vair buseh *[busy]* … What is it abite?'

'Something to do with BBC Television, he says … '

'Ay'll spik to him,' responded Roach, in generous condescension to the possibility of a career-opportunity. 'Interwupt meh, will yo', with en argent cawl awftah thwee minutes.'

Roach waited for the extension switch to finish its customary twitches and convulsions and intoned an expectant 'Hill-ooo.' A soft Indian voice greeted him.

'Ah, dear Professor, how delightful! I am Ranjit Krishnaswami of the Brotherly Peace Congress. We in the BPC are striving for the liberation of the human spirit, and we know that you, too, are much concerned with this great preoccupation of our age. May I please come and show you some of our publications in your office?'

Roach was understandably confused. 'Wa ...a...al, Ay *em* vair busy,' he said, cantering in unseen confirmation of his routine evasion. 'What was thet you said to may seckecheh abite BBC Television?'

'Oh no, dear Professor: BPC – Brotherly Peace Congress, Foreign Mission.'

'Ay wealleh den't think Ay cen hilp yo',' said Roach, primly.

'Oh, but esteemed Sir – '

'Esteemed or otherwase, Ay em cartainly a vair buseh men. Now if – '

The charming voice did not change, but said: 'Then, dear Professor, you are a stingy old imperialist bastard pig who should be despised by all right-thinking persons!' The caller rang off.

Professor Roach could hardly believe his ears as he weakly put down the telephone. This was too much! First Pine-Coffin, and now, he – Irving Hawwison Woach, of all people! – hed been interwupted and insulted by this ... *native* johnneh!

He went into his secretary's room.

'Did ... ar ... Mr Kwishnaswami leave an ajjess or phen numbah?'

'No, Professor. Is anything wrong?'

'Wong? Oh, er, neh. He was ... wather stwange and ... ar ... Ay think we wair cut orf. How vair upsetting ... Ay den't want to spik to him again if he cawls beck. Ay shell geh hem.'

He took his walking-stick, and, in his upset condition, was incautious enough to set off into the afternoon dusk at unwonted speed; but he fortunately remembered his infirmity, and which side to limp on, before being observed. He sought consolation for his distress in the reflection that Kwishnaswami could be converted into 'Chwist, he's slimy'. He savoured his own formidable wit and wished he had responded with it at the time. Before reaching home, he was inclined to think that he had done so, and, moreover, with devastating effect on that native johnny.

*

As Professor Roach let himself into his lonely house at the city's edge, he did not notice a car parked a hundred yards away; or see the man sitting in it; nor yet see or hear that the man was talking to himself.

'No!' the man was saying, as one who is struck by a flash of the obvious. 'Of course! He'd be the wrong one! Mustn't allow myself to be distracted! I'm not supposed to be enjoying myself, fun though it is! It's the other one I want, isn't it, Prof?'

The appeal for confirmation was addressed to a budgerigar in a cage on the floor of the car in front of the passenger seat.

'Seems I bought you for nothing, Prof! Shall I give you to his next-door-neighbour, then? He's got lots of your little friends in a big aviary, by the look of it ... No! you've given me an idea! You'll come in handy for the other one now. You're in a cage, and he'll be in a pine coffin. Though a cardboard one would be enough for the likes of him ... You don't say much, do you? Can you say 'Prof', Prof? Come on, give it a try! Prof! Prof!'

Laughing, he drove off, the bird clinging desperately to its perch.

'Well, if you've got nothing to say for yourself, I'll practise ... '

He continued in a woman's voice: 'That naughty little boy has put my dear little birdie through your letter-box. Please let me have him back – my sweet little birdie – please! Please let me in! I'm sorry about the nuisance! I'll come and catch him.'

The rehearsal in the car was replicated in performance. Dr Pine-Coffin let a lady in to catch a bird and was caught himself by a gentleman.

The non-lady did not take the bird, but left the back door to the kitchen open, with the door to the rest of the house shut.

*

The Melbury constabulary assumed the murder of Dr Pine-Coffin to be connected with those of Professors Peccary and Arlington – three were really too many to be single events! Their Chief Constable made a great show of magnanimity and inter-force co-operation when requesting Hooligan's secondment to assist them; though it was obvious that he scented an intractable case and wanted to share, and if possible displace, the obloquy of bafflement.

Hooligan found it ironic that he should now be investigating the murder of a man whom he had suspected, albeit on a mere whim needing to be satisfied, of having murdered his two predecessors on the list. He would otherwise have considered the possibility that Pine-Coffin had murdered Peccary and Arlington and then, for whatever reason, been murdered by someone new to the case; but the investigations of Pine-Coffin put in hand after the visit to the University of Melbury had cleared him with a perfect alibi. A possible suspect had been eliminated in both senses of the word!

And the third murder had brought little more to go on than before. An elderly man with an up-and-down kind of walk, but otherwise of no particular characteristics, was stated to have been walking his dog nearby, although nobody remembered having seen the dog. The unusual gait recalled the limping bogus porter who may have killed Arlington at Pagham, though the latest suspect did not limp. The non-dog was certainly reminiscent of the Peccary case. Of course, there may have been, in both cases, a real dog unseen about its canine pursuits; but a leash is an excellent prop in the assumption of a role. The latest murder indicated access via the back of the house. That might suggest a visitor on terms of familiarity with the victim; but enquiries by the local CID had identified alibis for all his known intimates. They had also established that the front door was working properly. The killing had taken place in the hall near the front door - so why was the back door open if it had not been used for access? Some pretext to get the victim to open it? Carelessness as the murderer fled? – though why would the killer not leave by the front door? Could just have been panic, I suppose ... But could it be a deliberate taunt by the murderer? – the use of the back door was a vague reminiscence of the Peccary case. The blows to the head had been delivered by a right-handed person. But so what? Bludgeoning was a common enough means of killing people; and being right-handed, or indeed left-handed, has no statistical significance. The local force had discovered that Pine-Coffin was neither liked nor disliked by colleagues and neighbours. Some of them had no alibis, but, again, 'So what?' Plumb jokingly asked Hooligan if he had an alibi, and it turned out that he did not.

Hooligan was intrigued by the budgerigar. How did it come to be fluttering around Pine-Coffin's house? {'Crappin' in the fruit-bowl,' suggested Groyne, with sage irrelevance, when they discussed the three murders on the telephone.} There was no cage in the house, and no bird seed. Had the murderer taken them and left an uncaged bird? Or brought an uncaged bird? In either case, why?

'Why *do* people do unaccountable things?' Hooligan wondered aloud to Plumb. 'Of course, if they're insane there's an explanation somewhere in their mad scheme of things, but there's no point in our trying to look for it. But perhaps he's trying to put us off the scent: it makes no sense precisely because he intends that it shouldn't. We're supposed to be distracted by trying to puzzle it out. The bird goes, in a way, with the glue in Peccary's lock and the torn page left with Arlington. Of course, the glue and the bird could each have been a coincidental prank by someone unconnected with the crimes. But *three* coincidental oddities? This bird ... Suppose it had some other intended use – in connection with some other victim who was then somehow not the one who was actually murdered?'

'Well, Roach is the local big cheese, sir' remarked Plumb.

'Yes, he's that all right – so a likely target, perhaps.'

'But, still, why would Roach have been thought of originally as a victim? If he was.'

'Good question, Ted? And – why switch victims? If there was a switch - that's just a wild guess.'

They visited Roach at his home and discovered that his next-door-neighbour had a large aviary.

'Yiss,' Roach began sit-trotting, 'she keeps bards. Swan of Evon in may hice end thezz demned twitterwahs in hars.'

The detectives visited the neighbour to ask if a budgerigar had been missed. They discovered that she kept no budgerigars, and was a semi-invalid old lady, quite incapable of hitting anybody.

The bird seemed, however, to link Pine-Coffin's murder with Roach, however tenuously; therefore to point to a professional connection; and therefore to reinforce the notion that Professors of English Literature, or at least specialists in it if not formally Professors, were being singled out.

Plumb's enquiries in local pet shops established that nobody answering their vague description had bought a budgie. Hardly a valuable discovery, but it reminded Hooligan of the same negative discovery about the bogus porter's new overall: it had not been bought locally. This confirmed the impression that the criminal thought ahead, was devious, and was mobile about the academic world.

What was there about Pine-Coffin to have attracted the murderer? He was the first victim not to have been a full Professor: but that difference may have no particular significance for he was, it was said, virtually certain to have been Roach's successor on the latter's retirement in the near future. That would have at least been a reason for suspecting Pine-Coffin if Roach had been killed and if Roach had not been near retirement. As for the alternative explanation of professional rivalry ... Roach had been cleared at Pagham by Groyne and had an alibi for Pine-Coffin's murder; so he's not our man. Suppose a colleague had wanted to succeed Roach and had murdered Pine-Coffin to dispose of the competition? That led nowhere. In the first place, Pine-Coffin had no obvious rival in the Department, and, in the second place, without Pine-Coffin they would now have to replace Roach when he retires by advertising the vacancy – for which anyone from outside could apply.

That still left the possibility that someone else in the Department simply resented Pine-Coffin's destined promotion, or that someone – whether a colleague or not – hated him as an individual. That was always possible, of course, but not a profitable line of investigation really. These people seemed to enjoy their hates too much to want to be deprived of them. Anyway, there was no obvious suspect anywhere in the dead man's professional or private circles, while the assumption that one murderer had embarked upon a series of killings was now much more soundly based.

The Melbury police re-interviewed Peabody, whose trial for his attack on Thurlow was imminent. But they drew a blank. The young man had no connection whatever with Pine-Coffin, was still as left-handed as when first arrested, even had an alibi of sorts, and was beginning to feel persecuted. His complaint was, 'They can't find their murderer, so they're trying to fit me up.'

Roach had mentioned to the Melbury police the two curious telephone calls which he had received: 'one at may hem, spouting indecipherwable wubbish, sounded lake bed poitcheh' and 'one in may awfice fwom a Mr Wanjit Kwishnaswami, an Indian. Neh, fwom Indiah, not one of the Wed vawiety in feathers. Neh, Wanjit with an 'r' ... Arse, thet's weight. He cleemed to wepresent a bodeh called the Bwotherly Peace Cawngwess.' Neither the caller nor the association could be identified, but a cranky-sounding organisation whose representative went in for non-violent name-calling was an unlikely clue in a murder-investigation. Hooligan, however, learning of these calls, was uneasy: to add to the odd features at the three murder-scenes, there had been literary-sounding gibberish, impersonations, and Roach's 'weal' Indian. There was a common theme of eccentricity, perversity ... derangement, even? But it had not been Roach who had been murdered: there was no getting round that!

Hooligan went through yet again the statements of everyone interviewed in connection with all three murders, and could find no unexplained facts or uninvestigated coincidences. He was left with one, and only one, incontrovertible fact: that all the victims were in the same subject and of similar age. That must surely have a meaning? But the same could be said of an isolated word in a foreign language. The case was still a tangle of loose ends tacked on to nothing.

Hooligan received a telephone call from Bertrand Pyle.

'I'm speaking to you from not quite beyond the grave,' he said, 'though I feel that's where I might rather be. To wit, I am at home with my leg in plaster, and have been for a couple of weeks. I broke it by falling downstairs drunk, celebrating after my mother-in-law went home. Thought I'd just mention it, in case you suspected me of doing for old Pine-Coffin.'

'Perish the thought, Mr Pyle!'

'Well, you would say that wouldn't you?'

'Of course I would!'

'Then, while perishing the thought, you can ask Dr Bossom, my GP. He's a bluff fellow, but I'm sure he can recognise a broken leg when he sees one, and that was *his* opinion when it bent the wrong way.'

'It certainly seems that you didn't do any of these murders for me, Mr Pyle.'

'So I expect you to check with Dr Bossom, Pillingham West Health Centre, and I do not expect a visit from you. Right?'

'As rain, Mr Pyle.'

CHAPTER 11

MEDIA, MUGGER, MELODRAMA, MURDER

After the third murder, public interest and news media activity were reawakened, with an intensified conviction that this was not a coincidental series of unrelated crimes but had a single perpetrator. The Phantom Porter of Pagham was, somewhat inconsistently therefore, ousted from common parlance by the Bird-Man Killer of Melbury, and in the latter guise entered many a child's nightmare as a feathery ogre.

Television's *On the Logan Beat* ('and here i ... i ... ... IS -- - JACK LOGAN!') played a major role in this process. It appeared on-screen twice weekly, and then invaded the public's days off with *Logan's Weekend Round-Up* ('wi ... iii ...TH – JACK LOGAN!). He took the view that the viewers could forget the news if they wished but should not be allowed to forget his name.

The eponymous commentator began his opening remarks to camera, with a dramatic shot of Melbury's manor house clock tower, shining in the February sunshine, sprouting from his shoulder.

'Hel-*LO*!' he said and took care to follow his trademark facial light-up with a solemn look as befitted his present topic. His repertoire of second expressions to match what he was about to say was a favourite target of television impressionists. So were his mannered introductory sequences - without punctuation, pausing without sense at the end of each line on his autocue, and permeated with his profession's *de rigueur* emphasis on prepositions

'Fear stalks the Hallowed. Halls OF Academe the dons the,' he announced gravely, 'degrees the dignity OF learning have?' (this would be transmitted over standard footage of a bishop receiving an honorary doctorate at Oxford, but who would know or care?) 'they become the. Hunting-ground OF an MA-maniac, a BA-batterer IN. Pursuit OF Professorial prey?' Mobile eyebrows proclaimed his razor-sharp intelligence cutting through non-essentials to the heart of the matter. He followed this display speedily with a down-to-business jut of the jaw and, demanded, as though about to chide the viewers for not knowing, 'What do the dons DOWN here. AT Melbury think?'

Waiting off-camera some yards away, Professor Roach stood at a slow trot, although his abdominal bulk made his legs look too thin for purpose and created the impression rather of an ostrich than of a horse. He had relinquished his walking-stick for the interview, because he had decided to be urbane, unflappable, and above all quietly commanding.

Logan had, while speaking, processed ingratiatingly towards the camera, which had retreated from him at a slightly faster speed. This intentional discrepancy would create an enlarged perspective by the time the introduction had ended and would allow the inclusion of the ostrich awaiting interview. At the last split-second, with his eyes on the lens, Logan trod on a loose stone, twisted his ankle, lost his balance, fell against the ostrich, and shouted, 'Shit! CUT!'

'By all means,' murmured Roach, amiably, for he expected the worst from television and therefore could not be disconcerted by experiencing it. He waited, like Patience on a monument, smiling at Grief, and took a couple of hurdles while the opening shot was re-enacted. Logan leered at the camera even more penetratingly than before as his preamble came to an end, this time without mishap, and began the interview – whereupon Roach suddenly froze into immobility for the camera's sake.

'Professor Irvingroach, you're the Dean OF the Faculty –'

'Yes, Ay kneh,' responded Roach, surprised at this statement, for he had not realised that this quasi-message to him was a standard television device to explain an interviewee's relevance for the sake of the viewers. 'But the neme is not double-bewwelled.'

'Professor, what do you think OF this danger TO dons?'

'Withite neighing exectly what is geng on, end whither thar is or is not a deenjah to – um, dons, es you put it – it is impossible faw meh to weach any conclusion in the mettah.'

'Would you say that the media has exaggerated the problem?'

'I would not say thet the media *hes* done anything at awl.'

'Why not?' Logan had hoped for at least an accusation of sensationalism.

'Becawse the ward "media" is a plurwal and cennot be the subject of a singular varb.' He began to canter slightly as he warmed to his explanation but immobilised himself as Logan's aide touched his shoulder off-camera in restraint. 'Farthermaw,' he continued, 'one wealleh must defane the media to which one wefars. I teke it that your usage sarves es a collictive leeble *[label]* faw the media of mess-communiceetion: nemely, the Pwess, wadio, television of cawss' – he smiled, as though conceding an irrelevancy for courtesy's sake – 'end, though it is pwobableh not jarmene *[germane]* to ar pwesent carcumstences, the cinemetogwephic film.'

Logan was on the point of becoming exasperated, and of interrupting in a desperate attempt to elicit a straight answer. His earlier meeting with Roach, to establish the general nature of the interview and to rehearse the important points, had left him enervated and despondent. This prevarication on-camera was the last straw. But Logan, for all that his detractors made him out to be a buffoon, was a professional, and suddenly received warning and guidance from his experience and instincts. This was one of those occasions at which he excelled – when the routine extraction of information from an interviewee would suddenly yield place to memorable entertainment. The interviewer had to be alert to the right moment when the interview, by apparently going wrong, could go better than right; and he had to be flexible enough to follow the unexpected new path. Logan just knew that the viewers would enjoy seeing this old varsity twit with a camp speech impediment quibbling about semantics while a homicidal maniac might be at large on the campus. He looked grateful for the correction, and repeated his question in correct grammatical form:

'Of course, Professor. So do you think those particular media OF mass-communication' (he leaned on the phrase, both to make Roach think he had learned under august tutelage and to let the viewers discern the sarcasm) 'have exaggerated?'

'Not heving studied thar wepawts [*their reports*], end withite neighing the wealiteh, if indeed there be one, which their wepawts hev allegidleh exeggerweeted, it is impossible faw meh to say if any exeggerweetion, or even underestimeetion, mee hev occarred, and, if seh, et whose instigeetion. Ay would hev thawt thet you war bettah pleced then Ay to awnswer thet quistion.'

Logan had all he needed, and pounced: 'Professor Irvingroach, thank you.'

Quickly turning full-face to the camera, he said, portentously:

'Nearly two years OF tension. Exaggeration? Or, Playing-Down? Just a. Case OF Professorial Panic? Or is there a campus-. Killer AT large? Certainly, some Professors have. Been "don TO death" and will there be. More? Is it a case of "Murder BY Degrees"? Will there – '

His fractured discourse was, however, ruined by an unwanted voice-over, confusedly saying, 'Ees thet awl, Mr Leggan? Ay thawt yo' wah geng to awsk meh abite ... ?' Roach was bundled aside by the aide, whereupon he frisked about in frustration as though scratched from the race while under starter's orders. Logan had to re-record his sign-off later.

Roach's colleagues, watching the broadcast in their lock-fast homes, wondered how it was that Roach had been induced to stand still, apart from his false start when Logan's subject and verb had failed to agree. They had confidently expected his head to be in constant transit from above camera to below and back again, and they were disappointed. Logan had, in fact, been temporarily disconcerted by Roach's mannerism. But, having been well-briefed about Roach's pedantry, and noting that he had written a book about sex and literature – that might do for an intellectually salacious programme some time – he had kept him immobile on-camera by a simple stratagem: on a sudden brainwave, he had told Roach during a preliminary run-through that the television jargon for any sort of fidgeting on-camera was 'masturbating.' Roach had, as intended, feared exposing himself to sniggering from technological *cognoscenti* – although the effect was dearly bought, for Roach had delayed the start by attempting to engage Logan and members of the crew in discussion of the processes of jargon-formation in language, with particular emphasis on sexual and lavatorial analogies 'since such enelagehs [*analogies*] are awften pawt of the cweative pwociss.'

*

The news media, as Professor Roach called them (and them; not it) were by now well-supplied with unacademic items from the academic world, which over the next few months descended several undignified steps into the bottomless pit of banality.

The feigning of old injuries, now supposedly giving trouble and therefore providing a spurious excuse to carry a walking-stick, had gone. The literary lion, and even the historical, sociological and scientific lion, was now disinclined to enter life's jungle without his claws, in the form of the heaviest stick available which might still have been sold as an aid to locomotion.

Some even carried actual weapons: in consequence of which, Professor Justinian Easedown (famed for his *Animal Symbols in Early Chaucer*) of Prince College, Oxford, spectacularly marred a lifetime's spotless legality. With not even a parking-ticket to his name, he was convicted of assault and battery and of carrying an offensive weapon. A remote colleague of his, from the social sciences and unknown to him, had been hurrying to the station to catch the late train to London, and, pantingly and clumpingly drawing level with Easedown, had been suddenly belaboured with a baseball bat. Easedown, while regretting his victim's injuries, was at great pains to point out to the court the parfict wectitude, as he saw it, of his logical pwocisses. A murdarwah of Pwofessahs, neh less, was at lawge; he had become awar of a wepid parsuit; he had tarned wound and had seen in the hawf-late *[half-light]* a demented-looking chemp *[tramp]* bearwing parposefulleh dine *[down]* upon him. He had difinded himself against the seeming inevitabiliteh of atteck. Cartainly he wealised thet en unusualleh lawge pwoportion of seshel *sarntists [social scientists]* did look lake demented chemps, es any political documentcheh *[documentary]* emply illustwated, but what wah the pleece doing abite the murderwah?

The magistrates took into account that Easedown's ineptitude as an assailant had inflicted insufficient damage to warrant a charge of actual bodily harm. They imposed a heavy fine and stated that they would have added a prison sentence, had it not been for the fact that the Professorial victim could, as Easedown maintained, easily be taken for a tramp, even after having smartened himself up to give evidence. They warned Easedown that he should not carry any article which might be used as a weapon except an umbrella when rain threatened, or a walking-stick if he were suffering from any medically verifiable and relevant infirmity.

Professors Shyce and Bally, back in Pillingham, were more fortunate, in that they belaboured only each other with their walking-sticks in a mutual misunderstanding, the exact nature and definition of which they attempted to discuss in court, to the Bench's obvious exasperation. Both having been charged with a breach of the peace, rather than assault and battery, they decided, upon being convicted, to pay each other's fines as a symbolic gesture of good will. This was a little sullied when Shyce's cheque bounced and Bally was rearrested.

*

Professor Arnold Bludger, a historian at the University of Pillingham, was less fortunate in his incursion into the realm of violence. So was one Alan Donovan of no fixed address, for he had looked forward to a free wallet from this old boy trundling along, but received instead a broken collar-bone, a broken arm, and a number of gashes to his legs. Every one of his injuries came from blows which would have been fatal, had it not been for Bludger's incompetent aim with the chopper which had suddenly appeared from beneath his coat.

On perceiving the would-be mugger to be indisposed to rise, Bludger made to leave, returning after a few paces – Donovan whimpered and tried to crawl away – to wipe his chopper clean of blood on his victim's clothing before departing.

Donovan's anguished cries attracted attention, and the luckless miscreant was soon in hospital being interviewed by Detective-Sergeant Plumb. He gave his name as Alexander Donnell and provided a plausible address. The gist of his statement was that he was going down to *The Legge of Muttone* for a pint when this old maniac had suddenly attacked him. His brief story at an end, he was leaning back on his pillows, the epitome of innocence ravaged by brutality, when, in mingled horror and disbelief, he saw, appearing behind Plumb, the policeman whose career had long been fatally intertwined with his own, in the form of three previous arrests.

'Hallo, Paddy,' said Hooligan. 'Bit off more than you could chew this time, did you?'

He took Plumb's notebook and read the statement, shaking his head, and laughing.

'What happened to the bit about your white-haired old mother and her Bible-class, Paddy?' he said, crossing out the page and initialling it. 'Start him off again, Ted. If it's any consolation, he fooled me the first time as well. Name: Donovan, Alan Patrick. He'll tell you the rest ... Won't you, Paddy,' he added, with sudden emphasis. 'And don't tell us you were going to a respectable pub like *The Legge of Muttone*, or I'll start looking for a conspiracy charge to hang on you. And right now, I'm just too bloody busy to bother, unless you make me ... '

The routine processes of enquiry into the cause of Donovan's injuries soon brought Bludger and Hooligan together. On learning that Bludger was a Professor at Pillingham University, Hooligan wondered, in a surge of excitement, if he had chanced upon the serial killer. The nature of Donovan's injuries spoke against that, for they seemed to indicate an element of chance rather than skill, and had been inflicted with a chopper, not with a hammer. On the other hand, perhaps Bludger-the-killer, taken by surprise as the victim, had not been up to his usual standard ...

Hooligan's immediate impression of Bludger reinforced his doubts; the man was a fool. But proper procedure must have its due, so he began by asking Bludger to account for his whereabouts at the time of the previous murders. Bludger had expected the opportunity to justify his attack on Donovan and generally to explain various niceties to an unenlightened, but appreciative flatfoot, and was therefore surprised at this opening gambit. It dawned upon him only now that his attack on Donovan had made him a possible suspect for the three murders in academe. It was his attempt to digest that idea, rather than any lack of co-operation, that made it difficult for Hooligan to extract the required information. But Bludger eventually descended from Olympus in the spirit of *noblesse oblige* and offered to consult his diaweh [*diary*] and his seckercheh [*secretary*] as soon as sarcumstences parmittid.

Bludger explained carefully the situeetion as he saw it, and what he hed done abite it. The fluency of his discourse suggested prior rehearsal in a state of self-righteous agitation.

'We live in a varlint eege [*violent age*],' explained the pundit and prophet-without-honour,' a *mal de siècle* in which sosarteh [*society*] naythah gives veectims the pwotection which would ensue fwom eeficcient diticion of cwame [*detection of crime*] end appwopwiate punishment of cwiminals, naw [*nor*] pwovades edequate compenseetion for ectual veectims. Whar the law wefuses to ect, aw [*or*] is uneble to do seh, the pwocisses of law do not applay, faw the law hes declard thezz aweas in which it does not ect to be neh lawngah [*no longer*] under its suzerwainteh. Ordinawy citizens tharfaw hev the weight [*right*] to difind [*defend*] thimsilves, including the weight to cawwy a weapon, pwovaded it hes demonstwableh enleh a difinsive parpose. Ay ceased to shchike [*strike*] the miscweant es soon es Ay was conveenced thet he was neh lawngah eble to continue his atteck upon meh. If he hes susteened any injuwies in the pwociss, he hes enleh himself to bleme. Es far es Ay em concarned, he is just seh much wubbish to be swept up end dispezzed of, and you may do with him what you wish.'

He leaned back in his chair. He had made the matter clear and required only that his slow-witted audience catch up and assure him that he had been understood before he could depart for pursuits both more interesting and more worthy of his time and trouble.

'Just let me see inside your coat, sir.'

Bludger obligingly showed Hooligan his overcoat-lining, into which his wife had sewn strips of tough material to hold the chopper firmly in position while also permitting its easy extraction.

'Ay took the aydeah fwom Waskelnikov *[Raskolnikov],*' he said, rather proudly. 'A feectional cherecter, of cawss, seh Ay den't think Ay cen cawl him es a witness, h'm, h'm!' Rising to leave, he added, 'Dostoevsky's *Cwime end Punishment*, you kneh' – though he did not expect Hooligan to 'kneh' anything of the kind.

To Bludger's chagrin, for he did not like people beyond his immediate circle to recognise literary allusions, Hooligan replied, curtly, 'Well, Professor Bludger, Raskolnikov was mentally unbalanced and I'm not Porfiry, so we'll get on with it,' and, to Bludger's utter amazement, charged him with carrying an offensive weapon and causing grievous bodily harm. Hooligan had wondered briefly about a charge of attempted murder but reflected that the jury might be influenced in Bludger's favour by Donovan's long criminal record. And, to be fair, there was no real evidence of intent to kill; indeed, Bludger's ineptitude as an assailant would easily be converted by his barrister into an intention not actually to kill.

Donovan assured the court that he was now a reformed character, thanks to the love of his mother, thanks to Inspector Hooligan's wise and friendly counsel during their long association, thanks to the devoted doctors and nurses who had demonstrated how rewarding a life of service could be, and thanks to the terrible warning against wrongdoing which his injuries had given him. He had used this enforced inactivity to re-examine the whole basis of his life, was horrified at what he had done, and was determined to put this understanding to good use in future. He was told to shut up, fined fifty pounds and given a suspended sentence of three months.

Professor Bludger was several times told to be quiet by a magistrate still irritated by the pedantic and hair-splitting garrulity of Professors Shyce and Bally and was given three months with no suspension. This period coincided with the Summer Vacation of 1984, so nobody noticed his absence from his Department. The University's General Purposes Committee considered the possibility that Bludger might be deemed to have been guilty of, as the standard contract of employment put it, 'disgraceful conduct such as to diminish the University's reputation' – which would have warranted his dismissal. But they decided instead that he had committed a 'reprehensible act which the University could not countenance if repeated.' The conceptual and terminological distinction between what they should have done and the nothing that they did took three hours in the Committee and may have seemed clearer to members than to normal people.

Hooligan sent Plumb to Bludger's Department to check Bludger's alibis for the three murders, and these were satisfactory. However, these events brought home to the detectives yet again that they were no nearer a solution.

*

Lieutenant-Colonel Sir Randolph McDowald-Stourbridge, MP (an undeclared cousin of Bludger), who occasionally demonstrated that he was still active by emitting salivating rumbles about Laura Norder, put down a Parliamentary Question, asking the Home Secretary if he would introduce legislation which would permit law-abiding citizens to carry weapons for defensive purposes. The Home Secretary replied that he had no such intention and wished to point out that a large proportion of those charged with assault claimed self-defence when pleading not guilty or when seeking a lenient sentence upon conviction. The Lieutenant-Colonel then wrote a letter to *The Times* and *The Northern Custodian*, in which he implied a distinction between law-abiding citizens and Labour voters. This stimulated a number of responses from Labour voters who neither thought themselves *ipso facto* criminals nor their Tory opponents entitled to carry arms with which to assail anyone who looked non-Tory.

The Bishop of Barking joined the correspondence, but regretted having done so when *The Northern Custodian*, printing his admonition that it would be imprudent to seek a change in the law without public debate, attributed to him the statement that it would be impudent to change the law with public debate. A series of letters excoriating the Bishop for his supposedly Fascist tendencies appeared, before it became apparent that the Custodian was not nicknamed the Cutsodian for nothing.

The Daily Reflector nearly published a leader which referred to 'the 75-year-old Bishop, gassing through his gaiters', but fortunately checked in time to discover its more intellectual rival's defective typography. It substituted yet another of its assembly-kit calls to Reason:

'Everyone's willing to love a University Prof.

OK, so they've got to make up for being geniuses. We don't mind them being a bit nutty. A shade absent-minded.

But what makes them think they've got the right to go laying about themselves with clubs and meat-cleavers?

Is that what we pay our taxes for?

Is that the sort of example our bright kids are to expect at College these days?

COME OFF IT, DONS!

GET BACK TO YOUR BOOKS, and <u>CUT THE ROUGH STUFF!</u>

The leader-column then invited the reader to 'See page 4' for a more recent news item giving rise to these words of wisdom. During the acrimonious misunderstandings generated by the bone-headed Lieutenant-Colonel and the *Cutsodian*'s slapdash compositor, two professors with long-cherished fencing experience had fallen out when their newly acquired Alsatian dogs had started to fight; whereupon the learned gentlemen had been arrested while duelling arthritically with walking-sticks amidst the quadrangle flower-beds. Page 4, however, had been changed in the *Reflector*'s editing process, and now carried an item about surgical advances in a medical school which, seeming to be related to the meat-cleavers of the editorial, called forth angry ripostes from consultants in a number of hospitals.

*

As intellectual life, in so far as it resided in the universities and the Press, began to disintegrate under the strain of apparently imminent homicide, academic enthusiasm for conferences dwindled. After all, the campus of a university had already provided unparalleled opportunity for the murderer to enter, kill, and leave unnoticed in the general comings-and-goings – and may well do so again! Those who, in their conscious minds, knew university residential and conference buildings to be, in the main, modern down-at-heel, out-at-elbow structures of the most prosaic kind, nevertheless turned them in their imaginations into crypts peopled by cautious killers, who would creep in with cat-like tread, kill, and creep out again. There was also a conviction that the danger applied to conferences in Britain, not to those held abroad.

Accordingly, conference-organisers, fearing that their events, if held in Britain, would be under-subscribed and therefore run at a loss, hastily attempted to switch to foreign venues. But this hope was dashed when the general shortage of university funds prevented many would-be participants from obtaining grants to attend.

The ingenuity of devious minds with no grip on reality sought to explain that their preference for foreign travel at public expense was not based on its superficial attractions, but rather upon its considerable academic merits. Professor Roach, for example, addressed the Senate of the University of Melbury on this vital subject:

'The sharwing [sharing] end compewwison of exparwience between one univarsiteh end enothah, including' – here, free once more from the inhibitions of Jack Logan's lies about television jargon, he began his equestrian self-approval at the chief concept of his discourse – 'including foweign ones, is a means of invigorwating and widening our wark, and the wark of colleagues elsewhar,' he intoned, jiggling his reins with pleasure at the recollection of paid travel abroad and the prospect of more to come. 'The ecidimic velue of joint sissions – in dipth – with one's opposite numbahs in a stwuk-sh'd [structured] excheenge of views with delegits of the hest-cuntchy [host-country] and from elswhar hes not hithahtoo been wecognised as beeng, which it ees, a cweative extension of the pwinciple which' – he took his last fence – 'hes undahpinned conferwence ectiviteh in ar en [own] cuntchy for many yars.'

He resumed his seat with an air of having been first past the post.

University Finance Committees up and down the land were, however, sceptical, and the conferences had to proceed in their usual British locations amidst uncertainty.

*

Professor Arnold Bludger, released from his summer in prison, somewhat leaner and greyer than before, looked forward to resuming his former life in the new academic year of 1983. He had, moreover, conceived a new interest: that of academics, distinguished ones in particular, whom oppressive regimes in various parts of the world imprisoned for their principles. That these brilliant, sensitive minds, upon whom the preservation and dissemination of culture and the progress of civilisation depended, he ruminated sorrowfully, should be condemned as common cwiminals and locked awee in company with thieves, embizzlahs, and depwaved villains of ev'wy imeginable kaynd (mest of them addicted to jink and jugs), was an outwage. That they should be given over to the chawge of overbearwing, uneduceeted petteh officials, who addwessed one bay one's sarname and expected to be called 'sir', and who thweatened cartain unspeakable and undetictable means of encouwagement – with whom Wetional Discussion was, in short, impossible – was an Affwont to Humeniteh. And he would nevah understend why the Pwison Governah, in whom the outah menifesteetions of educeetion were at least superficialleh appewwent, hed forbidden the esteblishment of a Pwisonahs' Committeh, particularly since he would have been invated to attend *ex officio*.

Mrs Bludger, whose little-girl voice and character belied her florid, flamboyant and perfume-reeking exterior, collected him from the prison gate, and told him happily that they had been invited to the theatre that very evening. It was to the recently re-opened *Cockatoo Theatre* in Binghurst-on-Sea, a little town some fifteen miles away from their home in Pillingham.

'And, Arnold dear, we could go to the cottage straight from here if you like,' she said, excitedly. 'Couldn't we? I've packed your things for a long weekend there, so we could go to the theatre in the evening ... You've no appointments yet,' she added, tactfully, 'and that nice Mr Omen from the BBC said he'd ring you next week when I told him I expected you home today.'

'Mr ... Omen?'

'Yes, dear. Tarquin Omen, he said his name was. He said he wanted to have you engaged as a consultant for a new history series on TV. Isn't that nice!'

Bludger nodded curtly, for such recognition of his eminence was his due, and wanted to know what the evening's play was.

'Here's the letter, dear. It *does* sound nice.'

She waited in hope while he read it.

He noted with satisfaction that it came from the manager personally – not from an assistant– and was not a circular.

Dear Professor Bludger,

I am approaching several distinguished people in the region in the hope of interesting them in the relaunch of our Theatre.

While we hope to provide entertainment – must, indeed, do so if we are to remain economically viable – I am hoping also to put on out-of-season performances of plays dealing with modern issues of the day. For the latter I hope to form a small Advisory Committee which would assist me in selecting suitable pieces to raise the public level of consciousness of the "Cockatoo" and to enable us to contribute to public debate of matters of public concern, and hope that you will accept membership of it.

As a first stage I am inviting you to attend our current performance – an entertainment, as I hope you will see, but one of a historical kind and will allow you to get the feel of the building. I enclose two tickets and a handbill, and I hope very much that you will be able to come.

With all best wishes
Yours sincerely
Tulip Anderson (Ms)
Manager and Artistic Director

Professor Bludger grunted, and Mrs Bludger was relieved to detect a preponderance of approval in the timbre.

'Stayle [Style] wepetitive,' he mused. 'Too much "hoping" – he pwobableh misuses the ward "hepfulleh" [hopefully] – people do nahdays, you kneh. His deshes are a pwoblem, end Ay see a tautologeh or two ... Howiver, he hes some useful aydeahs, end Ay em dispezzed to geh. Ay think thet the Committeh should sponsah a competition forw a jama dealing with the imparfect alaignment of the concipts of law end justice. Ay wonder who the Charman will be ... ' He assumed, of course, that he would be 'inveted to accipt this wel [role]'.

The flattery in the letter directed to such conceit would have been sufficient to bring him to the theatre that evening. The writer was not to know that, as a bonus making his acceptance doubly certain, Professor Bludger's new mission in life would so neatly match this invitation.

An enclosed handbill, advertising a Victorian melodrama, *Sir Jaspar and the Maiden*, explained that the performance would be given in Promenade Theatre style. There would therefore be no conventional auditorium, and no distinction between audience and stage. Spectators would be allowed to, even asked to, move around the auditorium, and the cast would pass amongst them at will as the story unfolded. Interaction between cast and audience was welcomed. Professor Bludger was convinced that his expert knowledge as a historian of the Victorian penal system would be extremely relevant.

'End whar are the tickets?' he demanded, coldly, fearing that a display of pleasure would undermine his image of suffering and resolution.

'In my purse, dear.'

But Bludger had been re-examining the letter as she replied, and exclaimed: 'By God, it's a woman! Et least, Ay hep seh! One cen niver tell, nahdees!'

'Who's a woman, dear?'

'The producah cheppie, or what-d'you-call-it. Still, we may as well geh.'

Mrs Bludger pointed to the handbill. 'It theth we're to go in Victorian dreth if we can, dear.' She forgot to control a lisp in her excitement: 'I'm going to wear Granny'th old shawl, and I've brought your *lovely* Norfolk jacket and deerthtalker, and ...' She nearly suggested that he could take a walking-stick but decided not to, and thus ended lamely, 'We'll look quite the part.'

Binghurst-on-Sea had been, in its time, a fishing village, a major port in the trade with Ireland, a minor port in the tragedies of migration to North America, and an Edwardian-and-Twenties holiday resort. In the latter capacity it had acquired the enticing but – in view of the extensive deposits of silt from the no-longer-navigable River Bing – disingenuous 'on-Sea'. A post-war attempt to go all big-dipper-and-holiday-camp had competed vainly for a while against package holidays to Spain. Then the increasing prevalence of cars allowed it to discover a leisure-centre-and-weekend-break role, and it was found to be ideally placed for short-term escapes by the inhabitants of the region's several interlocking conurbations. It was almost back to being a fishing village, but this time for yuppies, most of whom took their fibreglass rods to the pub and nowhere else.

The *Cockatoo Theatre* survived on a mixture of entertainments: nostalgic re-enactments from its music-hall days; bookings by amateur operatic and dramatic societies; and touring shows which the management somehow found ready-made or cobbled together. Photographs of such luminaries as George Robey and Marie Lloyd jostled for wall-space with posters of Binghurst Light Opera Society's renditions of *Rose Marie* and *The Merry Widow* – many of their own lions and lionesses already myths in their own lifetimes.

The Manager and Artistic Director, as Ms Tulip Anderson called herself (she rather relished the acronym of her official title) had perceived the proximity of a large middle-class population bored by theatrical kitchen sinks, sickened by rock musicals, and riding on a nostalgia boom. Her high hopes of the current production were certainly being fulfilled, if ticket-sales were anything to go by.

For this occasion, as on previous showings of *Sir Jaspar and the Maiden*, she had abandoned her habitual skin-tight black silk trouser-suit and red boots in favour of a stereotyped Victorian governess's grey uniform (though still tight-fitting). In this guise, and not quite unintentionally giving a few men an ill-defined frisson, she watched the arriving patrons as they slowly filled the auditorium, which had been cleared of its normal seating. The arrivals groped their way around various articles of furniture intended as props ('kindly lent by Bingham Reproduction Furnishings'), and, as they gradually lost their inhibitions at their unaccustomed antiquities of dress, seated themselves on those props or stood around in bemused groups and gossiped expectantly.

Professor Bludger, a passable impression of a country gentleman of his grandfather's day, and for once dressed to match his opinions, perched himself on an upturned barrel in a part of the auditorium apparently destined to be a wine-cellar when the plot required it. He awaited events. Mrs Bludger, as a blowsy granny, stood near him, but kept finding herself in front of, then beside, then behind him as he twisted this way and that, trying to decide which way he should face to observe the action when it began.

A rhythmic thumping stilled the buzz of conversation, and a group of actors and actresses in several classes of Victorian dress marched in, led by a young woman beating a drum affixed to her belly. The drum served as time-keeping for the procession as it wound its way amongst the knots of spectators, and the beat was joined by a low chant from the cast. These two sounds then became an accompaniment for a street ballad from their young leader, narrating the events of the forthcoming play, which was allegedly based on actual events. Bludger graciously nodded his confirmation, although it was all new to him.

During the evening, the wicked baronet Sir Jaspar Blackheart's cruel exploitation of his tenants, and unscrupulously lustful pursuit of the fair sex amongst them, came inexorably to a climax. Having paid unwelcome attentions of a most insulting kind to the virtuous and lovely Amelia Faithful, and having been rejected with that proud scorn which only offended purity could create in one otherwise so gentle, Sir Jaspar had so manipulated certain business affairs that Amelia's father, the good-hearted but helplessly moronic Albert Faithful, could, at the baronet's villainous whim, be consigned unjustly to a foul prison; Bludger shook his head in sorrow. The workhouse awaited Mrs Faithful, the fair Amelia, and a considerable army of innocent flaxen-haired rosy-cheeked younger sibling Faithfuls (the latter recruited from amongst the offspring of Binghurst Light Opera Society's membership, and so effectively disguised that their angelic appearances aroused fond emotions even in those who knew them). Sir Jaspar would desist from his vindictive intention only if he had his wicked way with Amelia, who would be required to swear on the Bible to keep the sordid bargain a secret. ('Misuse of weligion was awften a means of oppwession,' Bludger remarked to a passing yokel.)

Amelia's intended, the stout-hearted George Truelove (his energy on a level with that of Sir Jaspar, but his intelligence unfortunately no more than a healthily bone-headed version of Albert's) made various attempts to avert disaster: first he sought to take Albert's spurious guilt upon himself; then he tried to scare Sir Jaspar off; finally, he tried to kill him. All to no avail. Meantime, the damnable baronet had lured a number of other luscious maidens, less suspicious, or less plucky, or less fortunate than Amelia, to ignominy and death, for he was progressively revealed to be a species of Bluebeard impatient of the marriage-ceremony. He had also found time to send to their doom (usually in his wine-cellar, thereby intermittently displacing Professor Bludger from his perch) a number of bluff, honest members of the lower orders – variously fathers, brothers or affianced sweethearts of the rustic damsels concerned – who had sought, with more rhetoric than competence, to defend honour or life remaining, or to avenge that which had been lost.

The centre of the action moved around the auditorium, and the audience did likewise in order to see. They were occasionally apostrophised by members of the cast, who, however, did not wait for Professor Bludger to explain that the tarminologeh of the quistion requard clewificeetion. The players cleverly took advantage of the mobility and distraction offered by their setting, and of frequent plunges into shriek-laden darkness, in order to appear differently clad in different roles: an overriding practical necessity in any case, since each of them fell victim to several fatalities. The whole evening became a bewildering mêlée of dimly perceived comings-and-goings, poisonings, shootings, wallings-up, noyades, suicides and incarcerations in madhouses.

Not a few of the audience had responded whole-heartedly to the management's invitation to dress in period – the right spirit outweighed many an anachronism, though not for Arnold Bludger – and needed little encouragement to participate in the action, at least to the extent of providing hisses, boos, and other forms of spoken stimulus.

Professor Bludger was becoming extremely bewildered, for this was a strange and exhausting contrast to the drab, disciplined life which he had led for the past three months until that very morning. He was momentarily startled when, in the midst of the ill-lit tumult, a man wearing a brown derby and cape over a frock-coat, and with a huge beard and rimless glasses, whispered to him:

'Professor Bludger? How do you do, sir! Wilf Sassoon, Assistant Manager. Would you care for a comfortable seat elsewhere and a glass of wine, sir? I think we've had enough of "speeding glum heroes down the stairs to death", haven't we?'

Bludger rose, a little stiffly, trying to place what was obviously a quotation – though it didn't sound quite right – and looking forward to the proffered peace and refreshment with this properly respectful person. He did not see very clearly where they were going, or where they were, when they were suddenly in darkness. So profound was the darkness that the long steel blade did not glint. He howled in agony as the knife was thrust several times into his abdomen, and between his ribs, and into his throat. Tulip Anderson, at some distance, made a mental note to restrain the sound-effects from that corner tomorrow night.

This unscripted sub-plot coincided with the dénouement. The doughty George Truelove burst in and saved Amelia in the nick of time, and, though manfully about to do battle and expunge the villain from the face of the earth – and how could one so pure not have the strength of ten? – when he was himself saved in a further nick of time from the moral tarnishing and legal complexities of actually doing so. Sir Jaspar obligingly fell prey to his own evil passions and debauchery, and died of Victorian apoplexy, uttering his last imprecations.

So the wicked baronet had choked on his own evil fury; good old Albert Faithful and his family were saved; the fair and unsullied Amelia was united with that paragon of manly virtue, George; and the jumbled audience, frozen at the last stark horror of Sir Jaspar's dying curse, melted into applause, though with its appreciation mitigated by an admixture of amused condescension, lest anybody should momentarily doubt that they were above being gripped by such a tale.

The house lights were restored.

'This fellow over here,' remarked a young man, indicating the recumbent Professor Bludger, 'he's really entering into the spirit of it.'

His friends joined in, assuming Bludger to be one of the cast: 'C'mon, chum, you'll have to fight the good fight again tomorrow night, y'know.'

'No over-acting, please!' called another as he went past.

Mrs Bludger's scream, and the sight of the slumped corpse while their eyes were still unaccustomed to the light, made the audience assume that they were being treated to a trick-epilogue. But her little-girl vocal power was far less convincing than their recent experiences of scripted professional screams. This ultimate anguish is seldom heard from an adult in real life: for it dare not express itself fully, for fear of accepting and confirming the apparent reason. The real thing was judged by the degree of its conformity with the more familiar pretence and was found wanting.

CHAPTER 12

SOMEONE WHO IT WASN'T

Hooligan had been feeling pleased with himself. He had just cracked a conspiracy case by noticing a trivial point and gently dwelling on it endlessly until the weakest liar had collapsed and brought the others down with him. He had felt that the witness, when drawn into chit-chat, had spoken in a style which was not that in which he answered questions about the crime. His rather halting, rather ungrammatical conversational sentences sounded natural to him. In contrast, his replies to questions about the crime were fluent, stilted, and in the same words at each repetition. From that point, the longer the process went on, the clearer it became that he had been rehearsed for his interrogation by someone else. This someone else was obviously more intelligent and better educated and had done an excellent job in translating his directions into attitudes and linguistic forms prevalent in the social scale further down than his own, where the interviewee hailed from. It was a far cry from the fatuity of the middle-class actor in 'B' feature films, thinking to play a low-class villain merely by remembering to drop his aitches; but the pretence was essentially the same, and could be spotted sooner or later. Until Hooligan had realised what had happened, none of the police officers had even suspected the existence of a boss for the thugs whom they had arrested. Now, a simple affray at closing-time had become a conspiracy-charge, and the sentences would run into years instead of months.

All very satisfactory.

Then had come a telephone call from the Chief Constable. A Professor Bludger from the University of Pillingham had been murdered on the neighbouring constabulary's patch, and Hooligan was to go and liaise in the local investigation.

Hooligan seemed to see Peccary's leer as a symbol of the unknown killer's mockery.

'Up the ladder and down the bloody snake, Ted,' Hooligan remarked to Plumb, as he replaced the telephone. '*Cockatoo Theatre*, Binghurst. Another Professor murdered last night. That's four victims in two-and-a-half years.'

'Christ! Well, don't look at me,' Plumb fished. 'I was at the rugby club dinner-dance.'

'And I was in the shed, trying to repair that coffee-table I told you about. Well, don't look so shocked – I've only taken three months to get round to it. Three months ... he must be only just out.'

'Who, sir?'

'The victim: Bludger. Arnold Bludger. Remember the Professor who laid into Paddy Donovan? Of course you do: you took Paddy's two statements. Well, it's him. Bludger, I mean. Paddy will have an alibi, of course, and it's not his style anyway, but we'd better check him out.'

'What do you mean, sir – "his style"?'

'Bludger was stabbed – and pretty frenetically, too, by a right-hander. Now, Paddy does sometimes threaten violence, but only for show. What's more, he's a southpaw, and never uses a knife. Anyway, the choice of weapon raises another problem: Bert-the-Basher has always used a hammer so far.'

'Then it's someone else, sir?'

'Could be, I suppose.' Hooligan pondered and became more and more depressed.

'It could be the same fellow wanting us to think someone else is joining in. And there are other breaks in the pattern. Until Bludger, all the victims were in English Literature. But Bludger's a historian. And what's more, he's on the staff at the University here in Pillingham: he's never done two from the same University before.

'Does the Pillingham connection mean much, sir? After all, Binghurst's about as close to two other universities as it is to Pillingham.'

'True. If it's not the latest in our series, then it's either a random isolated killing or it's personal to Bludger. But if it *is* the same guy, is he just trying to confuse us with these new elements or does he have some purpose we haven't spotted? He's changed his MO, he's broken the pattern of victims and places, and he's made us wonder if he's going round the sequence again but doing historians this time.'

'Or was one of them the intended victim for personal reasons, and the rest, perhaps including this one, just camouflage?'

'Your theory again, Ted! But suppose Bludger is the intended one, and the earlier ones are camouflage – and the killer *wants* us to think that killing Bludger's a trick to throw us of the scent. Camouflage as camouflage ... Look, we can go round all day, if we let ourselves. Will you tell young Rafferty to check on Donovan? – he'll see through the blarney straightaway - and you and I will go for a country drive – what country's left between here and Binghurst ... '

*

A uniformed constable stood guard at the entrance to the *Cockatoo Theatre*, eyeing a long queue at the box-office; the real murder had enhanced the attractions of the sham ones. Hooligan noticed, as Plumb brought his disreputable beloved old Ford to a standstill, that the constable was neatly beneath the eponymous bird in painted metal over the doorway, and that some whiteish crumpled chips-paper thrown up by the wind and caught on a tail-feather was trailing from its rear-end as though the constable were about to be a target for more than dramatic criticism.

The visiting officers avoided eye-contact with their old friend, Beer-Belly, and entered the setting where eighty years of melodramatic blood, gore and corpses had now been outdone by reality.

The constable had directed them to Tulip Anderson's office, but once in the corridor they were intercepted by a bald man with a shoulder-length occipital fringe, wearing a sweater and jeans, both of which consisted to a considerable extent of holes, and with bare feet in non-matching open-toed sandals. This apparition stared past them, but his speech was more to the point:

'Y' can't come in. Like, no-go.'

Hooligan smiled amiably, produced his warrant card, and purred: 'Cool it, baby – we're da fuzz, like, know what I mean? So where's Toolip's pad, daddy-oh?'

The man reacted as though Hooligan had spoken normally and pointed them along the corridor.

Plumb hoped that Hooligan was not going to be an embarrassment today: he had peculiar moods sometimes, especially when anxious. As they walked the remaining few yards, Plumb reminded himself that Hooligan was an accomplished mimic. New York Jewish, hippy, or whatever it was, just then … and his Indian was better than average – could he have been Mr Krishnaswami, as reported by that old fool Roach? Would he make a convincing porter with an odd gait?

The sound of conversation became audible from the other side of a half-closed door. Tulip, hearing them approach, came out, followed by a man who introduced himself as Detective-Inspector Williams. She left them alone, and minced along to the box-office, her eyes on the profitable queue with no less lasciviousness than Plumb's as they followed her tightly-silked buttocks. Hooligan and Williams gazed more discreetly but with no less appreciation.

Williams had already carried out or initiated a number of enquiries. Mrs Bludger had been sedated in the nearby cottage hospital and could not be questioned yet. But he had established that the letter which had lured Bludger to his death was an obvious forgery, and local printers were being checked in the hope that one of them had made up the false letter-head.

Hooligan looked at the letter more closely – it had been pierced by the knife, and blood stains obscured some details – and shook his head.

'Surely it's a do-it-yourself job,' he said. 'You can get stencils on transparent sheets and make up your own notices. That makes an original, which can be photocopied if need be – as in the present case.'

Williams peered, and coloured slightly.

'The light's better now than when you first saw it,' Hooligan added. 'But you'll agree that anyone, really, could have produced it. Local stationery suppliers might be able to say who bought some stencils recently, but their customers could include just about any firm or society or individual in the area. We can check the typewriter, of course, but ten to one it's a common make. Have you considered his English style yet, Inspector? I find it rather poor. Someone whose English isn't very good, perhaps? Or someone with good English trying to disguise it?'

Williams peered again and made a gesture of indecision.

'My suggestion, said Hooligan, 'is the second possibility: someone wanting to disguise his better education. You'll see that there are no actual mistakes of spelling or grammar, yet somehow it sounds clumsy.'

'Then,' Williams said, 'how come he's let us spot it?'

'From the previous murders – if, of course they're connected with this one – I would say he's playing with us. Obviously, if he's that good he might have avoided letting us twig at all. So, yes, playing with us. And that goes with it's being the same man.'

'Certainly Paddy Donovan couldn't have written even this well,' put in Plumb, and, on a nod from Hooligan, explained to Williams how Donovan came to be mentioned. Williams, perhaps smarting a little at having been unobservant in the matter of the letter, resumed his account of their work at the scene of the crime. A 999-call, placed within a minute of the discovery of the body, had brought a patrol car to the theatre within little more than another minute. From that moment, nobody had left the building without being required to show proof of identity and address; and statements had been taken from a number of them. About a dozen unidentified people had, however, left before the police arrived; that figure was the doorman's impression, and also tallied with the ticket sales. Descriptions of some had been obtained, although the Victorian clothing they had been encouraged to wear was a hindrance. The theatre's financial records showing payments by cheque or credit card were being checked against the list of those known to have been present, in the hope of revealing anyone else who had left immediately.

'Our man wouldn't fall for that one,' said Hooligan. 'But he came well-prepared, so he must have seen the show before and figured out the best place to strike. And the best time – at the end of the show, when people would be leaving anyway. What I suggest that we should look for, Inspector, is someone who might have booked a single ticket for at least two evenings, but probably not at the same time ... and paid in cash ... and who might have booked three for last night – two for the Bludgers and one for himself. But ... would he have booked them all at the same time, do you think? That might attract less attention than coming back. He would assume that we'd wonder about this. Is he toying with us on that point, too? It might all depend on how confident he is in his disguise.'

He explained to Williams how the murderer had probably disguised himself in the previous cases. Tulip returned on the pretext of looking for a telephone number – but really from curiosity. She did an all-over flounce at having to release the box-office tickets clerk to answer questions, but took the hint when Hooligan mentioned, with an air of great sorrow nobly borne, that Inspector Williams might need to close the theatre for forensic examination of the auditorium if other lines of enquiry proved fruitless.

The tickets clerk came in, relishing the attention, and shook her wiry perm in contemplation without being very informative. Then, on the point of going, she turned and said:

'But – silly me! – I'm forgetting Mrs Somme. One ticket on each of two, or was it three, evenings, and three for last night. A little unusual, I suppose ...'

'Who's Mrs Somme,' Williams asked her. 'I haven't heard the name locally ...'

'Mrs M C Somme, so the gentleman said. He spelled out the name, S-O-double M-E, when he ordered by telephone, and said Mrs Somme's chauffeur would collect them and pay. And he did.'

'Paid in cash?' Hooligan asked.

The wiry perm nodded.

'And how was he dressed?'

'In his chauffeur's uniform! But in any case, he *looked* like a chauffeur. And sounded like one. *You* know ...'

'No.' Hooligan tried to look appealing stupid and waited.

'Well ... all polished and polite. And touched his cap. You don't see much of that nowadays, but I suppose Mrs Somme pays for it.'

Williams asked: 'What exactly was the uniform like? And how would you describe him otherwise?'

Hooligan could have predicted her reply. She told of a man of average height, average build, middle-aged, clean-shaven, 'sort of dark' hair – and *so* like a chauffeur.

Williams was glad to sum up thus far: 'So – you've had men walking their dogs that nobody saw, a porter who wasn't a porter, and now I've found you a chauffeur who probably wasn't a chauffeur. We'd better start looking for Mrs Somme.'

'I suspect she doesn't exist,' said Hooligan. 'Tell you why in a minute. But, first, is there anything much in the statements you've taken? I'd like to read them all, of course, in case there are any hints about the previous murders ... but did you form any impressions?'

'Not much, really. Some of them, as you'll see, saw nothing but the play. It moved around the place, you know, and the audience followed. Not a proper play at all. They're a funny lot round here ... And some witnesses thought they saw just about anything you could name, though that could be imagination after the event. Murderers behind every false beard, ladies with stilettos – the knife I mean, not the heels. But it was no stiletto – the doc thinks it's more likely some kind of hunting knife.'

'Hunting,' Hooligan mused. 'He's doing that all right.'

'Oh, and there was one lady who said she saw the theatre ghost from when this site was a workhouse.'

'Perhaps you'd like us to forget the stilettos and the ghost, then. But: some other questions. Did anybody recognise anybody else in disguise?'

'No. We've identified the people who came together or knew each other.'

'Were any too heavily disguised to be recognised even by people who knew them?'

'There were one or two with really enormous Victorian whiskers, presumed to be false. And one of them was in the dozen who left in the couple of minutes before our lads got here.'

'He's probably our man. Phantom Porter, Bird-Man, and now Phantom Chauffeur doubling as Whiskery Victorian – whom the Press will probably call the Phantom of the Theatre. They'll love this.'

Hooligan could see Beer-Belly's enthusiastically darting bulk and hear the shriek of headlines.

'Yes, we can take it that our whiskery killer was the chauffeur and that he placed the telephone order for the tickets. But you were asking about Mrs M C Somme ... '

'She's not in the local directory,' Williams confirmed, perusing the telephone book on Tulip's desk. 'We'll enquire further, of course ... electoral roll, for example ... public library membership ... But you were thinking there's no such person ...?'

'Do enquire, of course, because I could be barking up the wrong tree, and you'll need to satisfy yourself. But – Somme? As in Battle of, 1916? And Mrs M C? As in MC for Military Cross? Quite a few MCs were earned on the Somme, including some by famous people – George Butterworth, Siegfried Sassoon ... '

'It does sound fictitious,' Williams agreed, though he did not recognise the names. 'Does he intend us to spot that he's playing with us?'

'Very likely. After all, he could have used some other disguise or some other false name, but he chose to plant these clues. And if he'd just come in unannounced to buy tickets, he needn't have given a name at all. No, he's sending us some sort of message. A 'yah-boo, can't catch me' kind of message. But even this raises other puzzles. Is the murderer a historian, or did he just know that Bludger was? Or was it just a private obsession – such as his grandfather being killed at the Somme or decorated there?'

Williams was beginning to feel left out again. After all, this was his patch, and this man Hooligan was only a Detective-Inspector like himself, even if Them Upstairs had brought him in as a specialist in the series of cases. But he appreciated the respect Hooligan had shown for his position and decided to combine co-operation with taking control of what was rightfully his.

'I'll check with some veterans I know,' he said. 'They might have noticed a name like Somme, if she exists. And I'll put out enquiries to costume-hire agencies, with a list of the types of costume seen leaving last night before our men got here. And now we'll have to ask specifically about chauffeurs' uniforms. We're already enquiring about the sale of knives – though, of course, he could have owned it already …'

'Well, you've got everything in hand,' said Hooligan, sympathising with Williams's mastery of resentment. 'It's your case, so please don't let me interfere. I'm just looking for common features, as you know. More of an observer than anything. Will you let me know what you turn up, and what you learn from Mrs Bludger? I'll make some enquiries on your behalf in Bludger's university circles, and check on anyone in the family who might inherit. I'll be glad to report back to you on those points. Do you see this as the way forward?'

Williams was mollified.

Hooligan did not seriously expect anything of interest to emerge either in Binghurst or in the University or in the family. Even the chauffeur's uniform could have been hired in a place too remote to be relevant or could even have been in someone's private possession already. Perhaps the putative grand-dad won an MC at the Somme, then became a chauffeur, and left his uniform when he died to … No, that won't do. Officers win the MC, and don't become chauffeurs. Other ranks win the Military Medal – the MM.

Then - someone who actually is a chauffeur, but too far away to be tracked down? Or someone who owns a costume agency, or works in one? Or someone in a dramatic society? The successful impersonations do suggest someone in that line of country ... but societies hire costumes from agencies, so we come round in a circle ...

'By the way, Inspector,' Hooligan added, as they left, 'it occurs to me that the local dramatic society will know the building, perhaps the play as well, and may have their own stocks of costumes. Or hire them from a particular agency ... Just a thought ...'

It would be something else to do. Something else to say had been done when there were no results. A stone not left unturned ...

They strolled the gauntlet of the curious crowd and were accosted by the quivering eagerness of Beer-Belly and his photographic friend, the two-legged tripod. ('Is there such a thing as a "bipod"? Hooligan wondered. 'If not, there ought to be. The thing exists, and there should a word for it.')

'Is there a connection with the murder in Pillingham, Inspector?'

'I'm just an observer,' he insisted. 'It's Detective-Inspector Williams's case, so I can only refer you to him.'

In the car, Hooligan, aware once more of Plumb's occasional worried scrutiny and state of preoccupation, began laughing – to Plumb's confusion. When he had subsided, he said: 'Sorry, Ted, I can't keep this up. I really do have an alibi for last night: I was with Tommy Balham all evening. The grapevine says we're both going up to Chief Inspector, and Jeanie and I, with Tommy and Margaret, were bending the elbow a bit, to celebrate.'

'Oh, congratulations, sir!' Plumb was genuinely pleased, but also glad of the distraction away from the embarrassment which he felt was about to come.

'Thanks. You've propped me up very nicely these last few years, Ted, and soon we'll have to have a talk about your Inspector's exams. Anyway, you can now stop suspecting me of having flipped over Carolyn's problems with Arlington, can't you? What's more, Tommy Balham checked up on me at the time, as I would have done in his position, except that he doesn't know that I know.'

Plumb's jaw dropped. 'But ... really ... I ... But how ...?'

'It's what I would have wondered in your place, Ted. Your train of thought was most impressive. It so happened that you were on the wrong track, but never mind. I couldn't resist inventing that uncheckable story about the coffee-table as a tease. But, you know, you have been a bit obvious. All those oblique questions! But, then, I'm more secretive and furtive than you are ... like our murderer ... Maybe that's why he intrigues me so ...

'... Trouble is, we don't know whether we're after a fantasy-solution – one that sounds improbable but is a lunatic's reality – or a very ordinary one with a mass of false trails that we haven't identified yet ...

'... There are three new aspects to this latest one.' He began to count on his fingers but stopped himself hastily. 'Number One: This is the second of the victims to have a Pillingham connection: otherwise they're all from different Universities. If the murderer is from Pillingham, he would certainly find it easier to prepare and carry it out in his own home area. Though I suppose it doesn't mean that he's a university man himself. Hell, I suppose we haven't really considered the possibility that it's the entire population of the city to search through! Though he does seem to know the university world ... Point Number Two: He's changed subjects from English Literature to history, and that change is simultaneous with the return to Pillingham. So again, we assume he's local, and probably "gown" rather than "town." Number Three: It's a new MO – knife rather than blunt instrument. This might suggest that he's not a pro, set in his ways. Chances are, he's never had so much as a speeding-ticket in his life. He might have hoped the change of MO would confuse us, but probably wouldn't seriously expect it or rely on it. He'd expect us to guess that he's local. Or perhaps he doesn't care if we do.'

'Could he have contrived that point to mislead us, sir? I mean, he could make us think he's local to anywhere, just by doing another murder in the same place.'

'Damn you, Ted, you're right! We can only hope that he thought it more risky to go to a strange place, or to be away from home longer. Oh, who can tell?'

Hooligan brooded as Plumb drove them back to Pillingham.

'How did the murderer know when Bludger was coming out of prison? Exactly, I mean – just knowing the sentence was three months, which he would have known from the trial-report, wouldn't have been accurate enough to set this up. Perhaps Mrs Bludger can shed some light on that. Would you have a word with Williams for me? No, on second thoughts, I'd better contact him: I think his ego's a little delicate.'

He was silent again and then said: 'Ted, if you wanted to lure someone to a theatre, wouldn't you first have to know the show was on? And that the type of production favoured murder and escape?'

'Well, yes, sir, but the Press ... '

'Usually advertised only locally, surely? And local papers, even city ones, aren't easy to come by outside the area. No, just from the fact of the murderer's having known the show was on, he's probably local. Probably knows all the victims ... moves in their wider circles ... though with no obvious personal connections to them ... so he has no extra need to be careful except when actually committing the crimes. He's hidden in plain sight all the time, and very confident about being unnoticed. He's probably quite willing for us to connect his various impersonations – the porter, the man with the non-existent dog and perhaps with the bird, the telephone trickery, the bewhiskered man at the *Cockatoo*, and the chauffeur… Confident because he knows he's a vague nobody to us, probably a normal person to those who know him … probably well-educated, probably a university connection, possibly an interest in the First World War – but that might be personal, he doesn't have to be a historian – mobile, imaginative, quirky, lucky, acting ability, and probably a person of some consequence.'

'Are you sure it isn't you sir?'

'Thank you – I think!'

'Why do you think he's a person of some consequence, sir?'

'He can take time off during the day, not so much for the crimes but for the preparations and travelling. Though he could be unemployed, or on shift-work - except that the things he's capable of don't go with either.'

'Hospital doctors do shift work, sir. And Dr Bossom said that Peccary had made enemies of some doctors.'

'True. But the other victims have had no known medical quarrels. And the literary and historical connection doesn't go with the medical profession … Oh, hell, round in circles again!

'And we made checks on students who might have had it in for the victims. I suppose we'll have to go through that again with Bludger. I'll get on to that, sir?'

'We daren't not do it. But … '

Silence fell again, as Plumb's shabby old Ford sped them along. Then Hooligan said:

'We have to decide … Is Bludger the intended victim, with the previous ones as red herrings?'

'Unlikely, sir. He would have given us three red herrings. A bit excessive, perhaps!'

'Exactly! So: Is he after Professors of whatever at Pillingham with Arlington and Pine-Coffin as the red herrings? But surely he wouldn't produce even two red herrings? Isn't it more likely that he knew them or knew of them, and that they were intended victims. That argues an English Literature connection. But would that place our man in Pillingham or elsewhere?'

'Pillingham, surely, sir?'

'Yes. And why?'

'If he's in English Literature from elsewhere, how come he fixed on Bludger?'

'I hoped you say that. We've so little to go on, but we must assume that he's from Pillingham, that he's doing for Professors of English Literature, and Bludger's a blind.'

'So how can we predict what he might do next, sir?'

'God knows. What *does* make these funny university buggers tick?'

CHAPTER 13

ON THE TRACK, AND OFF IT AGAIN

Hooligan's Chief Constable, Mr – a surgeonly 'Mr', above the petty dignity of titled rank – Quincy Campbell, smiled amiably at Hooligan.

What a wealth of meaning was packed into that smile! 'I have a razor-sharp mind and immeasurable wisdom,' it murmured. 'Furthermore, I am irresistibly charming. Granted, I am modest and unassuming – I should not be, I know; it is merely one of my many virtues to be so - but, by all that's wonderful (me, chiefly), haven't I got charisma! Possessing these and countless other admirable qualities, all of which, despite my manifest lack of self-advertisement, are obvious to any but the undiscerning, whose opinion we may safely leave out of account – possessing these qualities, I say, I have no need of an overtly forceful character. Clearly, I could be forceful if driven to it; the incomprehension and unappreciativeness of the plebs can be so provocative. But, yes, most of the time I may safely eschew the path of forcefulness. For one thing, I have a natural authority. And beneath that, my rapier-intelligence, profundity of thought, and subtle but powerful personal magnetism – thence comes my common touch, by the way – provide not merely adequate, but superior means of achieving my objectives. I am the scalpel, the épée; I leave the battle-axe, the mace-and-chain to others.'

Mr Campbell then deigned to speak. He was, despite his smile and all it betokened, Not Pleased. Questions in the House and letters to *The Times* and *The Cutsodnia* – he preferred his own anagram – were still dwelling on sensitive issues. Embarrassing attention had been drawn repeatedly to the different constabularies' different views of the reasonable limits of self-defence and of such crimes as carrying offensive weapons and keeping dangerous dogs. And suddenly it was coming the way of Chief Constables, in the form of pressure from a most articulate sector of the population: a sector, moreover, with a love of and flair for publicity almost equal to that of small furry animals and children. Academe. What was more, Pillingham had had more than its fair share of those professorial murders – two to every other constabulary's one! And the local Vice-Chancellor had been on the phone, complaining that his fellow-Vice-Chancellors had nicknamed him 'Killer'. Hooligan with his outstanding record otherwise, should do something about it. Not just sit and brood about budgerigars, and dramatic societies, and the First World War.

And what about this latest victim? It began to look as though the murderer had gone to Scotland, and stabbed a Professor of Physics this time, right in the middle of his lecture in the ancient University of Strathreekie. Professors were going down like ninepins, and it had to stop.

'Actually, sir, I was trying to tell you: we've eliminated McClumpha, except for the one murder he actually committed in Strathreekie. Mrs McClumpha is half his age and looks like Marilyn Monroe' – Mr Campbell shifted slightly in his leather armchair – 'and McClumpha thought he had good reason for bumping that Physics Professor off. We're not sure that there *was* an affair, but there's no doubt that McClumpha thought there was and that he did that murder. Plumb – he's my Detective-Sergeant – has been liaising with our colleagues up in Sconnie Botland' – Mr Campbell winced – 'and has established that McClumpha was abroad for scientific visits when the other murders occurred.'

'Then,' Mr Campbell intoned, with the air of a precise mind meaningfully locating the crux of the matter, 'what are we to do?'

'The only thing I can suggest, sir, is that we assume he's going to have another go at the next English Literature Conference – which would mean we should stake the place out. That would, of course, need a lot of officers, preferably including some women, for several days.'

'We don't have the manpower, Hooligan. Have you *seen* the latest crime figures?'

Hooligan felt it unwise to mention that he was sufficiently well-acquainted with the figures to know that his own above-average success rate had reduced them.

'And an entire Conference!' continued Mr Campbell. 'Didn't he wait for the end of the play in the theatre so that he could escape more easily? So wouldn't he do the same again – kill at the very end of the Conference and get clean away?'

'He might and he might not, sir. He'd assume we'd think that, and then might or might not do it for whatever reason. We just don't know.'

'But the manpower!' came a lament from on high, followed by an eagle's swoop: 'In any case, my dear fellow, you didn't find anything when you went incognito to Melbury. Spent most of your time watching the wrong man!'

'If you recall, sir, I recommended guarding the place, but Melbury's Chief Constable wouldn't agree. Even though I was watching the wrong man, a mass effort at protection might have worked and saved a life. And I was right about its being Melbury, which was the only point you disputed at the time. Sir.'

'Lucky guess!' hooted Campbell. 'Atmosphere of violence there – easy to predict.' ('Then why did you dispute it, you prat!' Hooligan could put meanings into a smile deliberately, even if they were not perceived.) 'But guard a whole Conference? No, Hooligan, you'll just have to catch him by proper police methods. ('And what the hell do you know about them?') That'll be all.'

Hooligan could not resist the notion that the Chief Constable was turning into one of the academics he had been dealing with. Was there something about hierarchic seniority that damaged the brain?

*

One Sunday morning, Bertrand Pyle was clipping his front hedge for the last time before the winter. His leg ached slightly, but he found the hedge better company than that available indoors, and he liked particularly the decisive snip which sent each vigorous growth to the ground.

A car went past and pulled up a few doors along. He was vaguely aware that a man was coming from it to speak to him. He turned, and recognised Hooligan.

Greetings were exchanged, and Hooligan enquired about Pyle's leg. Then Pyle said: 'Well, there's two more you can't get me for! Pine-Coffin and Bludger ... Someone's doing for the buggers, for sure, but it ain't me, s'welp me, guv, bang ter rights.'

'That's right, Mr Pyle, it ain't you wot done it. You wouldn't have made it that easy.'

'I like to think so. Well, what can I do for you, or you for me?'

'I'm not quite sure ... Is there somewhere we could talk?'

'Ah! I've been missing my interrogations!'

'This is far from being one – except that I want to pick your brains about something to do with the case. The cases.'

'O K. But not in there, though.' He jerked a thumb at the house. 'I've heard the antennae being adjusted ever since you arrived. I was about to knock off and go to the boozer ... '

'Come for a drive, then? Where do they sell your favourite beer? The rozzers are paying.'

Pyle went round briefly to the back of the house to put his gardening tools away in the shed.

Fifteen minutes later they crossed the plastic wood and nylon-wool flooring of *The Legge of Muttone*, with its plastic leather chairs beneath low beams of plastic oak with moulded worm-holes and protruding plastic rusty nails. Hooligan was disappointed not to see some plastic bats hanging from the ceiling.

They drank real ale.

'So you're a Chief Inspector, now. Congratulations! You must be more successful with your other cases than with whoever-it-is.'

'I seem to have been.'

'I don't see how I can help you, but I'll drink anyone's beer, as you've noticed.'

'I don't see how you help me either, Mr Pyle, except rather generally ... Just tell me about academics as a category, so that I can understand them and their world better. You don't seem to like them, and often they don't seem to like each other. But tell me minus the side-swipes.'

Hooligan was not surprised when, despite his having urged objectivity, Pyle launched into a series of caustic and scurrilous remarks. That was not what he wanted to hear, not so much because he was already half-inclined to believe it, but because he had heard it before. However, some interesting train of thought might lurk in it – Hooligan often scratched around for ideas like this – or perhaps Pyle's storm might rage itself out and yield place to measured comment. In that vague hope, he fell into the role of appreciative audience.

'I get the impression that academics think they're rather hard done by these days,' he prompted, as Pyle sipped his beer for a rest.

'Hard done by?'

Outrage and scepticism demanded a repetition, louder and further up the scale:

'*Hard done by*? They've got sod all to do and all day to do it! You've taken them at their own valuation, I can see! Believed their publicity – which is good, I grant them that. But, knowing them as I do, I invariably disbelieve everything they say, on principle – the principle being, that they haven't got any principles, except that of preserving their own convenience and status. They're self-indulgent' – he began to simmer again – 'childish, overbearing, vain, mendacious to the nth degree, they've got jobs for life for half a year's unsupervised work, and still they're never satisfied!'

The tirade continued, and Hooligan, still hoping to learn something, cranked him up whenever necessary with such provocative comments as:

'Strange how the Professor-character in films and books is always a dignified old chap, brilliant intellectually, of course, absent minded, but very polite and honourable ...'

'Polite and honourable?' Pyle almost choked on his beer. 'Dignified?' He put his glass down, fearing that he might otherwise drop it.

'Yes, that's the popular image all right. But it's the nice ones you have to be wary of: just watch them turn nasty and abuse a trust when they don't get their own way. "Polite, honourable and dignified," you said. Boorish, ignorant, scheming, petty little crooks, more like! If you put a real one in a film, nobody would believe it ... And they're a useless bunch of buggers. The Professor of Economics says unemployment will come down, so it goes up. The Professor of Engineering says a bridge is safe, so it falls down. The whole bloody place is full of them – mathematicians who can't read a departmental balance-sheet, musicians who can't play their instruments, linguists who write bad English, and engineers whose machines don't work.'

Hooligan recalled how little his tutor in criminal law had known about criminal law. But he concentrated as Pyle's venom flooded on:

'Them and their bloody research! Into what nobody needs to know, most of the time! And that's how they get promoted! But not one of 'em will call the others' bluff - for fear of having someone call theirs. A conspiracy of silence about the conspiracy of crap! *I've* found that promotion just depends on whether your face fits. And you can see how deformed and twisted some of the faces have to be to fit the circumstances, and vice versa.'

Hooligan had lost Pyle's train of thought slightly (so, probably, had Pyle), so he risked a blunt question: 'Do you think the murderer is an academic?'

'Hardly credible. They're crooked enough - but too inept!'

'But he seems to know the academic world.'

'Obviously. But that could include librarians' - Pyle bowed, ironically - 'administrators, secretaries, students, ex-students ... all the various members of the public connected with universities, such as local bigwigs, top civil service ... even some obscure member of the public who applied to university and was rejected ... Now, if only Adolf Hitler had been accepted by the Vienna Art School, if you see what I mean ... I don't want to tell you your job, Chief-Inspector, because academic ignoramuses are always trying to tell me mine, and I know how galling it is ... By the way, did you know that Chairman Mao hated academics because he was a librarian as a young man and they treated him arrogantly, so that's why he sent them into the fields to be re-educated by peasants? ... Where was I?'

'You were about to tell me how to do my job because we can both see I haven't had any success with this one!'

'Ah, yes. Well ... it's my guess that this guy you want is an academic only in being a screwball and pretty nasty and seeming to know the academic world. He's different in being intelligent and a good planner. One or two of them *are* intelligent, of course, but they're an endangered species ...'

Hooligan suspected that another tirade of rehearsed vituperation was about to erupt from the obsessive Pyle, so he rose and bought another round of drinks. Seated again, he resumed his pumping.

'If it's not an academic I'm after, can I forget the idea that the murderer is trying to get a Professor's job by causing a vacancy?'

'I would think so. They would hardly appoint an outsider to the Chair. In any case, creating a professorial vacancy would only help the next-in-line, meaning Reader or Senior Lecturer. Nowadays, when a Professor retires, or has a compulsory retirement like my Rat-Pig friend, Peccary... '

Pyle launched into another digression: 'Did you know, by the way, that the peccary is a notoriously malodorous pig-like creature from the tropical Americas? No? I told our highly esteemed Registrar, John Boyle – you've met him? – I told Boyle, and the info ran around the entire Rudiversity. Not that you'd trace it back to canny John ... He couldn't stand Peccary, and can't stand most academics anyway ... Sorry, where was I? Oh, yes, you were asking about replacing people ... Yes ... When a Professor goes, nowadays, they usually promote someone already there and then freeze *his* post. Like they did with old Simmonds, whom your lot kept suspecting! It saves on the total salary bill. Universities are that short of funds these days – by courtesy of our dear government, which – '

'So nobody gets a job now except at the very top and from within?'

'Yes – and no. There was a stage, before things got really difficult, when there still were jobs at the bottom of the ordinary Lecturer grade. Internal promotion at the top to replace a Professor created a kind of suction-effect with a junior vacancy at the bottom end of it. Everyone moved up a notch. Silly buggers playing musical chairs. Then even that seemed to dry up, though there are signs of it coming back again, now that the contraction of the higher education industry's easing off a bit. Jobs for the boys, and girls, again …'

Hooligan wondered, but not aloud, if the murderer was trying to create a job at the lower end by stimulating what Pyle had dubbed the 'suction-effect'.

'What sort of people might these boys and girls be?' he asked.

'Recent graduates, almost certainly with a "first", and with at least most of a PhD finished. The low starting-salary wouldn't attract anyone older. And with scores, literally scores, of well-qualified applicants for every job, the one who gets it would probably be the Professor's pet, with his face fitting. Hence, unlikely to murder the old sod ... Oh, I see what you mean: a young graduate creates a vacancy by bumping a Professor off. And from whichever Rudiversity he wants to work in. Though there'd be so many applicants – his chances of getting the job would be pretty small …'

Pyle was seized with a new fancy: 'You know, two or more could join forces and murder a number of Professors, to improve the odds. A bit like the Hitchcock film – *Strangers on a Train*, remade as *Strangers in a Degree-Factory*.'

'Not likely in this case. I still think we want one man.'

'Will he have another go, do you think?'

'I hope not,' replied Hooligan, guardedly.

'Well, I can suggest a few victims if he comes to me for advice. There's a Chemistry Professor on our Library Committee who'd be greatly improved by an outbreak of sudden death.'

'As long as you don't do it or encourage anybody else,' said Hooligan, gently. 'That really would embarrass both of us. And it would ruin your splendid role as Greek chorus.'

'In which role,' Pyle chuckled, 'I suspect that you feel an affinity with this unknown fellow. Is he your Jungian shadow, I wonder?'

Two men, one a wizened little fellow and the other lean and of sardonic expression, entered *The Legge of Muttone* and made for the bar, waving at Pyle as they did so. Pyle explained that they were Mew and Clark, his drinking-friends from the Library, and Hooligan said: 'Perhaps I'll slip away … Is there any hope that they could drive you home? Otherwise you could get a taxi at police expense.'

'No, they'll take me all right.'

As Mew and Clark approached, Hooligan said, for them to hear: 'Nice running into you again!'

He felt that this parting remark was as good as a request to be circumspect in what Pyle repeated; and left Pyle free to tell his friends whatever he wished otherwise.

*

Hooligan drove home, rather depressed. Pyle's discourse, distastefully vitriolic at some times, entertaining at others, perceptive nonetheless, had made him feel tired, although it had been quite fruitful in clarifying his own thoughts.

So the purpose in murdering Professors of English Literature could be to create a junior vacancy? This theory would fit two other facts. One, that Pine-Coffin was murdered, while Roach, the actual Professor, was spared. Roach was about to retire, so there was no need to kill him; Pine-Coffin was his destined successor and therefore the obvious target. And the Department which had lost both Roach and Pine-Coffin was pretty likely to be allowed to fill a junior vacancy. Hooligan reminded himself to check on that point: was there a vacancy? And who applied for it? The second fact was that the victims came from different universities: once you'd bumped off the Professor and they'd filled the post from within the Department, and without allowing a vacancy further down, you had to go elsewhere for your next victim.

Or did you? Why not bump off the successor? Because these crimes were obviously prepared, and by someone who, though taunting them, was very careful. The successor was more use to the murderer as a police suspect: whereas, to go back to the same place to bump off the new appointee would increase the chances that the police might suspect applicants for the consequential junior post.

But, as Pyle had confirmed, there was no guarantee that the murderer would be appointed when that junior job was filled. That was the hole in an otherwise attractive theory.

It would follow therefore that the murderer was unusually well-qualified – not a beginner at all. And that would fit the description of the Phantom Porter and the Phantom Chauffeur – a middle-aged man, a bit younger than his victims. The old man walking his non-dog near Pine-Coffin's house could be an irrelevancy. Or a good disguise - not an old man at all. So the murderer could be – what? – a distinguished amateur in the subject? Doing some other non-university job, such as publishing, or teaching English or drama in a school? Or an actor, who may have done a literature degree? Whatever he was, he would need to be better qualified than a recent graduate, but not earning very much.

But what about Bludger? He wasn't in English Literature at all, so where did a historian fit in? He made sense only as a deliberately false lead: a change of academic subject, a return to a Pillingham connection, a change of MO – any of these could be significant. Or not! But possibly Bludger was put in the murderer's mind by the old fool's own misguided venture into violence. This again, suggested that the murderer was local.

And what was that about the Registrar, John Boyle? Hates academics, according to Pyle ...

As before, every seeming clarification replaced old uncertainties with new ones; revealed some possible lines of enquiry to be fruitless; and opened up bottomless pits of speculation. Including the speculation, which he had suppressed until Pyle had articulated it, that he was in some kind of vicarious relationship with this murderer. With his shadow-side.

Hooligan drove and reflected ...

He was suddenly, with no obvious reason, jerked by a sixth sense from his depressed fatigue into alertness. A lorry which had been following him in apparent contentment had suddenly pulled out. Its driver, seeing an oncoming bus, braked, and skidded towards Hooligan, who tried to accelerate out of danger. The lorry clipped his car, and sent it bouncing off a lamp-post. His car then slewed round and collided with the bus, which was itself skidding by then. The car overturned twice, while the bus struck a stationery car full of passengers.

The lorry roared off and was never found.

The lorry-driver's score was slightly higher than that of the murderer whose identity had preoccupied Hooligan a moment earlier.

CHAPTER 14

BOLTED IN, AND DEAD

In 1984 the annual English Literature Conference assembled at the University of Stockchester, its members free from the anxieties and its finances relieved of the absenteeism which had beset the event in the previous year. After all, that murder up in Scotland showed that nobody was safe anywhere, so what was so dangerous about a conference? Of the four murders – five, if you included McClumpha up in Strathreekie – only one had taken place at a conference, and that was two years ago. The power-vacuum left in their psyches by the ebb of panic was occupied by self-deception: in their desire to be a tribe, to be comforted, and to confer, they overlooked the fact that the Scottish crime which seemed to console them was – as the habitual murderer, gleefully reading of it in the newspapers, said to himself – obviously *hors série*. And surely, they reasoned, the murder of Bludger was, in its way, an encouraging sign. He had been a hishtorwian, not a lichacha shpecialisht; and he'd been shtebbed, not shtwuck evah [*over*] the head. So ill-thought-out was this view in their circles that they even spoke, with facile jocularity and with as much taste as wit or logic, of being 'bludgered' to death.

The slow, dithering arrival of participants passed off without incident; so did the routine approval of a motion calling upon the *Gumt* [Government] to pwovide more funds for them; likewise the opening sessions concerned with faynencial end administwative business. Shallow passions (the type which rage the most and harm the least) were aroused, and cardboard swords were crossed, on the vexed question of Conferwence Subscwiption Weets [*rates*]. Should these be a flet chawge [*flat charge*]? Or should the chawge varwy with the saze of the welevant Depawtment?

Or varwy with the saze of the Univarsiteh? Would one teek the saze of the Depawtment or Univarsiteh to be the numbah of its stawff, or pestgweduate students or undergweduates? What abite the fect that some Univarsitehs wair wicher *[were richer]* than others?

A compromise was agreed upon, and those who seemed to understand the statistics – an impression which owed more to the ineptitude of some than to the acumen of others – were entrusted with the duty of a complex calculation. The academic sessions, too, were charged with emotion masquerading as principled commitment. How, for example, could one equete the velue of degwee-cawsses of differwent content? Could one wealleh accept a degwee-cawss without Chaucah end Pairs *[Piers]* Plowman? End since they wair essential es owigins of the lichacha, surely they should be studied in thar pwopah chwonologeh, neemly, farst? Professor Easedown of Prince College, Oxford, having delivered himself of this mettah of pwinciple, glared in derision at the host-contingent from Stockchester: he was the blue blood of pure learning confronted by these Johnny-come-lately pragmatists. In all these disputes, long-standing enmities and alliances were reinforced or called off; real or imagined slights or favours from the distant past were punished or rewarded by today's stance; the prospects of favourable reviews of forthcoming books were improved or jeopardised. Some form of crude Darwinism created new alignments from the processes of argument, for this parasitic gathering was, in its way, a self-contained ecological system. Fortunately, the passions were entirely cerebral, the weapons merely figurative – else the homicidal diminution of their ranks so far had been but a drop in the ocean of the blood which would now have been shed.

The third and last evening of the Conference had come with no sign of trouble other than that engendered by playground squabbles. Members had relaxed, had even become free-and-easy, as any lingering tensions abated. The routines of meetings, coffee, meetings, bar, lunch, meetings, tea, meetings, free time, bar, dinner, and bar had established their own complementary routines of somnolence or aargent business elsewhar, particularly during formal lecture sessions.

Towards evening, Professor Waff, whose inner condition had been unsatisfactory and a cause of his solitude for years, was in a lavatory cubicle, emitting sounds more reminiscent of an outboard motor under test than of a venerable scholar. The building's air-conditioning hummed its white noise and the plumbing gurgled and reverberated, while his gaseous bowels challenged the former's capacity and rivalled the latter's sound-track. In one of the brief intervals of perception which his labours allowed him, he was aware that two men had come in, talking amicably. One of them sounded like Johnston-Baglinnet, newly appointed to the 'Char' here at Stockchester; he did not recognise the other voice. Waff's resumption of activity prevented him from correctly interpreting what he would otherwise have heard; he mentally reconstructed it the next day.

There had been a dull thud and a groan, followed by the same sounds, mainly in that sequence, several times. Then somebody had staggered into the cubicle next to his – he believed he had also heard a dragging sound – and had bolted the door. Scrabbling sounds had ensued, and then somebody had left the room – without even having washed his hands! He had wondered if someone were ill but had felt that his own circumstances precluded discussion through a partition.

Meanwhile, other events, unknown to Professor Waff, were in train.

Professor Gristmill, on his way to the bar, had reached the foot of the stairs and had realised that he had forgotten his tobacco-pouch and would 'hev to geh beck' for it. This fact seemed to him to call for an appropriate comment, for it was extremely inconvenient and he wished it had not happened. His erudite mind, stocked to overflowing with literary knowledge and honed in the subtleties and richness of the English language, could provide a no better exposition of his situation than would have occurred to, or perhaps shocked, the janitor.

'Shit-bloody-balls-bloody-fuck-bloody-sod-bloody-cunt,' he said, with perhaps a shade more sense of language than of logic, but precious little of either.

Then, finding such a sequence doomed to self-repetition which would not contribute to a solution of the problem, he fell silent and made his way back upstairs. Panting slightly with exertion and suppressed rage, he paused at the top of his climb, then stomped with resolute fury along the corridor.

The timing of these tiny events brought him face to face with a man in middle age who was emerging from the lavatory. Gristmill noticed that the man leaned backwards as he walked, like a pregnant woman or a man who had been obese until recently. Something in the man's reaction on seeing him – a nervous focus leaping into his face – made Gristmill hesitate. The stranger, seeing this, himself hesitated, and then said: 'Someone's ill in there.'

Gristmill assumed that this was the reason for the man's nervousness and was reassured. But what was to be done?

'Ill?'

'Yes. Can you come and see? What's your opinion? Should we do something?'

The stranger opened the door, and Gristmill, his newly attributed medical knowledge growing with this deference to his judgement, passed ahead of him into the lavatory room. Two cubicles were engaged, and it was unpalatably obvious that Professor Waff occupied one of them. As the main door closed behind him, Gristmill felt a blinding flash of pain radiating from the back of his head, followed by fiery blackness. He had no time even for a string of expletives.

His assailant dragged him into the vacant cubicle next to that of Professor Johnston-Baglinnet, placed him, like his dead and live neighbours, on the seat, bolted himself in, and turned to examine his victim more closely. Perceiving him to be still breathing – what a thick skull he must have! – he struck him again and examined him again. Blood might fly about if he hit him too hard in a confined space, and he wore no overall this time; so he gripped the unconscious and tiresomely still living Gristmill by the throat, pressed his thumbs to his victim's windpipe, and forced himself to count slowly up to sixty. Gristmill's involuntary gurgling was obscured by Waff's performance. Long before the minute was up, the murderer was rewarded by a protruding tongue, popping eyes, and a purple complexion not wholly unlike the porcine prototype in the garden shed. But he did not let go until the self-imposed count was complete. Pleasure then yielded place to prudence: with a conscious effort of will, he freed his thumbs from their orgiastic compression of Gristmill's windpipe.

His unlooked-for, but thoroughly welcome, extra murder successfully accomplished, he climbed over the partition and left hurriedly. He walked, as he had practised, leaning slightly backwards and with a rolling gait.

Professor Waff, drawing near to the end of his own equally unaesthetic exertions, was mystified by having heard the same strange and unpleasant-sounding events a second time. A few minutes later he, too, had left. Back in his room he found that a note, written in block capitals, had been pushed under his door:

ANTHEM FOR DOOMED GUTS
   What ancient bowels are these that fart like cattle?
      Only the sullen thunder of the bums,
   Drowning the quivering door-frame's rapid rattle
   Can splutter out their faecal origins.

Mortally offended, Professor Waff screwed the paper up and threw it away. Although an English Literature specialist, he took the verse to be merely bad poetry in its own right and did not recognise the Wilfred Owen parody. For him, lichacha ended with the Ettinth Centcheh *[Eighteenth Century]*.

The new lavatory-neighbours, whom Waff had deserted but had occasionally to revisit, sat there all night, their distorted faces streaked with dried blood, their eyes staring to an unperceived horizon.

The Conference was scheduled to end the next day; all rooms had to be vacated by half-past-ten in order to prepare for a gathering of economists coming in next. Overnight revellers, forced by their consumption of beer on expenses into frequent relief-treks, did not particularly notice that the same two cubicles were permanently occupied, though the perfect silence and inoffensive atmosphere for as long as a third was not occupied by Professor Waff revealed who was *not* there. The continued monopolisation of the two cubicles was found to be a little inconvenient the following morning, as was the increasing pungency of death, but the Conference broke up and melted away in collective self-congratulation.

*

The cleaners descended on the building in force to prepare it for the next Conference, and in due course reported to the Head Porter that two rooms still had property in them. He pronounced solemnly that he would undertake the Boxing and Tagging of Late Departers – a procedure less aggressive and less vindictive than its name, for it consisted only of storing items in labelled boxes. The ladies, their grievance at having been so obstructed by Late Departers now mitigated by the dignity of official action, went about their work with renewed zest, and in due course bucketed and mopped their way into the lavatories.

This building was a women's hostel, preferred as Conference accommodation because it was in better condition, with its graffiti more literate and less improbable than in the men's building. Most of the lavatories, consisting, of course, of cubicles only, had been redesignated for male use, since the majority of delegates were legally male. Nevertheless, the cleaners had fewer inhibitions, even during male occupancy, than their colleagues who worked the men's building next door.

Flo tore down the temporary label *MEN* with an air of avenging a violation and entered. Espying two closed doors, she shrilled, though not unkindly, 'C'mon, you two, can't sit there aw day!'

Receiving no response, she continued with a touch more asperity:

'Taken a lease on the place, 'ave yer?'; and then:

'Cat got yer tongue? Don't mind me, dear. 'Ad free chiwdren of me own, yer know!'

This last remark was not merely a claim to vast experience of bodily misfortune, but an oblique comment on the smell. The air-conditioning had long dispersed the contributions of Professor Waff, but had not prevailed against the fact that, in death, Johnston-Baglinnet and Gristmill had lost control.

Flo, irritated by the continued silence, and emboldened by her sense of right and wrong – for they should have been long gone by now – stopped and peered under the nearest of the two doors. She saw a pair of large brown brogues shiny with black polish, surmounted by shapeless corduroys, obviously fully up.

"Wossaw thissy nere [*What's all this in here*]?' she demanded and peered under the other door as though for reply. The shoes and trousers differed, but she discerned the same fully clad, seated, silent immobility.

' 'Oi'll fetch the 'Ead Porter!' she warned; then, on reflection, continued more gently: 'Are you aw right in there, dear?'

The silence continued. Flo reached under the first door and pulled at a corduroy leg. Professor Gristmill had been slipping imperceptibly all night and, now dislodged, fell sideways; then, turned by having rolled against the partition, he fell to the floor. His battered and bloodstained head appeared suddenly under the door, his unseeing eyes fixed on Flo, his dead purple tongue roguishly on view.

Flo screamed, recoiled, tripped over her bucket which went clanking off, fell heavily, struggled to her feet, and ran out, holding her heart and her head (though she had not struck it in her fall), and wailing. Her colleagues, their attention attracted by the din, met her.

' 'E's in there!' she intoned. 'Lookin' up at me!'

'What?' they demanded. 'What did 'e do? - you can tell us, dear. Dirty beast!'

They marched in resolutely, leaving the tearful Flo to the rear. This affront to one of their number, in whatever it may have consisted (and they intended to ascertain the exact details later with minute exactitude), had to be avenged. This groper-streaker-Peeping Tom-flasher-rapist, be he what he may, would cower in his miserable lair and take what was coming to him.

But the war-party, in turn, shrieked and recoiled. As Flo might have told them, Professor Gristmill's head projected beneath the door, displaying visionless eyes, yellowish teeth, protruding tongue, and hair matted with dried blood. Even had she prepared them for that, she could not have mentioned that his neighbour, Professor Johnston-Baglinnet, had also been dislodged and had slowly subsided when Gristmill had collided heavily with the partition. His face, likewise dark with dried blood, stared in an unseeing frown from beneath the cubicle door. The two mutilated heads, venerability transmuted into grim indignity by violent death, gazed with grisly furtiveness up the ladies' skirts.

'Get George!' wailed somebody, whereupon they all turned as one, like a hunting pack put to flight, and ran down the corridor, shouting for the Head Porter.

Flo was recovering from her first shock, but, finding herself now abandoned and her starring role inexplicably torn from her by this sudden exodus, sought to restore her lost status. She decided to be rediscovered sobbing by the dreadful scene when they returned. She re-entered to prepare herself for her come-back, found that the lone head had become a double-act, and fainted.

The Daily Reflector carried a headline DEAD DONS IN GIRLS' LOOS, with a picture of Flo looking, in consequence of several glasses of sweet sherry at an unaccustomed time of day, far less distraught than her quoted words would have led one to expect. A few unimportant details followed, with an injunction to *See back page*, where the same information was paraphrased. *The Reflector* was too interested in its salacious imaginings to include any reference to the earlier killings around academe. Their daily pundit, *The Man Who Sees*, was moved to wonder what the learned gentlemen were doing in the 'Ladies' in the first place; why there were two of them; what these bog-capers had to do with education; and whether this was what ordinary, decent hardworking people sent their kids to college to learn. They later had to apologise before the Press Council and pay an undisclosed sum to an educational charity in the Third World. 'O K, folks, British justice is good enough for us,' they proclaimed afterwards, as though this humiliating proof of incompetence were a victory.

The Cutsodian managed a factual report, but, true to its typographic tradition, unfortunately referred to the Ladies' Laboratories. A certain Ms Tulip Anderson wrote an angry letter to Stockchester's Vice-Chancellor, upbraiding him for the segregation of men and women in scientific work and demanding to know whether the women's laboratories were of the same quality as the men's.

Professor Waff learned of the murders from the news shortly after arriving home. Embarrassed by his involuntary not-quite-spectatorship of the proceedings, and feeling that his colleagues, including the two victims, had always been unaccountably unfriendly towards him, he kept his own counsel.

The police, in their search for evidence, picked up references to a nondescript man who 'sort of swayed when 'e walked – might of bin a sailor, if you arse me' – and who might have had nothing to do with the case.

CHAPTER 15

ON WATCH

That quality of Chief Constable Mr Quincy Campbell's smile which indicated his effortless superiority of mind and character was fast becoming artificial in substance and presentation. More and more was it the deliberate flash of eyes and teeth by which the politician or comedian encourages his audience to the desired response, or behind which he quaking hides the insufficiency of his argument or script and his faltering conviction. He could not disguise his predicament from himself: he had turned down Hooligan's renewed recommendation to stake out the Conference on English Literature at Stockchester, whereupon the gutter-Press, having long bayed for the blood of the Phantom Porter, the Phantom Chauffeur, the Bird-Man, and the Don-Basher, had gleefully invented the Bog-Bandit. Whoever and whatever the perpetrator was, he had struck again! And with two for the price of one! The police, particularly in his constabulary where it had all started, looked silly; the media were having a field-day; and the academic world had resumed its panic. More Professors had been prosecuted for carrying offensive weapons or keeping dangerous dogs; more letters to the Press and more pundits from the investigative sector of television ('I could strangle that bloody Jack Logan with his own microphone cable!'} dwelt on the inconsistency of the police and the courts in prosecution and sentencing. And the whole mess now had this unsavoury lavatorial aspect! If only he had let Hooligan, poor devil, have his way! Next year's Easter Conference at Doupminster would have to be staked out: with no useful leads at all, there was nothing else to do. And imagine the outcry if the next Conference were not staked out and another murder occurred there! These gatherings took place every year, but it wasn't too soon to start planning police infiltration – and after he'd been so against it, too! Damn Hooligan!

And suppose there was another murder before then! Hooligan's Sergeant, Crumb or whatever his name was, had pointed out that not all the murders had been committed at conferences. Perhaps the murderer wouldn't wait for another year. Or perhaps he'd reckon on a stake-out and stay away – or even cock a snook at them by striking during the Conference but elsewhere!

On the other hand, as Hooligan had pointed out some time ago, a conference was obviously an ideal place, with all those Professors doddering about and declaiming, and strangers legitimately coming and going. And Hooligan had said that this looney was probably playing with them and might relish the idea of a challenge.

Yes, damn Hooligan! Just typical of him: even though he hasn't got his man this time, he's been right about everything!

*

'Thank you for the flowers and the card, sir. Sorry I couldn't justify a wreath!'

While Mr Quincy Campbell, incapable of banter, and ill-at-ease by the compulsory affectation of grace and bonhomie so foreign to his nature, murmured a suitable platitude in reply, Hooligan, also stiffly but with a more valid cause, half-rose and reached out to take down from the mantelpiece another card.

'This was amongst the cards which came to the station when I was dead,' he explained, 'or I should say, when I was on the way back from being dead. A two-minute stay, but I didn't care for it ... If I hadn't had a flash of coming danger I would have hit the lamp-post head-on and wrapped myself round it. On the other hand, if I hadn't been preoccupied with the case I wouldn't have needed that forewarning. In one way I got lucky, though … I and one of the other victims would have died but for the coincidence of Dr Bossom – you know old 'Boomer' Bossom? – coming up behind. But that's by the way. Have a look at this card, sir. It'll go into the case-file now that I can see it belongs there, but I think you'd be interested in it just now …'

Mr Campbell took a conventional get-well-soon card, opened it, and read out a typed message:

THE LAST LAUGH
'O Jesus Christ! That's it,' he said; and died,
Whether he vainly cursed, or prayed indeed,
The lorry chirped – In vain! vain! vain!
Exhaust pipes chuckled, Tut-tut! Tut-tut!
But Hooli-Gun recovered!'

The Chief Constable frowned an anti-smile.

'What is it? What does it mean? Very bad taste, I would say. An anonymous crackpot, presumably.'

'Yes, sir, all of those things, of course - though the "bad taste" isn't as bad as it might seem when you read it more closely. But, more to the point, it's the same typewriter that bamboozled Professor Bludger into going to the *Cockatoo Theatre*.'

'Ah!'

'And there were no fingerprints on it. That in itself is interesting. It's impossible to send someone a glossy card like this and not leave prints on it, unless, of course, the intention is not to leave any. So he bought it wrapped in cellophane, and avoided touching it.'

'But why wouldn't he have got an ordinary unwrapped one, with dozens of prints on it and none of them his?'

'To waste our time, you mean? Yes, I wondered that, too. But I think he wants us to be absolutely sure it's him. This is more of a "Yah-boo, can't catch me!", wouldn't you say? We're to compete with him for the "last laugh".'

Mr Campbell sighed and looked again at the typed message.

'What is this reference to "Hooli-Gun"?' he asked. 'Does that mean he's going to shoot someone next time?'

'I doubt it, sir. The verse is a take-off of a poem by Wilfred Own – First World War poet – and the original mentions a gun at that point. But I think the whole thing is intended to tell us it's the same man.'

'I don't follow you'

'A First World War connection, sir – to go with that Mrs M C Somme at the *Cockatoo Theatre* who seems not to have existed. I've had a list of First World War specialists compiled by a contact of mine in the University Library – a former suspect, as a matter of interest! – but none of them seems a very good prospect from our point of view ... all in the clear in one way or another ... But surely it means also that he intends to be active again, or at least wants us to think so. Either way, we have no option but to take him seriously. Sir.'

'Which brings me' – his visitor took a deep breath – 'to the purpose of my visit. Apart from a natural interest in your recovery, of course.'

It was Hooligan's turn to be graciously platitudinous – an impulse which neither man possessed, except that Hooligan had technique and Campbell none.

'We'll need a plan of action, Hooligan.'

'I was wondering about putting some further information about me in the Press, sir. It needn't be true – just as long as it makes him communicate with me again and perhaps reveal something more about himself. I think I've figured out what kind of person he is, so the more we can – '

'Oh, we can't pussyfoot around, Hooligan,' returned the man of action; as Hooligan's vague proposal was intended to bring about, in order that 'Them Upstairs' would determine policy and take responsibility for it, rather than carp afterwards. 'No: immediately upon your return, you will be released from all duties in order to prepare a mass police presence at the next Conference at the University of Doupminster. My opposite number in Doupshire has already spoken to the Vice-Chancellor there.'

'I really don't think he'll strike there, sir, or at any conference now.' He relied on Campbell to dig his heels in. 'The time for that was ... What I mean is, he'll expect us to do that, so he'll take the, er, mickey: either he'll do one just before, and leave us wondering whether to call the surveillance off, or one somewhere else, or just after, to make us look like berks. Or he'll just do nothing for a while, for the pleasure of making us exert ourselves to no purpose.'

The Chief Constable was irked by this apparent contrariness. Rather than recognise a different point of view, or the effect of changing circumstances, he told himself that Hooligan had been ill. He choked back a retort, with determined tolerance in his smile.

'But we can't do anything else,' he said. 'What else is there to do which would look reasonable to ... er ...?'

Hooligan reminded himself that even Chief Constables had a 'Them Upstairs', just as the gods of Ancient Greece had Fate.

'I suppose,' he conceded, 'at the least we might save a life by deterring him from another murder there.'

Mr Campbell brightened. 'Exactly so! He's interested in you personally, and in playing a game, as you so rightly pointed out. He might come and look on and give himself away!'

'If that's what you want, sir, I'll be glad to set something up. We'll be looking for him looking for us ... but whether we'll see him as clearly as he sees us ....'

'Of course we will! Trained officers!'

Mr Campbell's resolute display of uninterest in alternatives, which was what Hooligan had wanted, gave way to relief that he had survived the ordeal of adopting Hooligan's earlier view, even though perhaps too late. He accordingly submitted to the further ordeal of tea as Jeanie entered. Mr Campbell preferred to condescend to women and was therefore unsure of himself when they were not his subordinates in the police force. Ex-WPC Hooligan's charm infiltrated his defences and nearly exposed a man who sensed his own limitations.

*

Hooligan was virtually convinced that the stake-out would not yield any tangible result, except possibly that of preventing a murder at the Conference itself and the concomitant displacement of a crime elsewhere. The murderer was wise to them; and was so well aware of their deductions about him that he had taken to feeding them scraps of useless information in a spirit of mockery. He would expect them to attempt an ambush: for he would know that there was nothing else left for them to do and that they dared not, as Mr Quincy Campbell had made clear, neglect the obvious. And he would assume that they would credit him with having realised this. Since his actions had indicated to them that he knew the academic world and dwelt in it, they would expect him to spot any irregularity in the Conference arrangements and to stay his hand. Each side knew that the other side knew, and so on ...

Hooligan fumed to himself. All this should have been done two years ago. Now it was pointless. Like picking up the fallen bottle when the blood-red wine was all over the carpet. Still, they might save a life, and might prevent the murderer from setting up any more Conference panic. And there was always the hope that he might overreach himself through arrogance or carelessness. There even remained the faint chance, to be fair, that Campbell was right: that the murderer might decide to strike at this Conference precisely because of the improbability that he would so.

Mr Campbell, over-reacting against his own former obduracy, and cherishing his image as one who thinks big, had at first insisted on saturating the place with several dozen police-officers. Perhaps he also wished to absolve himself of the possible charge of not having taken preventative measures to the limits of his capacity if another murder should occur there.

But he was finally persuaded by Hooligan's argument that this would assuredly be spotted by the killer and only warn him off and might become grounds for operational criticism later. After all, the murderer had been successful at his trade for four years and was no amateur. They must decide between a large and easily detectable police presence as a deterrent and a smaller one which might catch the criminal. If he spotted a large police presence at the Conference and decided to kill anyway, he would probably arrive only towards the end, and even more probably not commit the murder until the last minute – so that by the time the body was discovered, the Conference would have dispersed, and the cleaners would have interfered with the clues. That lesson he must have learned at Pagham and at the *Cockatoo Theatre*. And the deployment of many officers would have been wasted. The solution, Hooligan urged, was not to put a great hulking bobby, even if in some sort of disguise, on every stairway, as the Chief Constable seemed to envisage, but to have a smaller number of officers unobtrusively present. They would be able to ascertain who was entitled to be there, especially towards the end of the Conference; and would more easily spot any unforeseen callers, legitimate or otherwise. Mr Campbell took a deep breath and decided to go on leave at Easter. Hooligan took a deep breath and went ahead with his arrangements.

Some of the police would arrive before the Conference and would be accommodated in hostels not used by the Conference members. They would masquerade as janitors, or as building workers and maintenance men supposedly working on a variety of jobs at or near the doors to the buildings being used for residence or meetings. Each building would have only one entrance and exit in operation, so that everyone who came and went was sure to be seen. At first, all the spurious building jobs would be where the arriving members registered, so that all members could be recognised by most of the officers. Each of the officers had a block of names to learn by heart; those impersonating janitors at Reception would match up names with faces as members arrived and would surreptitiously instruct colleagues. This, too, would help with the monitoring of comings-and-goings and indicate the presence of strangers.

The fictive artisans would then be employed on other non-jobs at relevant buildings, and doubt would attach to any visitor whom they did not recognise.

Three officers would arrive on time, but not together, as though they were attending the Conference itself, and would spend the whole time mingling with genuine members; they had been placed on the list of participants. Hooligan had hoped for some female officers to make the infiltration more low-key and, he believed, to improve the standard of concentration and guesswork. Unfortunately, all women officers were suddenly requisitioned for a spate of child-related cases, and he had to have all men.

He called a final briefing meeting the day before they set out for the Conference. There could be no instructional tour of the buildings: Hooligan even doubted that they could remain unrecognised at the Conference itself by his wary prey, but certainly a sudden visitation by a party of large fit men would warn the killer off if he were making his own prior tour of inspection. In default of a visit, they studied architectural plans showing their positions marked in.

The briefing was also intended to be dress-rehearsal quite literally, for Hooligan suspected that, if left to themselves, the officers would turn up too well-dressed. He was right.

'Those of you in overalls,' he said, 'use your heads! Every now and then, a man who wears an overall for his work does get a new one. But not the whole flaming gang on the same day! Dawson, it's your birthday tomorrow, so we'll let you keep your pretty brand-new one. As for the rest of you, I want those overalls creased and messy before you're seen in public. And don't forget – bits of wire, screwdrivers, anything like that, should be seen sticking out of your pockets. Holmes, wander around with a clip-board and a pencil occasionally, and don't forget to scribble something on it with an air of importance. Obscenities if you can't think of anything else, as perhaps you can't.

'Detective-Sergeant Plumb and I will join the Conference as members. A few of them saw the two of us a few years ago, but we'll chance it – anyway, I doubt if some of them would recognise their own reflections – though I also doubt whether most of them look into a mirror very often. Once the events have started you won't be able to reach us except in an emergency, so refer to Sergeant Padley who'll be making a convincing drains-inspector.'

'The drain-brain!' said somebody.

Hooligan chose to ignore the interruption, which he thought not unfair, and continued: 'Now, along with Ted Plumb and me, three of you will be inside as academic visitors from overseas ... that's Page, Rafferty and McTavish – I've just noticed, you sound like the beginning of a rude joke – an Englishman, an Irishman and a Scotsman - but you three don't know each other or the two of us, OK?

'You three academics ... These people you'll be mixing with ... They may wonder who you are; but not for long, because they're not interested in anything but themselves.

You'll probably find yourselves rudely ignored, rather than having to fend off questions. Every Conference has its wandering visitors, and they've been told on their Conference papers who you're supposed to be. But they'll have forgotten, and, as I said, they're not really interested. You've got your background papers, giving your identities and the cover-plan: study them! You've been sent from your home universities by the Commonwealth Cultural Exchange in Canberra because there's talk of setting up a Commonwealth Literature Conference. The real members will think a Conference on anything is a good idea, and they'll only want to know how they can get a free trip to it. Stall them with the answers on page four of your briefing-papers ...

'Let them talk, listen respectfully – that will go with their self-image – and get them to say what they think of the murders, and what kind of people they think the likely victims are, and why. Normally we try to calm people's fears, but this time we want them to talk ...

'Now, all of you ... As for the murderer, we don't know if he will be paying us a visit at all. If he does, all we know about him is that he's unobtrusive, middle-aged, average height, clean-shaven, and convincing in different roles – he's appeared as a caretaker, a chauffeur, a Victorian stage-villain, and also on the telephone as an Indian, we think. So look out for anyone who's doing what you're doing – trying not to get noticed, or trying to seem what he isn't, and not necessarily a workman. He might have an odd manner of walking – a limp or leaning backwards or forwards. We haven't seen long strides or little mincing steps yet, but they're possibilities. But he may not use an odd walk, so don't get it out of proportion.

'I don't think he'll disguise himself as a woman but watch out for any middle-aged woman whose shoulders and manner of walking seem unfeminine. And don't make that an excuse to eye up girls – I don't want them complaining to the local police about workmen annoying them.'

The men wondered why he had suddenly paused and why he nearly, but not quite, giggled. He had, in fact, just realised out of the blue that this occasion was a perverse mirror-image of his first parade when doing National Service. For the police officers had assembled, not as shambling raw recruits, but as trained men, fit and alert. Their overalls were crisp and spotless; the three who were to join him and Plumb at the Conference were wearing neat suits or sports jackets, with trousers pressed, ties straight, shoes gleaming.

Hooligan's task was to turn them into something that would make a Sergeant-Major weep with despair. How could he create for their perception and emulation that impression of academics' mode of dress and demeanour? ... Reminiscent of janitors skyving, scruffy, unwholesome, with a caretakerly mixture of narrow-browed resentment and officiousness ... that slovenly gait ... that shambling immobility of body and soul ... Even the odd academic who was a snappy dresser looked like an unreliable bookie or the proverbial pox-doctor's clerk ... How on earth could he disabuse his men of some preconceptions about the sartorial elegance of academe?

'You've got to look like what you're supposed to be,' he began. 'If you must wear a suit, make sure it looks as though you slept in it. But preferably jeans, corduroys, or slacks provided they're baggy. Any jumper or pullover you like as long as the colour or pattern clashes with your trousers. Trainers or sandals. Wear shoes if you want to, but make sure they're well scuffed, don't clean them while you're there, except that if you opt for brown shoes, clean them with black polish. Comb your hair only once a day, and don't worry if you forget – just do it at the dinner-table, or not at all if you don't feel like it.'

The officers looked at each other in amazement. They had always thought Hooligan a little odd, even though he got results. But this sounded half-cracked. Was it an elaborate leg-pull? Or the after-effects of his accident?

Rafferty took courage: 'But we're to be at a university, sir. We're supposed to be Professors.'

Plumb, sensing the gap in understanding, intervened. 'Some of you might be a bit surprised,' he said. 'But Mr Hooligan and I have seen these guys at meetings. Most of them really do look like what he said.'

Rafferty was won over. 'I didn't hear you mention jackets, sir...?'

'Good point ... Preferably don't wear one. If you do, ask your wives or girlfriends which of your jackets they'd like to throw out, and wear that. And as with the jumper, it shouldn't match your trousers.

'And by the way – anyone you don't recognise and looks like a workman might be an academic arriving late for the Conference. Check before you think of nabbing him.'

Hooligan had enjoyed his performance and his audience's reaction and had appreciated Plumb's support. But his private thoughts were more sombre. His retirement loomed, and this major case, which had been dragging on for years, was no nearer a solution. His record of success had this tiresome blot on it.

But – no stone to be left unturned ... A thought had struck him while he had been adding his name and those of his colleagues to the list of Conference participants. This time there was something different from before, which might have been overlooked; which could now be investigated, as a light in the gloom. Previous murders at Conferences had been committed by a non-participant who had arrived from outside: the Phantom Porter and the Bog-Bandit, as the Press described him. And all participants had been cleared of suspicion. But suppose the killer was to be a participant this time? The Conference attendance-list would inevitably include some names that had not turned up before in their enquiries. Something for the redoubtable Plumb to look into ...

*

For three days a dozen or more police officers in overalls wandered around the Doupminster University campus with screwdrivers, lengths of wire, clipboards and conveniently-sized lengths of metal tubing – all as props to the contrived theatre of occasionally walking in and out of cupboards, tapping walls, measuring things, solemnly inspecting the functioning of taps and lights and the contents of drains. Being younger, taller and fitter than many men who did such work, they soon became the object of flirtatious curiosity to a few of the cleaners. One of them, a lady of substance, playfully groped Constable Dawson, who prevented himself only in the nick of time from delivering a caution about conduct likely to cause a breach of the peace. With great presence of mind, he sought to deter her by asking very earnestly if she would like to become a Jehovah's Witness, and was dismayed at her religious toleration.

*

In the Conference sessions, Professor Roach, now an *éminence grise* brought from retirement for a valedictory *pas de cheval*, scandalised most of the policemanly pseudo-academics by delivering a lecture which referred, with evident relish, to the pissing-contest in Pope's *Dunciad*. They were just as scandalised, though in a different way, by the fact that the audience, far from being either scandalised itself or dissolving into sniggers and innuendos, as any red-blooded constable would do, sat in solemn silence, and then engaged in turgid discussion about 'the welation between yurwin [urine] end cweativiteh' and 'whether the liquid of woistering dwinking songs were symbolicalleh connicted with yurwin'.

Constable Dawson, transferred at his own urgent and embarrassed request to Conference duties and hence transformed, by the mere relinquishment of a screwdriver and the donning of an ill-fitting jacket into a scholar for the duration, leaned over to McTavish and whispered incredulously:

'What does he mean – "Sim bollockly connected"? Who's Sim?'

'Tell you later,' muttered McTavish, like an old lag through the side of his mouth; though he had no idea.

Dawson listened with renewed attention and reflected that if they couldn't catch the murderer this time they might at least get that obscene old bugger, spouting up there, on some kind of indecency charge.

The constables, slouching and sartorially inelegant as instructed, and therefore camouflaged into their background, listened, with even more amazement and with even more rapidly dwindling comprehension, to the Report of the New Techniques Group. Predisposed by the discussion on Pope to expect something salacious, they were chagrined to discover that the title contained no *double entendre* of any kind: it referred only to the application of computers to literary research. A flicker of hope that they might have misheard the phrase 'textual abewwations' died, when mindless pedantry turned from its literwawy hewitage to seize the New Eege of Technologeh, too, in its death-grip.

Hooligan's innate respect for scholarship as an activity both drawing upon and enhancing personal experience had survived the mediocrity of most of his law tutors but had been shaken by his contact with academics ever since the Peccary case. It was now assaulted and battered with a blunt instrument in the form of a disquisition by a speaker who looked like an unmade bed. This contributor was too young to be a Professor, and therefore still pronounced his words properly. Unfortunately, he spoke like the computer specialist he was, and, for example, announced that money spent on computers 'will fructify on the research front'. Rafferty shifted in his seat hopefully. The droning voice then praised himself for having used a computer-program to set up a 'Repetitive Wordage Quotient - RWQ' with which he had counted and classified Shakespeare's references to animals. ('Give it a rest!' thought Hooligan. 'We've got the plays and a few books about them. How far does this sort of thing have to go?') The accompanying handout urged the identification of categories of research which were and were not 'terminal-consumptive', as though a need for more computer terminals were a fatal disease attacking literature, with withered circuitry emitting oscillating electronic coughs. Looking at his copy, Hooligan concluded that literacy was evolving a new No-Man's Land: the document had been written by someone who could count but not write and was intended for people who could read but not count ('wead but not cunt,' as many of them seemed to put it).

'This guy doesn't need Puck to give him an ass's head,' he thought. 'So ... our murderer ... Could he be simply exasperated? Driven insane by their folly? I could see myself bashing old Nick Bottom over there just to shut him up ... No, exasperation may come into it – but our man must have a conscious and enduring purpose to keep him doing it ... Just a general "Look what fools these mortals be" isn't enough ...'

He looked around, wondering what the audience, lounging in armchairs, might be thinking. Many may have been engaged in thought; but, if so, their thoughts had no impact on posture, demeanour or expression. Not a few had closed their eyes, and several unsynchronised wheezes betrayed that this was not in all cases an intended aid to concentration. Being fully visible and semi-recumbent, they looked less like the newels of his recollection, and more like discarded exhibits from a travelling waxworks. He heard himself whisper 'uglydemics'; and without realising that his neologism followed in the footsteps of a couple of his erstwhile suspects.

The impostor-academics from the constabulary were present in and around the Conference proceedings for three days, waiting for what might happen. Hooligan was relieved, though not surprised, that nobody from Pillingham or Melbury seemed to remember him or Plumb. He thought that one of them was giving him some funny looks, but he avoided eye-contact. He thought it safe to socialise a little between sessions and inched his way into this group and that. But, true to their habits of a lifetime, nobody took any notice of him, except that in the bar Simmonds, still dressed as though at random, and slightly drunk, suddenly turned to him and said, with a joviality never discerned in his sober state:

'We waa wonderwing whey evwybodeh twies to pee exectleh on the little disinfectant cube in the urwinal.'

'Ay den't think Ay could hit it at awl,' boomed a robust baritone woman smoking a cheroot at the far end of the group. She relished the schoolboy frivolity she had provoked.

Hooligan, assuming that alcohol had formed an alliance with Pope, tried to divert himself by counting ties, and had got as far as four, and two of them on women, when the Hissing Hippo of Melbury rushed up, excitedly waving a piece of paper.

'We've gort it!' he exclaimed. 'The Tongue-Twistah Chellinge fwom the Lenguage end Phonitics Siction!'

He read it out, slowly:

' "Two nuns, cawled the Fun Nun and the Dumb Nun, beth hed numb bums. The Fun Nun's numb bum was a number bum than the Dumb Nun's numb bum." But one is ixpicted to wesate [recite] it alide at gweat speed.'

'Just a memment,' objected Simmonds, searching for a pen. 'Ay can do these things bettah when Ay wate [write] them dine end wead them ite.'

'Thet's cheating!' the Hippo complained.

'Neh, it's not cheating, wealleh. It's just a differwence of methodologeh. In any case, you hed to wate it dine farst of awl.'

'Neh – they gave it to meh alweadeh witten dine. They hed to wate it dine while compezzing it. But for us, it's suppezzed to be the chellinge of a wecitation.'

'Ay den't see what awl the fuss is abite. Ay simpleh wead bettah then Ay wesate [recite]. What was the Text again?'

The Hippo said, 'You pwobableh cawn't even wead it wepidleh anywee,' breath-sucked in derision, and began dictating, while several members whipped out little notebooks and began to write.

Roach, gee-upping over the Hippo's shoulder, remarked: 'You've put a *b* on the end of bum. It *is* English Lenguage you specialase in, isn't it?'

After general guffawing, Simmonds, scribbling, asked: 'Surely it wasn't "fun bum"? Awltheh [Although] Ay suppez it could beh, if that wair the nun's pwedilection ... '

'Or as a twansfarred epithet,' added Roach, cantering behind Simmonds in a manner which Dawson was increasingly inclined to misinterpret. 'Lake [Like] "doves in a silvah-feathered sleep" in De La Mare's pem, *Silvah*.'

'Ah, yes, got it – Fun Nun! The joviellity of the leedy's postewwiah [joviality of the lady's posterior] is enleh attwibuted.'

'Are you sure?' queried the Hippo, joining the literary contingent's disregard for the prescribed mechanical task of

recitation in favour of the joys of exegesis. 'Does the part necessawileh wesemble the whel [whole]? Does enatawmical [anatomical] synecdoche wealleh exist, Ay wondah.'
'Whey not edd a Glum Nun?' somebody suggested.
'Or a Wum [Rum] Nun?'
'Or a Yum-Yum Nun?'
'With a Yum-Yum bum!'
There was a communal attempt to lengthen the text and to perform preferred variants as a sufficiently impressive speed. The conversation degenerated into a subdued cacophony as, in waning sobriety, they witlessly repeated combinations of sounds featuring the desired rhyme, timed their own and others' recitations, lost concentration, and squabbled about a count of seconds.

The disguised constabulary, already bemused or scandalised by the formal sessions, and further taken aback by the informal gatherings, watched and waited for something to happen.

But nothing at all happened. A search of the residential buildings on the last morning, which, both as a matter of logic and as confirmed by experience, was the probable time for a murder, yielded nothing but one genuine, still living but not fully conscious Late Departer – the estimable Professor Irving Harrison Roach naked in bed with a hangover and a soft porn magazine.

*

Back in the police station, Detective Chief Inspector Terence Hooligan held a debriefing meeting with his special squad, which yielded nothing of value; wrote up his report, which contained nothing of value; then attended, and in his ironic way, enlivened a drunken party in *The Legge of Muttone* in honour of his retirement. Paddy Donovan gatecrashed it, drunk, declared himself to be Chief Inshpector Hooligum'sh Number One Fan, and, while being carried out, delivered himself of a largely incomprehensible peroration, the fluency of which was marred only by several attempts to pronounce 'poleeshmanly virtuesh and dishtinctionsh' by whom it had 'alwaysh been an honour to be arreshted'.

Hooligan, amidst the jollity while creating his memorable hangover, could not forget that the unknown 'Doer-in of Dons', which *The Daily Reflector* now seemed to prefer as a tag, had eluded him. Next day, as his hangover receded, he had to agree with Jeanie as she reminded him of his achievements: the long list of villains whom he had put behind bars – some vicious and cunning, some stupid or unlucky, some really quite likeable. She pointed out that having missed just this one was his only major failure, and he should not get it out of proportion, because it was also the failure of the combined efforts of several constabularies. 'And the greatest pianist plays a wrong note sometimes!'

'True,' he thought, 'but a "full house" would have been nice ...'

But perhaps not all was lost. Old files never die; they only gather dust ...

Plumb, newly promoted to Detective-Inspector, and huffily rejecting suggestions that he could now afford a new car, would follow up any new leads with his usual meticulousness. But the trails had gone cold. If only their quarry would make a mistake! They usually do, sooner or later, though not all their mistakes are noticed - because they don't reach the eyes and ears of anyone who would interpret them correctly. And sometimes villains who've got away with it are accidentally gathered up in a net cast for some unrelated purpose ...

Vain hope!

CHAPTER 16

A MATTER OF LOVE AND DEATH

'Do I have to?' Hooligan said, with a tetchy expression when Jeanie broke the news.

'It's not much to ask! You've only got to stand there and give the bride away. And you did it splendidly for Carolyn.'

'A daughter's different. This girl, Sharon – I'm only her umpteenth cousin, removed God knows how many times. In fact, I'm not even that. She's your umpteenth cousin, not mine!'

'Yes, I know, but since her father, well, you know, ran off with that little tart half his age, you're her senior male relative. All the rest are dead.'

'Which hardly makes me want to cultivate the relationship. Anyway, I haven't seen her for years. Odious little brat, as I recall!'

'Was, maybe. Now she's a very attractive and sophisticated girl. Just nineteen. I've met her. Hour-glass figure, face like an angel with mischief. And you'll be the first to kiss the bride – so think of the reward and stop being such a grouch.'

'If she's what you say she is, I'll not give her away at all – I'll run off with her myself.'

'Don't be tasteless!' Jeanie had conveniently forgotten that it was she who had first alluded to Sharon's charms for her own purpose. 'And she and her mother will be here soon to settle one or two details. Don't look surprised: I told you yesterday.'

Hooligan, already at the end of his post-retirement power-drill phase, was nursing a lifelong distaste for decorating – about which Jeanie had been dropping hints like a Biblical sower of seed. So he decided to look on the bright side. No mean wedding present would be expected from such a distinguished familial office-bearer as the Senior

Male Relative Who Gave the Bride Away. This duty would assuredly prevent, for a while at least, any splashing-out on paint on the scale evidently envisaged by Jeanie.

Sharon turned out to be everything that Jeanie had promised, and Hooligan was instantly under her spell. But he tore his attention away from their glowing younger visitor and attended politely to her mother instead. If Sharon fulfilled a girl's supposed destiny of turning into her mother, he thought, she could do a great deal worse. The father must be stupid, as well as a louse.

The actual details of the ceremony and accompanying hysteria had been settled already, as he inferred from the way their pat explanations followed on from each other, like the narrative dialogue in an American soap. Or like two villains who had got their story straight before interrogation and thought the police too dense to notice. The purpose of this meeting was purely social; and, of course, predatory, with his acceptance of the substitute paternal role as prey. He let it all wash over him; when he needed an opinion, Jeanie would tell him what it was.

'Wake up, dreamy,' said Jeanie. 'That's probably the postman.'

He went out into the hall and opened the front door. A parcel addressed to him, New Zealand stamps, Carolyn's handwriting. She never forgot birthdays, though the cards and presents which she sent, and herself liked to receive, usually had a mildly sarcastic flavour.

This offering was light in relation to its size. Did it consist largely of polystyrene packing for something fragile? Or was it the traditional Large Parcel Joke, in which the seemingly endless removal of wrappings eventually revealed a tiny object? If the latter, an audience was necessary for the fun. But the consistency of the surface suggested the former explanation; and in any case, there would be a letter inside. He opened the parcel in the hall, and with pleasure saw a letter on top. As he looked beneath a protective wedge of packing, his attention was distracted by a grinning pig's head in delicate china, which an accompanying advertisement identified as a piece of work commissioned from a craftsman somewhere on the Canterbury Plains.

Laughing, he bore it all into the sitting-room.

'Look at what Kiwi-lyn has sent me!' he said, holding it up for all to see.

Jeanie, who straightaway discerned its significance for her husband, also laughed with pleasure, and said: 'Trust her to think up something like that!'

Sharon, unaware of the reference to a family joke, and suddenly with a preoccupation of her own, said, 'Flippin' heck!'

'Sharon! It's a very nice ornament!' remonstrated her mother.

'It's a kind of standing joke in our family,' Hooligan explained. 'I'm supposed to be a pig. I suppose they mean my lack of elegance. At least, I'm not one of the male chauvinist variety – '

'– you were, but you've improved' Jeanie interpolated.

'– yes, after seeing what women police officers can do,' he responded, with mock self-ingratiation.

'Anyway, that's supposed to be me, so I, I mean he, can sit up there and keep us all in order.'

He patted his birthday present, placed it carefully on the mantelpiece along with the letter to be opened later, and resumed his seat.

The pig beamed down in cheerful benevolence. Its manner of eyeing Sharon suggested that it was a heterosexual boar.

'Yes, it *is* very nice,' said Sharon, feeling that she had committed a *faux pas*, and added, hastily: 'We didn't know it was your birthday. Many happy returns! But it reminded me of something else. I once had a terrible fright with a pig's head. Someone threw one at us – a real one, not an ornament. Yes, he's very sweet, aren't you, Piggy? It was a great big one, with dried blood, and hammer-marks all over it.'

She paused for effect, and they waited for the rest of the story.

'You never told me,' said her mother, suspicious that she would not hear the complete story even now.

'Well, no. It was four or five years ago. Damian – that's my fiancé, Uncle Terry,' – Hooligan winced inside at having passed in a few seconds from feeling like a Lothario to being named as an avuncular teddy-bear – 'you'll meet him ... we've been ... er ... since I was eight and he was ten ... '

Two maternal nods confirmed the romantic perfection of marrying one's childhood sweetheart.

'Anyway, we were up in Pillingham West Woods, bunking off school, but we weren't ... I mean, we didn't ... er ... not at all ...'

'Sharon!' Her mother, suddenly leonine with disapproval, had cut across her daughter's floundering.

'I said: nothing happened!' Sharon retorted, sharply. 'You have to move with the times, you know! We're not monks and nuns!'

A row seemed imminent: this strong-willed young woman obviously had ideas which were not to her mother's liking. Jeanie, hoping privately that Damian was patient and resilient, quickly asked:

'What happened, Sharon? With the pig's head, I mean.'

'Well, there we were ... and suddenly, there *he* was, and he didn't see us, and he came over and threw this box into the bushes right over our heads.' Her mother, perhaps on some kind of ostrich-principle, closed her eyes in embarrassment at the implication of recumbency, as the girl continued: 'And suddenly, when he'd just gone, the bush gave way, and this great pig's head fell out.'

'Well, what do you make of that?' asked Sharon's mother, intent on discussing the mystery of the pig's head rather than having any attention paid to Sharon's presence at the scene with her boyfriend.

'I wondered if he'd killed it himself,' said Sharon; and added, 'And he looked so angry.'

The *non sequitur* was fortunate:

'Angry, you said?' Hooligan's memory responded, as so often before, to a key-word. 'And you said "hammer-marks". How did you know they were hammer-marks?'

'Damian said they were. Different sizes, too. Damian's always done carpentry, and he's taking over his Dad's joinery business. So he'll know,' she explained, as one with access to unparalleled expertise.

'Of course.'

Hooligan began to wonder if a few unidentified pieces of a jigsaw puzzle had been almost within his grasp the whole time. He tried to sound casual.

'What did you do next?'

'Screamed and ran, of course!' She giggled, because that was not quite true. But there was no point in setting her mother off again by referring to the comfort which Damian had imparted before they left. Or to her having prolonged her brief fright so that he would do so. Material for some later provocation, perhaps, when another occasion might demand or justify it.

Jeanie assumed that her husband was about to tackle this mystery just as he might have embarked upon a crossword, and decided it was time to revert to more important matters.

'You'll need a new suit for the wedding,' she said to him, 'and not before time, either.' She proceeded to talk past him, woman to woman: 'Getting him new clothes is like drawing teeth.'

He confounded them both by saying, 'Yes, you're right – I do need a new one.' His private gleeful thought had been, 'That will mean no decorating for some time!'

But by now Hooligan was fully a policeman again. What he had just heard could be no more than an interesting bizarre tale, as Sharon evidently thought. But if it was relevant, her belief had to be preserved for just a little while longer: otherwise, her view of it, and her information to him, might be distorted.

While the women were still reeling from the shock of his ready agreement to buy a new suit, he asked Sharon, as a by-the-way: 'What was *he* wearing?'

'Who? Damian or Dr Brisley? Ooh, I wasn't going to tell, because, well, we sort of know him, don't we, Mum? Still, I don't suppose it matters, really.'

'What ...?' queried her mother, as though rejecting the whole story, 'what would a man like Dr Brisley be doing with a pig's head in the woods? Really, Sharon, your imagination runs away with you sometimes!'

'No, it doesn't! But that's a good question. Would he have killed it? And why? And where was the rest of the pig?'

'Perhaps he was practising,' thought Hooligan, and asked: 'Did you report this to anyone?'

'Not likely! I can get into hot water without going looking for it. But now you'll solve the mystery, won't you, Uncle Terry. C'mon, Lootenant, gimme da t'oid degree!'

Hooligan still valued her ignorance more than any speed of progress.

'Perhaps you're looking for a fanciful explanation when an everyday one would do,' he suggested, as boringly as he could. 'Perhaps he bought a whole pig for the freezer and wanted to dispose of the head.'

'Our Mums would have made pig's head broth with it during the war,' remarked Jeanie, and returned to the main topic: 'But why wouldn't he just put it in the dustbin?'

'And have the neighbourhood dogs come and mess up the drive? And perhaps the head wasn't his. Suppose some idiot who had bought himself a whole pig threw the head into Dr Brisley's garden, and simply passed the problem on.'

'Why the hammer-marks?' Sharon persisted.

'I don't know the answer to that. We've accounted for Dr Brisley's possession of the pig's head and his wish to dump it. Perhaps the slaughtering-process produces marks like that. As I said, I don't know.'

'There you are, Sharon!' said her mother, as though winning an argument; she had forgotten her earlier denial of the entire story. 'There's your explanation! You and your mysteries!'

Hooligan circled round the point a little further.

'How come you know Dr Brisley?' he asked.

'He used to be in my drama society,' said Sharon's mother.

'What did he do?'

'Wonderful actor!' she explained. 'Actions, walks, voices – the lot. You'd hardly know him in a part.'

'In costume, I suppose? That must be quite a problem. Do you supply your own?'

'No – there's a costumes specialist. She makes some herself, and tells some of us how to make them, so we build up a stock. And sometimes we buy or hire, though we don't need to very often. It's Mrs Brisley who does the costumes, as a matter of fact.'

'So they're the master and mistress of disguise, then. Now, that's an ability I'd like to have had! Disguise myself as a little old lady, creep up on the villain, and then – grab!'

They laughed obligingly at Hooligan's contrived distraction, and Sharon's mother added:

'Though he wasn't that sort of actor. He's just one of those people who looks like whatever he's supposed to be.

As though there're nothing there except what he's made you think he is. Uncanny, really.'

'Pity he left then – you said he "used to be" in your drama society.'

'Yes. Pressure of work, so he said. Such a pity – but he said he needed time to do more literary work. He's really clever. Seems he's just published a book about these First World War poets. Must know more about them than the Professors do now.'

Jeanie was increasingly aware that her husband, retired or not, would never stop being a policeman. She knew only too well that affable manner which made his interrogations sound like polite chat in which the interviewee said something unintended. He was obviously on to something, and as far as she was concerned it was not going to get in the way of the wedding. She stamped firmly on this digression by producing tea and cakes.

The china birthday pig presided with gregarious geniality.

*

Hooligan checked himself from making an immediate call on Brisley: this was Plumb's case now; he telephoned his erstwhile subordinate.

'... Well, that's the story, Ted. I'll ... er ... leave it with you, then?'

Plumb, however, needed Hooligan as a sounding-board just as Hooligan had needed him when they had worked together. 'My gut reaction – try this on for size - is that it's a first-rate clue, or better than that, for an investigation - but it wouldn't be thought relevant in court. Procedure would want a statement from Sharon and her young man, but I wouldn't want to stir things up by drawing attention like that. And if the evidence about the pig's head's inadmissible, what use is a statement about it? And a young girl getting married, and so on ... Wouldn't want to upset her to no purpose ... What do you think?'

'I was hoping you'd take that view.' Hooligan was silently amused at Plumb's having, for the first time that he could recall, relied on a gut reaction.

Plumb continued: 'But it's hard to let it go just like that. I suppose I might have Brisley in and see what I can get out of him. But since we've got nothing and he knows it, that might just warn him to be more careful. And we do need him to slip up ... Preferably before killing again. Look, Terry, would you be prepared to go and have a go at him informally? He's obviously latched on to you – that card he sent, for example ... If anyone can make him open up, it's likely to be you.'

'I was hoping you take that view, too. Still your case, of course, but If I have your blessing ...?'

*

Hooligan telephoned Brisley's office to arrange an appointment. He rather regretted that he could no longer turn up unannounced, show his warrant card, and, if co-operation were not forthcoming, watch those fascinatingly varied reactions to the phrase 'murder investigation'.

The secretary accepted the vagueness of 'It's personal' when she asked his purpose and put him through. A man's voice spoke the one word, 'Brisley'.

When Hooligan gave his own name, but without police rank, and asked if he might call, Brisley agreed and suggested the coming afternoon.

'You haven't asked me what it's about,' Hooligan remarked, and thought: 'I bet *he* never looks down the telephone. No cheap theatricalities for him.'

'Oh, we'll find plenty to talk about, Chief Inspector.'

Hooligan remembered the campus and the building from his visits - five years previously, after Peccary had been bludgeoned to death, and then two years ago after Bludger had been stabbed. He sat briefly again amongst the volumes of *Who's Who* and *Who Was Who*, while Brisley's secretary knocked on a door and entered.

At the very outset he had been a couple of yards away from the murderer's office door! - just as he had been only a couple of questions away from the truth when he had interviewed Pyle! But the right direction is needed for the yards and the questions ...! And now he was about to meet this man with whom he had been preoccupied for so long. Who thought rather as he did. His Jungian shadow, as Pyle had put it. Himself in a parallel universe, even.

He noticed during his brief wait that both sequences of volumes had been kept up-to-date. More unknowns would have become *Who's*-worthy for the current volume; some formerly deemed to be eminent must have been revealed as nonentities and omitted from the latest *Was* ('must check on those murdered Professors when there's time'); and death would have banished the obscurity of some and granted posthumous *Who*-dom by entry into the Kingdom of *Who Was*-dom.

He was assailed, as he had been ever since he and Plumb had discussed this approach to Brisley, by a sense of futility: what they now had on Brisley was pretty flimsy.

How should the interview be handled? How does one go to a man whom one has never met - even to a man who has reacted dead-pan to a request for a meeting from a known policeman - and ask him if he is a serial killer? Does one lead up to it? Or jump right in? Fortunately, there are too few such cases for a reliable body of experience to have been accumulated. An interrogation specific enough and tough enough for a guilty party will be too much for an innocent victim of circumstance. Conversely, a line of questioning vague enough to allow peaceable retreat from an encounter with an honest citizen will have no impact on a seasoned criminal. So there had to be a way in, or round the point, with the options of a bull's eye if guilty or an amicable withdrawal if innocent. But the first few seconds can be crucial to progress. Tone, manner, gesture; or the absence of these; or their presence in different combinations and sequences – all these factors had to be right. As though the first chord of the overture governed the entire opera. And many an overture turned out to be just that – with nothing to follow.

So much in the course of the interview would depend on Brisley's attitude to his guilt - which Hooligan did not seriously doubt. The problem would be that a psychopath, as Brisley probably was, doesn't 'do' guilt.

The secretary emerged, followed by Brisley himself. He was a man of late middle-age, average height, average build, and nondescript appearance generally. Hooligan reflected that, despite his thirty years in the police force, he would have found it difficult to describe him distinctively in a way that would not depend on what he was wearing – as it might be, an overall, or a chauffeur's uniform, or Victorian fancy-dress, or Lord knows what else.

They sat down in Brisley's office, which was small, almost devoid of books, and littered with papers.

'You've been wondering how to begin this conversation, Chief Inspector!'

Hooligan took a slow breath which was not quite a pause.

'It will begin itself, Dr Brisley. I'm back to 'Mr' these days, by the way.'

'Of course. You retired recently and you are here alone, so this is obviously a personal visit. But then, murder can be rather personal, I suppose.'

'Not entirely in your case, I believe. Your motive was personal advantage, as you saw it – and I'd like to hear more about that – but you had no particular animosity against the victims as individuals. Is that correct?'

'It would be correct if I were your man,' Brisley agreed. 'In that hypothesis I might reply that I disliked those of the victims whom I happened to know personally, but it didn't actually matter who they were ... that it was necessary to dispense with them, and they were dispensable. So: in so far as an act of will was needed, it would not have been difficult for me to find the resolution to act. That would appear to be a satisfactory theory for you.'

'Let me see if I can understand you a little better, Dr Brisley. Your idea went like this ...'

As Brisley smiled and raised an admonitory finger, Hooligan amended his wording:' ... your idea would have been like this. You wanted a job as an English Lecturer – you're an expert on several branches of it, including your latest revealed interest, the First World War poets – and it was the fact that you wanted an ordinary Lectureship, not a Professorship, that fooled me. Still does, in fact. You're in a Professor-equivalent job now, aren't you? Why seek demotion?'

Brisley smiled again, and said: 'Of course, in your line of business you only think of going upwards, which I don't criticise for one moment – but I had, *would have had*, of course, several reasons, really. How can I put it ...? ... I think one has to be a fairly limited person to be satisfied with being a librarian. You spend half your time fussing about details chiefly of interest to other people, or having ignoramuses telling you what you ought to think and do. So I might, in your theory, have wanted to be the gamekeeper-turned-poacher.'

'Yes,' Hooligan agreed, 'clichés often satisfy the other way round. But it's still demotion.'

'It's about life-style. They have so few compulsions except those they set for themselves. Much of the time they come and go as they please, and just yell "Academic Freedom!" if they're criticised for it, or, indeed, for anything else. For anyone not bothered about making Senior Lecturer the heat's never on. Now, being a Professor *and* accepting the responsibility that ought to go with it - running a Department, serving on their damned Committees – that's another mug's game. Not a few of them manage to avoid the duties – just keep their heads down, enjoy the freedom and status, and just coast along – but that's not right, is it? If you take the perks you must do the job. That's why I have never aspired to being a Professor, either in real life or in our hypothesis. And, in our hypothesis, smiting the Unworthy would have been an added pleasure, but not the significant motive.'

'Could you have afforded demotion?'

'A recent legacy ... The lower salary wouldn't have mattered. But I dare say you'd find it difficult to prove a link between being able to afford a salary-cut and bumping people off.'

'None, obviously; though they're not mutually exclusive ... Continuing with our hypothesis, I think I know your next problem: you found that University expansion had ceased, so you decided to create a vacancy.'

'That *is* how I *would have* thought.'

'You understand what you're saying? In our hypothesis, you are admitting premeditated murder.'

'Of course. I would have taken the view that you can't make an omelette without breaking eggs. Or egg-heads, in this instance! Just by being in their jobs they would have been obstructing me - an important point for your hypothesis, Mr Hooligan? - in relation to the ambition you ascribe to me, I mean. Therefore, I would have wanted to remove them. Yes, it all fits together rather well.'

Hooligan grasped the extraordinary detachment from good and evil, the lack of any thrill of horror, of success, of fear, of furtive evasion, of vindictiveness, or of whatever emotions usually accompanied murder.

'I haven't come across anybody like you before, Dr Brisley. Could we explore your state of mind? OK, your *putative* state of mind. You hated and despised them and, quite apart from your hypothetical ambition, wanted to kill them, just for that reason?'

'Not really. They're not worth hating. Now Bertrand Pyle, whom you know and once suspected – amusing, that! – really does hate them. But he's got reason to. I haven't, not really. Oh, I've had my troubles with them, but that's true of any job. To me, they've been what criminals must have been to you, Mr Hooligan – things that shouldn't be as they are or shouldn't be there at all and have to be cured or disposed of – but only the odd one warrants any genuine hatred. Would you agree?'

'I would say that you've been worse affected than Mr Pyle,' said Hooligan. 'You surely can't believe what you say?'

'Oh, yes.' The urbanity was unruffled, even by the imputation of madness. 'As a category they have exactly what they want, grind down those they can grind down, and batten on parasitically when they're the weaker party. Don't get me wrong: some of them are quite nice people as individuals, some even good, hard-working. But their collective function is the one I've described: a pleasant life, occasionally useful, often useless. I wanted it, too, and would have gone after it – in our theory, of course! It's a crude Darwinism, if you like. They have certain characteristics which interact with those of their environment and favour their success as a species. Our murderer would be one of a more successful species in the struggle for supremacy: success being defined as the achievement of the will's will ...

'... They're very blinkered, you know. You must have noticed. Those generals who never went within ten miles of the front, wouldn't listen to reason, and sacrificed tens of thousands of men by their stupid orders – they didn't know or care what they were doing. Those are the academics. The soldiers marching slowly into machine-gun fire, thinking that it was a good cause to fight and die for, thinking that their self-styled betters knew best ... enduring trench-foot, gas attacks, drownings in mud ... the academics think that's everyone else. It's the same mentality. They don't hate the rest of us either, except when we doubt their wisdom and right to rule ...

'Bosses – business moguls – generals - Chief Constables,' thought Hooligan. 'It's a state of mind.'

'... Anyway,' Brisley continued, 'it was time for a little judicious mutiny in the interest of humanity and progress. That's how your elusive criminal must have thought. If you catch him, you can ask him. I can only guess.'

Brisley smiled and waited for his visitor's reaction.

Hooligan, listening to Brisley's disquisition, could not help recalling how he himself had felt on hearing of Arlington's murder: that the art of coarse justice had been well and truly practised on a deserving bastard who had upset his daughter. He tore his thoughts away from that to the present problem of inducing Brisley to explain himself – or perhaps merely guiding him along, since there was no sign of reluctance. He must get him away from these general propositions, away from the long-term after-effects of whatever critical incidents must have warped his mind in earlier life, and back to the crimes themselves. But easy does it ...

... Or was Brisley half ham-actor, admiring his own ravaged sensitivity and then getting carried away by hatred of people whom he had declared to be hardly worth hating? Hating can be such fun, with the right targets ...

'But, Dr Brisley, we've found ourselves talking about the incidental pleasure which our murderer would have derived from his plan. Can we get back to the plan itself? You – he - intended to create, first, a Professorial vacancy, which you would *not* apply for, and for two reasons: one, you didn't want it, because you'd have to do it properly and therefore take on a responsibility you didn't want; and, two, to avoid the suspicion of having created your own opportunity.'

Brisley nodded, and added, 'In our hypothesis, of course.'

'The Professorial position,' Hooligan continued,' would then have been taken by a Reader or Senior Lecturer from elsewhere, and *his* job would have been downgraded to an ordinary Lecturer vacancy in that other place. You would have applied for that, and would probably have got it in earlier times, because your rivals would have been younger men and women without your academic achievements. Right so far?'

'Excellent! You've put your hypothesis very well!'

'Thank you. Then the failing economy intervened. The process you had envisaged was halted because universities had to save money on salaries. So they kept promoting a Reader or Senior Lecturer already on the staff to Professor, and then didn't make an appointment of Lecturer further down. They just abolished the post. Am I still on the right track?'

'In our hypothesis, perfect! And it's still happening. I'm retiring early myself, Bertrand Pyle's getting the job, and even if he's replaced as Deputy it will be by internal promotion. The last vacancy at the low level will then not be filled. So old Bertrand's going to be respectable at last! But, reverting to our main theme, you haven't told me how our man, whoever he was, went about it all. I mean, it sounds quite a performance ... '

Hooligan again tried to conceal his horror at the extent of this man's detachment from the normal concepts of good and evil. Ordinary criminals, even savage ones, usually showed some emotion other than mere pleasure at an exposition of the plan. They might show indifference – but always of a dull, bored kind, certainly not this sinister animation. And more usually either defiance or remorse. One might even expect a mixture in an unstable make-up. But Brisley just offered his good-humoured endorsement of a simple narrative. Obviously he would never stand trial: deemed unfit to plead, no doubt. The trick-cyclists would declare him to be cycle-path; his score on Robert Hare's checklist of psychopathic symptoms must be through the roof.

'I think I know how you actually started,' said Hooligan.

'*Would have* started, Mr Hooligan. I merely conjecture, you understand.'

'OK, "would have". You would have decided to use a blunt instrument, for whatever reason, but you had no experience of violence, or no recent experience. Did you do National Service, by the way? That's where one's memories of hitting and stabbing things often hark back to … '

'Clerk in the Pay Corps. The only blunt instruments we had were army-issue pens and the minds of ex-public-school officers.'

'Without experience, you would have needed to experiment … to practise hitting flesh and bone to see what it felt like … and you somehow got hold of a pig's head. From a butcher, perhaps? Or an abattoir?'

'Now that's really good! I might well have done that! How did you think that one up?'

'Pure chance, I'm afraid. Someone saw you dumping the head, and it had hammer-marks on it – of different sizes, so I suppose you bought a few hammers to try out and dumped the rejected ones. Unfortunately, I found this out only yesterday.'

'If, indeed, you found it out at all, Mr Hooligan. You would wish our murderer, whoever he is, to fear that you had something more than guesswork. I would wish that, in your position ... But this witness, if he exists, obviously thought it was me. Wrongly, of course. Who on earth could it have been? And why does the witness come forward after so long? But I know you wouldn't say. Or couldn't. You didn't say exactly where he dumped the pig's head.'

'We both know where, Dr Brisley. Anyway, in our hypothesis, various other points join forces. You found out two things. One: you must have heard around the University, or perhaps had some other way of finding out, that Professor Peccary had to use the back door of his house, because his new carpet was blocking access to the front door. Two: you also learned that he would be out that evening and would be returning to an empty house because of his wife's absence. To ensure that we didn't know whether or not the murderer knew those two facts, you put glue in the front door lock and in several others down the street. Then the marks on the rear window put us in the same dilemma as the glue did: it might be what it seems and might not. I really must congratulate you: your little web of ambiguities was very well-woven!'

Brisley gave an ironic and pleased little mock bow.

'You credit me, in your theory, with great ingenuity,' he said. 'Everything would have seemed to favour my beginning – if, of course, I had actually begun at all. How might one imagine my first day "over the top"? Let me think ... Like all such operations, one has to prepare. First, I would have inspected the premises – as surreptitiously as possible, of course, and doing my best not to look like myself. I imagine that at the same time I would have procured a pig's head - perhaps pretending to be an artist or art teacher, would you think? I would have bought the hammers in different shops, to avoid being noticed and remembered ... How am I doing so far? But if this were my story, I would say you've missed something out. I would have felt the need to kill something live myself, by way of preparation. Perhaps a stray cat would have co-operated by being experimentally killed? Our man might not have done anything like that since his early teens. And then, though I would have decided to do for Peccary, and had prepared myself mentally, wouldn't I still have needed the right circumstances? Let me think ... Suppose that I had been going to avoid Peccary at lunch, as anyone with any sensibilities would, but suppose that somehow I couldn't avoid him – and from the conversation I learned that he was to be out that evening, would be returning to an empty house, and was having to use the back door. I would think that Fate was handing me the opportunity on a plate. It was that discovery that would have been the real moment of commitment: everything thus far would have been just playing at it. Only then would I have made, improvised almost, that plan you outlined – about the glue and the marks on the window, I mean. I would have felt that Peccary was just asking to be processed.'

'Processed?'

'As our man would think of it. Once they're to be disposed of, you process them. And, having processed Peccary, I would have felt constrained to carry on and process another, because to have stopped would have made a mockery of all my efforts thus far. In our hypothesis, of course.'

'I see,' said Hooligan, for want of any other rejoinder, and continued: 'After Peccary, with the subsequent murders we couldn't be sure of a connection until there had been several. I mean, two could have been a coincidence, though I did feel that there was a connection ... '

'How, if I might ask?'

'I ... sometimes seem to know things, as I believe you do ... but too imprecisely to be much use, at least on a big case where superiors in the Force have to co-operate over manpower and demand more than hunches. Anyway, in due course we knew we wanted a man in middle years, with first-rate but unobtrusive acting skills, good mimic ... You were Mr Krishnaswami, I take it? And Dr Kemp?'

'Who are they, may I ask? Odd people who turned up in your investigation, I presume? For the sake of our hypothesis, let's say I might have invented another persona or two. You see how obliging I am!'

'I expect nothing less ... And our man obviously has intimate knowledge of the university world, and an interest in the First World War poets. Of course, I got hold of a list of experts on that subject, but you weren't on it: you've published on Victorian literature, but only very recently on the First World War. Another of your ingenious non-clues: Wilfred Own parodies, and Mrs M C Somme, indeed!'

Brisley smiled, and said, 'That does sound interesting. But I confess you've lost me there ... Your theory grows under its own dynamic.'

'And you ripped out a page from a copy of Professor Simmonds's book - yes, ok, *would have ripped* it - just to taunt and confuse us.'

'You've lost me again. Do I infer that a page was left at the scene, or was sent to you? I know his book, though I don't know which sentence you mean. But I imagine that our man would have hoped that you'd pin the crime on a First World War specialist.'

'That certainly occurred to me.'

'I would have intended that. As to the actual list of First World War specialists, Bertrand mentioned it to me - without knowing of my own interest in those poets, of course, so my name wasn't on it. He's such a good reference librarian – can identify anything in print and get hold of it – but he's not clairvoyant. Anyway, if you'd pinned these murders on someone whom Bertrand listed, that might have created a vacancy, which our man would have welcomed.'

'That was why you tried to frame Professor Simmonds as well?'

'Would have tried! But the murderer would have known that you had already cleared Simmonds – and that therefore you would instantly have recognised the attempt at framing him as a tease, intended to keep your minds wandering to no purpose. And, trivial though it might seem, it would have been such a pleasure for a librarian to take a book and rip a page out. One of my recurring fantasies!'

'Yes, I suppose it would be a thrill, of sorts. As for Simmonds and all those on Mr Pyle's list, they turned out either to have alibis or to be unsuitable as suspects in other ways. Of course, we also tried to check out people who might have hated Professors as a category, but that was too big a job – they do little to endear themselves to people' – Hooligan hoped that some casual jocularity would draw Brisley out – 'though I don't think I found anybody who dislikes them quite as much as you seem to do.'

'No, not "dislike"; not really ... After all, I was trying to become the subordinate of one! As I said, as individuals they can really be rather pleasant, if unintelligent, and with an education that's restricted rather than specialised. The only source of trouble to me, and it's been a major one, has been when rationality and the sense of system demanded by my present job has conflicted with their selfishness and innate irrationality. They are simply the Lords of Unreason. But yes, you're right, getting rid of a few, if I'd gone down that route, would have been an agreeable and stimulating pastime – a good clean-out of the sludge at the bottom of the barrel. That's what a lot of them are, you know – the bottom of the barrel that thinks itself the top drawer. Oh, dear!', he chuckled, 'not only a mixed metaphor, but beginning to sound like poor old Bertrand. I mean, "lucky old Bertrand". Or do I?'

'Eventually,' Hooligan prompted, 'I realised that it had to be someone without an actual job in English Literature but unusually well-qualified in it. But the red herrings and the lack of any precise clues prevented me from getting any closer. You – our man - laid some effective false trails.'

'And "evwy tame the chale [*trail*] hes gawn keld," as these idiots put it,' said Brisley, pleased with his success and with Hooligan's obvious relish of his imitation.

Hooligan suppressed his inner alarm at finding himself getting on so well with Brisley, and concentrate.

'Our man might nearly have supplied you with another red herring, Mr Hooligan. It occurs to me, just as we speak, of course, that he might have considered doing for old Roach at Melbury. If that had happened, you would have seen it as confirmation that somebody was bumping off Professors of English Literature just for its own sake. Or perhaps you would have thought that our murderer was getting side-tracked – beginning to enjoy his work too much – and doing Roach in just because he was such an appalling man?'

'It might have done, yes.'

'It might have been a good idea, from our murderer's point of view, to have processed Roach. Remember that Roach was close to retirement, so not worth killing according to the career-plan we impute to our murderer. You would have been even further from realising that the purpose was to create junior vacancies in Universities other than those of the victims. But our man would have reckoned that you were nowhere near the truth, so the processing of a genuine target, Pine-Coffin in Roach's Department, would have told you nothing. Your hypothesis is really very productive, Mr Hooligan!'

'It was you who brought the budgerigar into Pine-Coffin's house?'

'I read about that in one of the scandal-sheets ... I imagine I would have put the bird through the letter-box first, to get Pine-Coffin to open up off-guard. Nobody expects to be savaged to death by a budgie, or even a budgie-owner. Our man collected another nickname in the popular press, didn't he? – the "Bird-Man Killer", indeed!'

'It was a very effective piece of mystification. I wondered at the time if it had anything to do with the change from Professor down to Reader, as Pine-Coffin was, and if Roach had been the original choice. But I couldn't figure it out then.'

'Well, you were nearly there, I would say. Suppose Roach was to have been killed as an optional extra. According to the Press, his next-door neighbour has a considerable aviary, and I would have discovered that when "casing the joint" – does one still call it that in real life or just in the B-movies? But Roach, being about to retire, was an irrelevancy. Pine-Coffin, his inevitable successor, was the necessary target. It seems that Pine-Coffin did open up, most obligingly, perhaps with his wonderful name as fate, and, as your hypothetical killer, I would have hoped that the bird would provide you with another little distraction.'

'That could have been thought through a little better, Dr Brisley. The neighbour is a frail little old lady and doesn't keep budgies, so it did instantly look like a deliberately false trail. Not all red herrings are equally good, and this one was counter-productive, by telling me a little more about you.'

'Pity! But you mean "about *him* ", of course. You still didn't catch him, though! Bludger had you confused for a bit, surely?'

'For a bit. A change to History, back to Pillingham, a change to stabbing. But then I concluded that his murder was a blind, and I really felt I knew as much as I could expect to: without that little detail of our man's identity. Did you practise stabbing, by the way?'

'Oh, I certainly would have done. A half-pig bought ostensibly for the freezer - minus head, of course! - would have served the purpose. I would have dressed it in some formal clothes that I was going to throw out, so I could get the right feel of stabbing through the material into flesh. A noble creature, the pig! Tasty, easy to buy dead, easy to dress, and such an apt symbol! And would our man perhaps have enjoyed the actual entry of the blade into flesh? It would have been all much easier than that business you described with the pig's head and the hammers – though I imagine that he would have felt a certain affection for his chosen hammer. But would he have been better advised to stab all the victims? It's more stealthy ... and if you have to get behind people and then raise your arm to hit them over the head, isn't it a bit risky? They might turn round at the last split second. So I surmise. You would know of course.'

He paused and Hooligan decided to let the silence continue, hoping that Brisley would reminisce further. But Brisley was waiting for the next question, so Hooligan asked, 'Why would our man have stopped?'

'Good point! I can only guess ... He might have been thinking of giving up. They kept freezing the Lecturer vacancies – university assets were more frozen than the half-pig he might have practised on! – and the plan would have seemed to be blocked. And obviously every occasion of processing carried some risk of detection. Ironically, it seems to have been a clue from the very first murder which brought you here – erroneously, of course – if I interpret your story of the pig's head correctly. Then there was your terrible accident, which I read about in the papers. Bertrand told me that it had happened just after you had visited him. Our murderer might have been afraid that you would think he was behind it: that wouldn't have been fair play at all! You were given up for dead, apparently, and I'm glad to see you fully recovered. By the way, I don't think I've congratulated you on your promotion and retirement.

'Your absence from the investigation, Mr Hooligan, would have encouraged the murderer to have another go during the Conference before last. As I imagine it, he was seen quite by chance after processing Johnston-Baglinnet – by the way, why do so many of them have silly names? Think of any daft word you like, and put "Professor" in front of it, and it sounds entirely convincing ... Where was I? Ah, yes, I imagine that the murderer was seen, and therefore had to process that other old bastard Gristmill on the spur of the moment. When somebody comes on stage who shouldn't, you just have to act natural, stay in character, and ad-lib. He would have been in Raskolnikov's position - a man in your position will know Dostoevsky, of course – though in this instance two Professors made two old crones – I don't see Gristmill as the innocent step-sister! By the way, I gather that Bludger used Raskolnikov's idea of sewing tapes into his coat to carry the chopper. Curious coincidence – two people copying the same misguided fictional character!'

'So that's why you killed two on the same occasion?'

'Yes, though you mean "he killed, as I imagine it". Have you ever been to any of these conferences, by the way? Yes, silly question, of course you have – you waited in vain for him at the last one. Load of conferoponces, all conferoponcing around at public expense. The old men are a lot of old women, and vice versa. Whoops! That's one of Bertrand's, I'll be bound!'

'But you - all right, "he" - didn't succeed in his chosen task, Dr Brisley. Broke all those eggs and didn't make an omelette. Didn't create the vacancy you wanted.'

'Sent them into a blind panic, though! Before long they were all expecting what that tiresome windbag Jack Logan called "murder by degrees".'

'Then it all had to stop.'

'Yes – a decision to stop. There wouldn't have been any point in continuing: they froze those last two vacancies as well ... and our man would be getting older and no longer a plausible candidate for junior posts ... And anyway, he would have realised – perhaps gone to check – that you would have been watching for him at the last Conference at Doupminster. Which he would have found inconvenient: you see, conferences must be the ideal place for our man to strike. Otherwise, he would need to get to know the victims' personal circumstances for a domiciliary visit, and not all of them would be suitable on their home ground. Planting bobbies at the Conference must have scared him off.'

'You've told me enough to put you away,' Hooligan said, 'and I don't mean jail – I mean "during Her Majesty's pleasure". You'll spend the rest of your days with lunatics like yourself.'

'Only upon conviction. And ... well ... why should I care, anyway?' The tone and manner remained amusedly detached and urbane.

Hooligan felt that more was to come. Why had Brisley paused? And why had he said 'Anyway'? He prompted Brisley to continue: 'Are you telling me that you don't care because ... you won't be available to stand trial?'

'Precisely,' Brisley confirmed. 'Her Majesty will have to forgo her pleasure in my case. Your investigation and legal processing of me, Mr Hooligan, will take long enough and will lose the race.'

'Against ... against what I think you mean? Some sort of illness?'

'Yes. Incurable cancer. So who gets the last laugh? Goodbye!'

Brisley stood up, his hand extended. To his surprise, Hooligan remained seated.

'Dr Brisley, I'm still learning how your mind works, and I just learned something else. If you were terminally ill, you would not have been so insistent that the truth was a hypothesis. You would have admitted it. You would have led me to an apparent triumph and then demolished me with your announcement. Only then would you have challenged me to have you convicted before your death. The two halves of your reaction don't fit together – in fact, I think that the story of cancer occurred to you only during our conversation and you had not thought it through in your haste to wrong-foot me. No, Dr Brisley, you're a fit man, and you're not out of the woods yet.'

'There is the little matter of proof.' Brisley sounded anxiously defensive.

'True. But you've made two other mistakes that give me confidence in the outcome, however long it may take. You revealed that you know about a particular sentence in the torn page – that detail was never made public. And you stated that Johnston-Baglinnet was killed before Gristmill – which even the pathologist couldn't tell. You'll deny having said all that, of course ...

'... But remember this, Dr Brisley: the file on these murders will never be closed in your lifetime.'